ROOM
TO MOVE

The Redress Press Anthology
of Australian Women's Short Stories

EDITED BY SUZANNE FALKINER

UNWIN PAPERBACKS
Sydney   London   Boston

First published in Great Britain and Australia by
Unwin Paperbacks 1985.
Second impression 1986

UNWIN® PAPERBACKS
40 Museum Street, London WC1A 1LU, UK

Unwin Paperbacks
Park Lane, Hemel Hempstead, Herts HP2 4TE, UK

Allen & Unwin Australia Pty Ltd
8 Napier Street, North Sydney, NSW 2060 Australia

British Library Cataloguing in Publication Data
Room to move: the Redress Press anthology of women's short stories.
1. Short stories, Australia — Women authors I. Falkiner, Suzanne
823'.01'089287 [FS] PR9617.32
ISBN 0-04-820025-5
ISBN 0-04-820023-9 (pbk.)

National Library of Australia
Cataloguing-in-Publication entry:
Room to move: The Redress Press anthology of Australian
women's short stories.
ISBN 0 86861 526 9
ISBN 0 86861 749 0 (pbk.)
1. Short Stories, Australian. I. Falkiner, Suzanne, 1952–.
A823'.01089287

Library of Congress Catalog Card Number: 85-71024

Set in 10.5/11.5pt Bembo by Graphicraft Typesetters Ltd, Hong Kong
Printed in Hong Kong

Contents

Contents

Foreword

There are thirty two stories in this collection and according to my cherished principles, which are against discrimination and segregation in the literary life, sixteen of them should be by women and sixteen by men. However, there is a strong case for giving women the luxury of their own collection. It has to be said that men have had the best publishing chances in this country from the time of colonisation up to the second World War, and that it is still easier for a second rate male writer to get into print than it is for a first rate female writer to do the same.

So that although one would ideally prefer writers to be just writers, without dividing them into sexes, it is popularly accepted—not only by publishers themselves but by the people who buy books and borrow them from libraries—that there are writers and 'women writers' or possibly 'lady writers'. Nobody uses the term 'men writers'. Women writers are also supposed to write for women; to call a book a 'woman's book' is not to pay it much tribute.

This assumption, that the creative genius belongs to the male, goes wide and deep in society, is not news any more and is not especially Australian. There are thought to be artists and women artists, and composers and women composers, though not many of the latter and they probably have a less rewarding time then even the men composers. The attitude is not historically mysterious and does not need debating here.

What is genuinely mysterious is why anybody should write short stories when they could be writing a novel or a film script or even a play, because financially the short story is a waste of time. The great market places for English language short stories, Britain and the United States, have shrunk. Home markets in Canada, Australia and New Zealand have not expanded to fill the gap. The market declined because of the arrival of television, especially colour television, and of the picture magazines (*Life*, *Picture Post* etc). The 'little reviews', the small format magazines which attract no advertising and publish infrequently, living precariously on subsidies, by no means take up the slack.

The short story is sometimes (erroneously) seen as being 'easier' to write than is a novel (and a poem easier than either) but in fact it is a form that requires considerable technical skill from an author, who has to make a point and develop a theme in a few hundred or a few thousand words. The short story should not be seen as 'less' than the novel. It is of a different shape and intention and it is certainly not something that can be dashed off at the kitchen counter while the dinner is cooking, although I expect many a good short story has had its original theme jotted down in just such a fashion.

Events move quickly in Australia. It may be that the time is now right for women writers, that they will emerge as an element equal to the men, or even stronger, on the literary scene. This will have its dangers, especially as they will be exposed to the relentless onslaught of the communications industry. But take away the trendiness and the polemical claptrap and women have a real chance, if publishers will also take a chance. Having retreated from writing what men wanted and expected them to write, they must decide to let intellect and intelligence take over.

If one asks, where are the women writers, some of them are in this collection, and others can be identified on bookshop shelves around the country. One also gets the impression that many others are waiting to come on the scene, working as magazine writers and specialist journalists, testing their need to write something better than 'indulgence' articles, and testing also the likely span of their concentration and the quality of their ambition.

There are stories in this book that adhere to the strict forms of the classic short story and those that are more open in treatment, depending on evocation to make a point. But almost all, the reader will find, are about relationships. This reminds me of the saying that when you ask a man how he is he will tell you about his work, and when you ask a woman she will tell you about her husband (or lover), relationships being of concern to most women above work and sport. Relationships examined here are between women and men, women and women, women and children. Not men and men, and only a flicker of reference to men and children.

This is interior writing. There is not much to be found about ambition, or war, or industry, or party politics, or even the practise of the arts. The emphasis is on what characters feel rather than what they do. In work scenes the emphasis is not so much on the work but on the relationship between the workers. While noting that many of the themes are about the relationship between mothers and daughters and other adults and children, one has to remember that a lot of the European and Australian literature with which we grew up was about the relationship between fathers and sons and teachers and pupils. These are persistent themes and not likely to be abandoned.

As a footnote to this, the critic who complained about a 'proliferation of aunts' in stories by Australian women writers will be gratified to find Aunts Flo, Eva, Prissie, Mags, Ally and Gwen in this collection.

The ages of the writers collected here range between the seventies and twenties, the youngest twenty two. Seven of them were born outside Australia: one each in Germany, Britain, New Zealand, Greece, Italy and the United States and two in Ireland. Only one story is translated from its original language. Some names, such as those of Thea Astley, Elizabeth Jolley, Nancy Keesing, Kylie Tennant, Fay Zwicky, Helen Garner, Gwen Kelly and Nene Gare will be known to readers. They may also have encountered work by Vicki Viidikas, Leone Sperling, Olga Masters, Kate Llewellyn and Finola Moorhead in the past few years or months. Other names will be unknown because they belong to new writers or to those who have never attracted the critical acclaim or popular interest they deserve.

The stories run from just over one thousand words up to eight thousand, according to the writer's fancy, or view of what treatment her subject deserves. They are very personal stories, often told in the first person and in the present tense (which may lead to a confusion of pronouns). Many of the women who figure in these stories are displaced, disoriented, dislocated or have been so at some time of their lives—Thea Astley's ageing Sadie in 'The Scenery Never Changes', stranded in rural suburbia; the not-quite-traveller, not-quite-tourist, rather left-over woman, always leaving and returning in Inez Baranay's 'The Saddest Pleasure'; the girl called Pud in 'Nothing Happened' by Margaret Coombs; Lindy Lou in Freda Galloway's 'Vida's Child'; Louise in Kate Grenville's eerie 'Dropping Dance'; in Nene Gare's 'The Child', poor Hannah, the quintessential victim; Hetty in 'Summer of a Stick Man' by Kathryn Stone. In 'The Ring of Kerry' the roles are reversed; it is the man who, having intruded on the woman and delivered his 'soft toothless kisses', slips away, uncommitted. There is not a strong element of humour in these stories, apart from Jeri Kroll's 'The Electrolux Man', Jennifer Paynter's 'Fifty Eight Cents', Robin Sheiner's 'Brass on the Cannon', Kylie Tennant's 'Lady Weare', but a strong satirical note is sounded in several of the others, along with disenchantment. Many of the writers are especially good at setting up a character in a few brushstrokes.

But good fiction, while needing good observation also needs to dig below the surface, and it needs to take nothing for granted. Women writers who are busily questioning masculine assumptions and who write accordingly will also have to avoid the trap of facile feminist assumptions if they are to succeed. Taking nothing for granted is the key note to this.

Elizabeth Riddell

Preface

Late in 1984, in response to an invitation to submit material for an anthology of women's short stories, some 270 writers sent examples of their work to Redress Press, a Sydney women's packaging and publishing collective. The submissions, a result of notices in the media and personal approaches to new and established writers, numbered over 700 and came from as far afield as New York, London, and all states of Australia. There were no limitations as to subject matter; the only conditions were that writers should be women, Australian citizens or resident in Australia, and that the stories should be original fiction between 500 and 10 000 words.

From the 700, thirty two stories have been chosen as representing a balanced selection of modern writing by Australian women. Most of the stories have never been published before, and for some of the writers it is their first publication. A little under half of the stories have appeared in literary magazines and journals, but with few exceptions they have never appeared in book form. Almost all have been written in the last five years. No effort was made to select stories that represented names, categories or political beliefs: these are simply the best of the stories submitted, as perceived by the editor and readers.

The editor, who read all the stories at least once, and some many times, would like to thank Kate Grenville for providing a balanced second opinion in the final selection, and Venetia McMahon and Margaret Coombs for help in the exhausting task of reading and evaluating the almost overwhelming mass of initial submissions. Thanks is due also to all the writers who responded so positively to Redress Press's invitation, resulting in a short list which would have come close to filling another book of similar length.

Acknowledgements

At the time of selection, the following stories have been previously published in these sources:

'Coral Dance' by Glenda Adams, in *Meanjin* December 1984;
'The Scenery Never Changes' by Thea Astley, in *Coast to Coast* Angus and Robertson 1962;
'The Saddest Pleasure' by Inez Baranay, in *No Regrets 2* Sydney Women Writers Workshop 1981;
'Nothing Happened' by Margaret Coombs: a short extract from an earlier version of this story appeared in *Canberra Times* in November 1976;
'Vida's Child' by Freda Galloway, in *Echoes of Henry Lawson*, edited by Hilarie Lindsay, Ansay Pty Ltd 1981;
'Night Runner' by Elizabeth Jolley, in *Meanjin* December 1983;
'The Ring of Kerry' by Rosemary Jones, in *Patterns* Vol. 2, No. 2
'The Holiday House' by Gwen Kelly, in *Southerly* June 1982;
'The Electrolux Man' by Jeri Kroll, broadcast on Radio 5UV, Adelaide
'The Dowry' by Penelope Nelson, in the *Bulletin* 25 December 1984;
'Only a Little of So Much' by Fay Zwicky, in the *Canberra Times* 15 December 1984.

The editor would like to thank the publishers of the following stories for permission to include them in the collection: 'The

Acknowledgements

Lang Women', Olga Masters, from *The Home Girls*, University of Queensland Press 1982. 'The Child', Nene Gare, from *Australian Voices: Poetry and Prose of the 1970s*, edited by Rosemary Dobson, Australian National University Press 1975.

Night Runner

Elizabeth Jolley

NIGHT Sister Percy is dying. It is my first night as Night Runner at St Cuthbert's. Night Sister Bean, grumbling and cackling, calls the register and, at the end, she calls my name.

'Nurse Wright.'

'Yes Sister', I reply, half rising in my chair as I have seen the others do. The Maids' Dining Room, where we eat, is too cramped to do anything else.

'Night Runner', she says and I sit down again. The thought of being Night Runner is alarming. Nurse Dixon has been Night Runner for a long time. All along I have been hoping that I would escape from these duties and responsibilities, the efficient rushing here and there to relieve on different wards; every night bringing something new and difficult.

The Night Runner has to prepare the Night Nurses' meal too; one little sitting at 12 midnight and a second one at 12.45 and, of course, the clearing up and the washing up.

Every night I admire Nurse Dixon in the tiny cramped kitchen where we sit close together, regardless of rank, in the hot smell of warmed up fish or mince and the noise of the jugs of strong black coffee, keeping hot, in two black pans of boiling water. We eat our meal there in this intimacy with these two hot saucepans splashing and hissing just behind us. The coffee, only a little at the bottom of each jug, looks thick and dark and I wonder how it is made. Tonight I will have to find out and have it ready when the first little group of nurses appears.

When I report to Night Sister Bean in her office, she tells me to go for the oxygen.

'Go up to Isolation for the oxygen', she says without looking up from something she is writing. I am standing in front of her desk. I have never been so close to her before, not in this position, that is, of looking at her from above. She is starch-scented, shrouded mysteriously in the daintily severe folds of spotted white gauze. She is a sorceress disguised in the heavenly blue of the Madonna; a shrivelled, rustling, aromatic, knowledgeable, Madonna-coloured magician; she is a wardress and a keeper. She is an angel in charge of life and in charge of death. Her fine white cap, balancing, nodding, a grotesque blossom flowering forever in the dark halls of the night, hovers beneath me. She is said to have powers, an enchantment, beyond the powers of an ordinary human. For one thing, she has been on night duty in this hospital for over 30 years. As I stand there I realise that I do not know her at all and that I am afraid of her.

'Well', she says, 'don't just stand there. Go up to Isolation for the oxygen and bring it at once to Industry.'

'Yes, Sister', I say and I go as quickly as I can. The parts of the hospital are all known by different names; Big Boys, Big Girls, Top Ward, Bottom Ward, Side Ward and Middle, Industry, Peace, Chapel and Nursery. I have a room on the Peace Corridor, so named because it is above the Chapel and next to Matron's Wing.

Industry is the part over the kitchens. There are rooms for nurses there too. Quite often there is a pleasant noise and smell of cooking in these rooms. The Nurses' Sick Bay is there and it is there that I have to take the oxygen.

I am frightened out here.

For one thing, Isolation is never used. It is, as the name suggests, isolated. It is approached by a long, narrow covered way sloping up through a war-troubled shrubbery where all the dust bins are kept. Because of not being able to show any lights it is absolutely dark there. When I go out into the darkness I can smell rotting arms and legs, thrown out of the operating theatre and not put properly into the bins. I gather my apron close so that I will not get caught by a protruding maimed hand.

When I flash my torch quickly over the bins I see they are clean and innocent and have their lids firmly pressed on. In the torchlight there is no smell.

The sky at the end of the covered passage is decorated with the pale moving fans of searchlights. The beams of light are interwoven with the sounds of throbbing engines. The air raid warning might sound at any moment. In the emergency of being made Night Runner so suddenly, I have forgotten to bring my tin hat and gas mask from the Maids' Dining Room.

I am worried about the gas mask and the tin hat. I have signed for them on arrival at the hospital and am completely responsible for them. I will have to hand them back if I leave the hospital or if this war comes to an end. Usually I never leave either of them out of my care. I have them tied together with thick string. I put them under my chair at meal times and I hang them up in the nurses' cupboard in the ward where I am working.

It is hard to find the oxygen. My torch light picks up stacks of pillows, shelves of grey blankets, rolls of waterproof sheets, and some biscuit tins labelled Emergency Dressings, all with dates on them. There are two tea chests filled with tins and bottles. The chests are marked Emergency. Iron Rations. Doctors Only in red paint. There do not seem to be similar boxes marked for nurses or patients.

At last I find the oxygen cylinder and I rush with the little trolley up to Industry.

Sister Percy is dying. She is the other Night Sister and is very fat. She is propped, gasping, on pillows, a blue trout with eyes bulging, behind the floral screens made by Matron's mother for sick nurses.

It is the first time I have seen someone who is dying. Night Sister Bean is there and the RMO and the Home Sister. They take the oxygen and Sister Bean tells me I need not stay. She pulls the screens closer round Sister Percy.

In the basement of the hospital I set about the secrets of making the coffee and having it come only so far up the jugs.

Later Night Sister Bean comes and says why haven't I lit the gas, which, when you think about it, is a good thing to say as they will surely want that potato and mince stuff hot. Before she leaves she makes me get down on my knees to hunt behind the pipes for cockroaches. She has a steel knitting needle for this and we knock and scrape and rattle about, Night Sister Bean on her knees too, and we chase them out, the revolting things, and sprinkle some white powder which, she says, they love to eat without knowing it is absolutely fatal to them.

It is something special about night duty, this little meal time in the middle of the night, with everyone sitting together even Night Sister Bean, herself, coming to one or the other of the sittings. She seems almost human, in spite of the mysterious things whispered about her, at these meals. Sometimes she even complains about the sameness of them, saying that one thing the war cannot do is to make these meals worse than they are and that it is sheer drudgery to eat them night after night. When I think about this I realise she has been eating stewed mince and pounded fish for so many years and I can't help wishing I could do something about it.

This first night it takes me a long time to clear up in the little pantry. When at last I am finished Night Sister Bean sends me to relieve on Bottom Ward. There is a spinal operation in the theatre recovery room just now, she says, and a spare nurse will be needed when the patient comes back to the ward.

On my way to Bottom Ward I wish I could be working with Staff Nurse Ramsden.

'I will play something for you', she said to me once when I was alone and filled with tears in the bleak, unused room which is the nurses' sitting room.

She ran her fingers up and down the piano keys. 'This is Mussorgsky', she said, 'it's called Gopak, a kind of little dance', she explained. She played and turned her head towards me nodding and smiling, 'do you like this?' she asked, her eyes smiling. It is not everyone who has had Mussorgsky played for them; the thought gives me courage as I hurry along the unlit passage to the ward.

There is a circle of light from the uncurtained windows of the office in the middle of the ward. I can see a devout head bent over the desk in the office. I feel I am looking at an angel of mercy who is sitting quietly there ready to minister to the helpless patients.

Staff Nurse Sharpe is seated in the office with an army blanket tucked discreetly over her petticoat. Her uniform dress lies across her lap. She explains that she is just taking up the hem and will I go to the kitchen and cut the bread and butter. As I pass the linen cupboard I see the other night nurse curled up in a heap of blankets. She is asleep. This is my friend Ferguson.

I sink slowly into the bread cutting. It is a quiet and leisurely task. While I cut and spread I eat a lot of the soft new bread and I wonder how Sharpe will manage to wear her uniform shortened. Matron is so particular that we wear them long, ten inches off the ground, so that the soldiers do not get in a heightened excitement about us.

Sharpe comes in quite soon. She seems annoyed that I have not finished. She puts her watch on the table and says the whole lot, breakfast trays all polished and set, and bread and butter for sixty men, must be finished in a quarter of an hour. I really hurry up after this and am just ready when the operation case comes back and I have to go and sit by him in the small ward. I hope to see Ferguson but S/N Sharpe has sent her round changing the water jugs.

Easily I slip into my dream of Ferguson. She owes me six and sevenpence. I have written it on the back of my writing pad. I'll go out with her and borrow two and six.

'Oh Lord!' I'll say, 'It's my mother's birthday and I haven't a thing for her and here I am without my purse. Say, can you lend me two and six?' And then I'll let her buy a coffee and a bun for me—that will bring it to three shillings and I won't ever pay it back and, in that way, will recover some of the six and sevenpence.

'Cross my heart, cut me in two if my word is not true', I say to myself and I resolve to sit in Ferguson's room as soon as I am off duty. I'll sit there till she pays me the money. I'll just sit and sit there till it dawns on her why I am there.

5

The patient, quite still as if dead, suddenly moves and helps himself to a drink of water. He vomits and flings the bowl across the room. He seems to be coming round from his anaesthetic. I grope under the bed clothes. I should count his pulse but I am unable to find his wrist.

'Oh I can't', he groans, 'not now I can't'.

He seems to be in plaster of Paris from head to foot. He groans again and sleeps. Nervously I wait to try again to find some place on his body where I can feel his pulse.

High on the wall in the Maids' Dining Room is an ancient wireless. It splutters and gargles all day with the tinny music of workers' playtime and Vera Lynn plaintively announcing there'll always be an England. Sometimes in the early mornings, while we have our dinner, the music is of a different kind. Sometimes it is majestic, lofty and sustaining.

'Wright!' Staff Nurse Ramsden calls across the crowded tables. 'Mock Morris? Would you say?' She waves a long fingered hand.

'No', I shake my head, 'not Mock Morris, it's Beethoven.' She laughs. She knows it is not Beethoven. It is a little joke we have come to share. It is the only joke I have with anyone. Perhaps it is the same for Ramsden. She has a slight moustache and I have noticed, in her room, an odour, a heaviness which belongs with older women perhaps from the perfumed soap she has and the material of well-made underwear. Her shoes and stockings, her suits and blouses and hats have the fragrance of being of a better quality. Ramsden asked me once about the violin I was carrying. She has said to me to choose one of her books, she has several in her room, as a present from her to me. Secretly I think, every day, that I admire Ramsden. I love her. Perhaps. I think, I will tell her, one day, the truth about the violin case.

A special quality about working during the night is the stepping out of doors in the mornings, the first feeling of the fresh air and the sun which is hardly warm in its brightness.

We ride our bicycles. Not Ramsden. There is a towing path along the river. I, not knowing it before, like the smell of the river, the muddy banks and the cattle-trodden grass. Water birds, disturbed, rise noisily. Our own voices echo.

Though we have had our meal we want breakfast. Ferguson hasn't any money. Neither has Queen. Ferguson says she will owe Queen if Queen will owe me for them both. We agree and I pay. And all the way back I am trying to work out what has to be added to the outstanding six and sevenpence.

Ferguson's room, when I go to sit there, looks as if it should be roped off as a bomb crater. Her clothes, and some of mine, are scattered everywhere. There is a note from the Home Sister on her dusty dressing table. I read the note, it is to tell Ferguson to clean her hair brush.

Bored and sleepy I study the note repeatedly, and add 'Neither a Borrower nor a Lender be' in handwriting so like the Home Sister's it takes my breath away.

I search for Ferguson's writing paper. It is of superior quality and very suitable. I write some little notes in this newly learned handwriting and put them carefully in my pocket. I continue to wait for Ferguson, hardly able to keep my eyes open.

I might have missed my sleep altogether if I had not remembered in time that Ferguson has gone home for her nights off.

I do not flash the torch for fear of being seen. I grope in the dark fishing for something, anything, in the cavernous tea chest, and hasten back down the covered way.

Night Sister Bean says to me to go to Bottom Ward to relieve and I say, 'Yes Sister', and leave her office backwards, shuffling my feet and bending as if bowing slightly, my hands, behind my back, clasping and almost dropping an enormous glass jar.

It is bottled Chinese gooseberries, of all things, and I put one on each of the baked apples splashing the spicy syrup generously. Night Sister Bean smiles, crackling starch, and says the baked apples have a piquant flavour. She has not had such a delicious baked apple for 30 years. 'Piquant!' she says.

S/N Sharpe sits in the office all night with nursing auxiliary Queen. Queen has put operation stockings over her shoes to keep warm. Both Sharpe and Queen are wrapped up in army blankets. Sharpe has to let down the hem of her dress. Sister Bean asked her to stay behind at breakfast.

Whenever I come back to the office Sharpe says, 'take these pills to bed twelve' or 'get the lavatories cleaned', and, 'time to do the bread and butter—and don't leave the trays smeary like last night'.

At the end of the ward I pull out the laundry baskets and I move the empty oxygen cylinders and the fire equipment; the buckets of water and sand. I simply move them all out from their normal places, just a little way out, and later, when Sharpe and Queen go along to the lavatory, they fall over these things and knock into each other, making the biggest disturbance ever heard in a hospital at night. Night Sister Bean comes rushing all the way up from her office in the main hall. She is furious and tells Sharpe and Queen to report to Matron at 9 a.m. She can see that I am busy, quietly with my little torch, up the other end of the ward, pouring the fragrant mouthwash in readiness for the morning.

The tomato sauce has endless possibilities. The dressed crab is in such a small quantity that the only thing I can do is to put a tiny spoonful on top of the helpings of mashed potato. Night Sister Bean is appreciative and says the flavour seeps right through. Tinned bilberries, celery soup and custard powder come readily to my experienced hands.

I do not see S/N Ramsden very often. She has not asked me in to her room again to choose the book. Perhaps she has changed her mind. She is, after all, senior to me.

There are times when an unutterable loneliness is the only company in the cold early morning. The bicycle rides across the heath or along the river are over too quickly and, because of this, are meaningless. With a sense of inexplicable bereavement my free time seems to stretch ahead in emptiness. I go to bed too soon and sleep badly.

I am glad when Ferguson comes back; very pleased. In the pantry I am opening a big tin, the biggest thing I have managed

to lift out so far. I say 'Hallo', to Ferguson as she sits down with
the other nurses; they talk and laugh together. I go on with my
work.

'Oh, you've got IT', I say to Ferguson. 'Plenty of S.A. Know
what that is? Sex appeal, it's written all over you.' And seeing,
out of the corner of my eye, Night Sister Bean coming in, I go
on talking as if I haven't seen her.

'How you do it beats me Fergie', I say. 'How is it you have all
the men talking about you the way they do. You certainly must
have given them plenty to think about. They all adore you.
Corporal Smith's absolutely mad about you, really!' Uncon-
cernedly I scrape scrape at the tin. 'He never slept last night.
Sharpe had to slip him a Mickey Finn, just a quick one. He's
waiting for another letter from you and I think he's sending the
poem you asked for. Who on earth is your go-between?' So I go
on and scrape scrape at the tin.

I know why there is silence behind me. I turn round.

'Oh, here you are at last Sister', I say to Night Sister Bean.
Ferguson is a dull red colour, pity, as she was looking so well
after her nights off.

'Here we are Sister', I say, 'on the menu we have pheasant
wing in aspic. Will you have the fish pie with it?' I serve all the
plates in turn. The coffee hisses and spits behind us.

'Matron's office, 9 o'clock', Night Sister Bean says to Ferguson.

'Yes, Sister.'

Ferguson is sent to Big Girls for the rest of the night and I am
to relieve, as usual, on Bottom Ward. I wake Corporal Smith at
4 a.m. and urge him to write to Nurse Ferguson. 'Every day she
waits for a letter', I tell him, 'she'll get ill from not eating if you
don't write.' S/N Sharpe finds me by his bed and sends me to
scrub the bathroom walls.

'And do out all the cupboards too, and quickly', she says.

In the morning when I see Sharpe safely in the queue for letters
I rush up to the Peace corridor and find her room. I cram her
curtains into her messy wet soap dish and leave one of my neatly
folded notes on her dressing table.

Elizabeth Jolley

Do not let your curtains dangle in the soap dish. Sister.

There is not much I can do with the cherry jam. I serve it with
the stewed mince as a sweet and sour sauce. It is a favourite with
the royal family, I tell them, but I can see I shall have to risk
another raid on my secret store.

The next night I have a good dig into both chests and load
myself up with tinned tomato soup, a tinned chicken, some
sardines and two tins of pears.

Nurse Dixon is mystified. Her eyes are full of questions.

'Where d'you get all . . .' her lips form whispered words.

'No time to chat now, sorry', I say. I am hastily setting a little
tray for Night Sister Bean. I have started taking an extra cup of
coffee along to her office. It seems the best way to use up a tin of
shortbread fingers. Balancing my tray I race up the dark stairs
and along the passage to Night Sister Bean's office.

'Bottom Ward'. Night Sister Bean says without looking up.
Again I am at the mercy of Sharpe.

'Wash down the kitchen walls', she says, 'and do all the
shelves and cupboards and quickly—before you start the blanket
baths.' She gives me a list of the more disagreeable men to do;
she says to change their bottom sheets too. All the hardest work
while N/A Queen, who is back there, and herself sit wrapped
up in the office, smoking, with a pot of hot coffee between them
on the desk.

I go into the small ward and give the emergency bell there
three rings bringing Night Sister Bean to the ward before
Sharpe and Queen realise what is happening.

'Is it an air raid?' Queen asks anxiously.

'Nurses should know why they ring, Nurse', Sister Bean says
and she makes them take her round to every bed whispering the
diagnosis and treatment of every patient. Night Sister Bean
rustling and croaking, fidgeting and cursing, disturbs all the
men trying to find out who rang three times.

'Someone must be haemorrhaging', she says, 'find out who it
is'.

Peering maliciously into the kitchen, Sister Bean sees me
quietly up the step ladder with my little pail of soapy water. The

10

wet walls gleam primrose yellow as if they have been freshly painted. She tells Sharpe and Queen to report to Matron's office 9 a.m. for smoking on duty.

Once again Sharpe is in the letter queue. I take the loaded ash tray from the Porters' Lodge and spill it all over her room.
  Your room is disgusting. Take some hot water and disinfectant and wash down Sister.
The folded note lies neatly on her dressing table.

I try listening to Beethoven but it reminds me of my loneliness. I wish Corporal Smith would write to me. I wish someone would write to me. Ferguson is going to The Old Green Room for coffee. She is popular, always going out.
  In my room I have a list.

1 Listen to Beethoven
2 Keep window wide open. If cold sleep in school jersey.
3 Ride bicycle for complexion. (care of)
4 Write and Think.

'I can't come out', I say to Ferguson, 'I'm listening to Beethoven', I say, ignoring the fact that she has not asked me.
  'It's only one record', she says, 'you've only got one record.'
  'It's Beethoven all the same', I beat time delicately and wear my far away look.
  Ferguson goes off out and I add number 5 with difficulty to the list. The paper is stuck in at the side of the dressing table mirror and uneven to write on.

5 Divide N.S.B.'s nature and discover exactly the extent of her powers.

I take my white windsor, bath size, to the wash room and fill a basin with hot water to soften the soap. I set to work with my nail file and scissors. I'll take my torch tonight, I'm thinking, a tin of powdered milk would be useful. Whipped up, it makes very good cream; delicious with the baked apples.
  The likeness is surprising. It is the distinction of the shape and the tilt of the cap, the little figure is emerging perfectly. I work

11

patiently for a long time. I am going to split the image in half very carefully and torture one half keeping the other half as a control, as in a scientific experiment, and observe the effect on the living person.

The idea is so tremendous I feel faint. Already I foresee results, the upright, crisp little blue and white Bean totters in the passage, she wilts and calls for help.

'Nurse Wright! Help me up, dear. What a good child you are, so gentle too. Just help me to that chair, thank you, dear child. Thank you!'

The Peace corridor is very quiet. Another good thing about the night duty is that we all may sleep in our beds during the day. Every morning I long for this sleep. Up until this time I, like the others, have had to carry bedclothes down to the basement every night because of the air raids. There are no beds in the basement, only some sack mattresses of straw. There is no air there either.

I love the smell of the clean white windsor. I am sculpting carefully with the file. The likeness is indeed perfect. My hands are slippery and wrinkled and I am unable to stop them from shaking. I feel suddenly that I possess some hitherto unknown but vital power to be able to make this—this effigy.

And then, all at once, Night Sister Bean is there in the doorway of the washroom, peering about to see who it is not in bed yet and it is after 12 noon already. Because I am thinking of the moment when I will split the image and considering which tool will be most suitable for this, the sudden appearance of Sister Bean is, to say the least, confusing.

I plunge my head into the basin together with Her I am so carefully fashioning, saying:

'Oh, I can never get the soap out of my hair!' delighted at the sound of weariness achieved.

She says to remember always to have the rinsing water hotter than the washing water. 'Hot as you can bear it', she says.

'Thank you Sister.'

She is rustling and cackling, crackling and disturbing, checking every corner of the washroom, quickly looking into all the lavatories, saying as she leaves:

'And it is better to take off your cap first.'

So there I am with the soaked limp thing, frothed and scummed all over with the white windsor, on my head, still secure with an iron foundry of hair grips and useless for tonight. My work of art too is ruined, the outlines blurred and destroyed before being finished. It is a solemn moment of understanding that from a remote spot, namely the door, she has been able to spoil what I have made and add a further destruction of her own, my cap.

My back aches with bending over the stupid little sink. These days I am missing too much sleep. In spite of being so tired I go down to the ramp where the milk churns are loaded and unloaded. It is the meeting place of the inside of the hospital with the outside world. The clean laundry boxes are there, neatly stacked. Fortunately Ferguson's box is near the edge. I open it and remove one of her fresh clean caps. My box is there too but I don't want to take one of mine as it will leave me short later in the week.

The powdered household milk is in the chest as I hoped, tins of it and real coffee too. I find more soup, mushroom, cream of asparagus, cream of chicken, vegetable and minestrone. I am quite reckless with my torch. Christmas is coming, I take a little hoard of interesting tins.

I discover that Night Sister Bean has a weakness for hot broth and I try, every night, to slip a cup along to her office in the early part of the night before I start on anything else.

Several things are on my mind, mostly small affairs. For some time I have Corporal Smith's love letter to Ferguson, sixteen pages, in my pocket. It is not sealed and her name does not appear anywhere in the letter. It is too long for one person so I divide the letter in half and address two envelopes in Corporal Smith's handwriting, one to Sharpe and one to Ferguson. Accidentally I drop them, unsealed, one by the desk in Night Sister Bean's office and the other in the little hall outside Matron's room. We are not supposed to be intimate with the male patients and I feel certain too that Corporal Smith is a married man ... but there is something else on my mind; it is

13

whether a nurse should send a Christmas card to the Matron. It is something entirely beyond my experience.

In the end I buy one, a big expensive card, a Dutch Interior. It costs one and ninepence. I sit a whole morning over it trying to think what I should write.

A very Happy Christmas to Matron from Nurse Wright
Nurse Wright sounds presumptuous. I haven't taken an external exam yet. She may not regard me as nurse.

A very Happy Event . . . that would be quite wrong.

A very Happy Christmas to You from Guess Who. She might think that silly.

Happy Christmas. Vera. Too familiar. *Veronica.* I have never liked my name.

A Happy Christmas to Matron from one of her staff and in very small writing underneath *N/V Wright*.

I keep wondering if all the others will send Matron a Christmas card. It is hardly a thing you can ask anyone. Besides I do not want, particularly, to give Ferguson the idea. She will never think of it herself. And who can I ask if I don't ask her.

I put the card in Matron's correspondence pigeon hole. The card is so big it has to be bent over at the top to fit in. I am nervous in case someone passing will see me.

Again I am relieving on Bottom Ward. Always it is this Bottom Ward. This time I have to creep round cleaning all the bed wheels.

'And quietly', Sharpe says, 'Nurse Queen and I don't want everyone waking up!'

The card worries me. I will take it out in the morning. The message is all wrong.

One of her staff! I can't bear to think about it. The card is still there, bending, apologising and self-conscious in the morning. I want to remove it but there are people about and correspond-ence must not be tampered with.

Twice during the day I get dressed and creep down from the Peace corridor, pale, hollow-eyed and drab; all night nurses are completely out of place in the afternoons. I feel conspicuous, sick nearly, standing about in the hall waiting to be alone there so that I can remove that vulgar card and its silly message. It is still bending there in the narrow compartment.

Even when the hall is free of people there are two nurses chattering together by the main door. Why ever do they stand in this cold place to talk. I have to give up and go back to bed, much too cold to sleep. Ferguson has my hot water bottle for her toothache. It seems I can never get even with her. Never ever.

The card is still there in the evening when we go down to the Maids' Dining Room for breakfast. I can hardly eat as I am thinking of a plot to retrieve the card.

The register is finished.

'Nurse Wright.'

'Yes Sister?' half rising in my chair as we all do in that cramped place.

'Matron's office 9 a.m. tomorrow.'

'Yes Sister', I sit down again. It can't be to thank me for the card as it hasn't been received yet. A number of reasons come to mind, for one thing there are the two deep caves of dark emptiness; perhaps they have been discovered ...

In spite of a sense of foreboding I go, with my little torch hidden beneath my apron, up the long covered way. I need more powdered milk. The path seems endless. The night sky has the same ominous decoration; throbbing engines alternate with sharp anti-aircraft guns and the air raid sirens wail up and down, up and down. The soft searchlights move slowly. They make no noise and are helpless. I feel exposed and push my hands round the emptiness of the nearest tea chest. Grabbing a tin of powdered milk I rush back down past the festering bins and on down towards an eternity of the unknown.

I have a corner seat in this train by a mistake which is not entirely my fault. The woman, who is in this seat, asks me if I think she has time to fetch herself a cup of tea. I can see that she badly wants to do this and, in order that she does not have to go without the tea, I agree that, though she will be cutting it fine, there is a chance that she will have time. So she goes and I see her just emerging from the refreshment room with a look on her

15

face which shows how she feels. She has her tea clutched in one hand and I have her reserved seat because it is silly, now that the train has started, to stand in the corridor being crushed by army greatcoats and kit bags and boots, simply looking at the emptiness of this comfortable corner.

I have some household milk for Mother, it is always useful in these days of rationing. I have the tinned chicken also. At the last minute I could not think what to do with it as Night Sister Bean will not be naming the next Night Runner till this evening, and, of course, I shall not be there to know who it is and so am not able to hand on either the milk or the chicken.

There is too the chance that the new Night Runner might be my friend Ferguson. It would not do to give her these advantages.

This is my first holiday from St Cuthbert's, my nights off and ten days holiday. Thirteen days off.

'Shall I take my tin hat, I mean my helmet, and my gas mask?' I ask Matron.

'By all means if you would like to', she says and wishes me a pleasant holiday and a happy Christmas.

The tin hat and the gas mask are tied to my suitcase. My little sister will be interested to see them.

My father will be pleased with his Christmas card. He has always liked the detail and the warm colours of a Dutch Interior. He will not mind the crossing out inside. The card will flatten if I press it tonight in the dictionary.

For some reason I am thinking about Staff Nurse Ramsden. Last night, in the doorway of the Maids' Dining Room, I stood aside to let her go in first.

'Thank you', she said and then she asked me what my first name was.

'First name?'

'Yes, your Christian name, what is it?' her voice, usually low, was even lower. Like a kind of shyness.

I did not have the chance to answer. We had to squeeze through to our different tables quickly as Night Sister Bean was already calling the register.

If Ramsden could be on the platform to meet my train at the

16

end of this journey I would be able to answer her question. Perhaps I would be able to explain to her about the violin case. I would like to see Ramsden, I would like to be going to her. Thinking about her and seeing her face, in my mind, when she turned to smile at me, the time when she played Mussorgsky on the piano in the nurses' sitting room, makes me think that it is very probable, though no one has ever spoken about it, that Night Sister Bean might very well be missing her life-long friend Night Sister Percy. Missing her intolerably.

The Electrolux Man

Jeri Kroll

THE doorbell rang. It wasn't just a random ring. It was the Electrolux Man, and I knew he was coming.

For the first time since I was single, I had gone to the Royal Show. I was lonely after my husband left, so I thought, why not? He'd never have gone. 'All fairy floss and glorious home', he'd snipe. I had been wandering around Centennial Hall, looking at all of those things which once might have concerned me. But now I couldn't have cared less whether half my house was uninsulated, and Pink Panther Batts were discounted 10 per cent. Living alone with a bloody husband somewhere who had emptied our joint account, I had to hang onto every cent.

So I drifted down the aisles, just glancing at the coffee grinders, juicers, and food processors, and then at furniture and draperies and aluminium windows, all designed to make the average Australian home into a dream. And the Bankcard bill a nightmare. I had given up those dreams with my Bankcard. I did stop at the textured ceilings just to feel a bit. Ridges and hollows and swirls. I could have used swirls to cover my bedroom ceiling. But I really preferred it cracked as it was. Lying in bed at night, I'd drift away from my book and explore the river that flowed out from my window to just near the light. Anyway, fancy ceilings were another thing I couldn't afford.

I wandered on till I came to the Electrolux Exhibit. A man in a bright blue shirt crouched over a carpet piled high with dust. And as I stood there, his machine sucked it right up in no time. Really, it was amazing. The couple watching were impressed,

18

too. They put their names down for a home visit. 'And you, madam', he said turning, 'would you like to see exactly how this marvellous little machine works?'

'Why not', I said, before I could stop. It must be ridiculously expensive, I thought. I could never afford one.

'What kind of carpets do you have?'

'I'd rather not remember', I said. I hate cleaning. His smile waned. 'Though I certainly do need a new vacuum cleaner. My old one's got no power.'

His eyes brightened. 'That's just the problem with most other machines. But Electrolux probably has a better tuned motor than your car.' He had a slow smile, it took a while to get going, kind of like honey dripping from a spoon. But not at all sticky. I probably didn't explain that well. Let's just say it was a nice, slow smile.

With a twist of his wrist, he upended the orange and brown vacuum, dumped out the contents on the carpet square, and resettled the machine. 'With just a tap here', he said, toeing the on switch, 'this silent model is ready for action'. And he scooped up the dirt in no time. I know I said that before, but the thing really did work. 'That's very good', I nodded, 'but I don't get dirt like that'. He whisked out his pad. 'Can I come round to your house then, to try out this model on the dirt that you do get? There's absolutely no obligation. But, if you do purchase the deluxe 720, we provide lifetime service, you know. And there's a monthly instalment plan if you prefer not to pay in a lump sum.'

Well, I was home most of the day doing nothing anyway. I couldn't find a job. My typing wasn't too bad, neither was the rest of me. But I didn't know shorthand. And if you're in your thirties, companies just don't want you. They'd rather try the girls fresh out of school. They're cheaper, and look better serving coffee. I used to be interested in pottery and gardening, but I couldn't seem to get myself out of the house. Yet I couldn't have cared less what happened to his house, oh, now my house. After all, he left, and he wasn't going to get back in.

So I gave the Electrolux Man my name and address, and on the Monday, right on the dot of eleven, the doorbell rang. It was blue shirt. 'Pleased to see you again', he said. No 'Gidday'. 'Pleased to see you again. I'm your Electrolux Man.' Your Electrolux Man. And he smiled that nice slow smile.

'Come in', I said, 'I'm afraid that the place is in a bit of a mess'.

'Oh, you don't know how many times I've heard that, and in the most immaculate houses. But then, that's why I'm here, to introduce you to the clean, clean world of Electrolux.'

'No really', I was embarrassed, 'I don't bother cleaning much, but then, there's just me'.

'Such a nice big house, too', he admired, craning his neck into the spare room, then my bedroom. 'Pardon me, but it's sort of a hobby of mine.'

'What?'

'Figuring out people's personalities from their houses.'

'Oh.' I flushed.

'But I have to have a good look round first', he qualified. 'I'm not always right.' Then he became all business. 'Now, where's your dirtiest carpet?'

And he set to work right there doing the whole lounge-room carpet. He didn't have to. This was just a demonstration, after all, and he wasn't sure I was going to buy. He showed me how to use all the attachments, the one for getting dust and cobwebs in corners, the one for blinds and upholstery, the one for thick carpet. It really is an amazing little machine. The upholstery attachment even clips in right under the main wand, so you can't lose it. And it handled so easily, even when I used it, though I didn't have the verve he did. He flicked his wrist so that the carpet attachment whipped over onto its back to suck up the stubborn bits, then, with a matador's grace, he flicked it back. I'm not given to flowery speech, and matador might not be right, but I have to give you an idea of his skill. Smooth, even strokes, and the lounge was clean. When he began on the blinds, I had to say something. 'Really, you don't have to do that. That's my job.'

'Oh, it's nothing at all, these haven't been cleaned in a while, and it's bad on your back.'

'Well then', I could only offer, 'would you like a cup of tea?'

While the kettle was boiling, I whipped round to the corner deli for a Tahiti Cake. After all, he was doing all that work for me. But that time he wouldn't really stop to eat. He vacuumed the cobwebs off the ceiling with the special long rubber thing with one hand and ate with the other. I followed him around, holding his tea. He came at eleven and left at one. 'I have another appointment at 1.30 in Unley', he apologized, 'but the carpet in the hall needs a thorough going over. Can I come back on Thursday?'

That first time we didn't talk much. You know, the obvious small talk. On Thursday, though, when he was doing the moulding in the hall, he told me he was an amateur artist. 'It's really hard to find time to paint. I use real paints, oils, not water colours. Water colours are cheaper, but they've got no substance. I need something that I can mould, that's responsive.' I asked him what he painted. 'Oh, so far mostly houses, the insides. They're what I know best, and an artist should always paint what he knows best. But someday I hope to do a complete house, inside and out.'

It seems that his family didn't like his painting. His wife complained about the cost. She also complained when he shut himself up in the bedroom to paint after tea. And her sheets smelled of turpentine. But the bedroom was the only quiet place in the house. They didn't have a shed. His two children were always blaring music in the lounge, or had the TV going. They were fourteen and sixteen, old enough to show consideration for others, he said.

When he came back on Monday, at eleven sharp, he brought the special accessory I hadn't been able to afford. Oh yes, I forgot. I did buy the Electrolux on their special terms. With a lifetime guarantee of service, at $18.75 per month. But this accessory, the Luxafoam Shampoo Unit, cost another $150. 'Just a loan', he grinned, adding the sample shampoo and water, then he zipped into the thick pile in the lounge. It was there that he told me most people thought he was a bit strange. 'You know, guys at the pub. You'd think I was the only artist in Elizabeth', he sighed. 'They kid me about becoming famous, exhibiting at the Royal Show alongside my machines. My kids keep asking if I'm going to cut my ear off. I told them if it would shut out their bloody music, I would. I go twice a week to the local, I like footy, just the same as they do. We have the odd barbie, and the wife and I even go dancing at the footy club sometimes. They still think I'm strange.' He considered for a moment. 'Maybe it's the banjo.'

He had to leave then, but came back next day about four to start on the spare room. It was dark by the time he was done. I was heady from all that dust and shampoo. I asked him to tea. I had enough, I explained, since I often cooked double portions. Then I didn't have to fuss every night. He phoned his wife, and stayed. He didn't say anything when I served up the grill, two chops and one sausage for him, one chop and one sausage for me. I did my special mashed potatoes with butter and milk and a dash of chives. There was custard for dessert. We had some beer, too. He nipped out to the pub while I was cooking.

'Do you get much commission?' I asked. 'Not bad', he said, 'but I haven't been able to put my heart into selling lately. Not many people seem interested in the beauty of the machine. It really is a fine little machine.' And with a faraway look he studied the ceiling. 'You've got cobwebs in here, too. I'll fix those tomorrow.'

He was a sensitive man. He put his heart into things. He wanted people to care. Afterwards, as we lay together on the bed, he pointed out the ingenuity of my spiders. I had webs with such unusual patterns. Together, we went exploring down the crack from the window. We only got as far as the tributary near the wardrobe, when he had to leave. I felt a bit guilty. He had a wife and two children. But he needed some support. He worked hard, and he didn't get much help from his family or friends.

The next morning he arrived with the garbagemen. It was 8 a.m. I had just showered, and was in my robe. 'You've got carmine cheeks', he beamed, 'or maybe cerise', as he followed me into the shadows.

My kitchen was de-webbed as promised. Before he left at four, he told me he thought the bedroom would take quite a while, since the carpet was thick and dirty, and there were so many cobwebs. It was time for a new order. The spiders had had their way too long. He came back that night with some more paper dustbags for the Electrolux and a suitcase. 'I like to do a job properly', he said. Although he wasn't outspoken, he had only done the baseboards when he told me he had grown quite fond of my house. I told him he wasn't like other men. He said he knew that.

That was a month ago. Since then, he's done each room in the house four times, about a week on average for the entire house. He's got it down to an exact science. I'm enjoying cooking again, mixed grills, soups, and a roast on Sunday. On Sunday, he only does the kitchen before I start cooking. Every night during the week he sets up his easel in the lounge and paints. It will take him, he estimates, about a month to get it right. Then he'll start on the spare room. Then the kitchen, then the hall. He's saving the bedroom for last. It's the most interesting architecturally, because of the old fireplace and narrow double windows.

Sometimes I feel a bit guilty about his family. But he's so happy. He even has time now to take a night off, so Sundays we go to the drive-in. My car is always spotless; he vacuums it every Saturday. But the theatres are shocking. They must either use a very inferior brand of machine, or they haven't had a cleaner in there for years, he says.

I worry sometimes though. What will happen when he finishes painting each room in the house? Will he leave me? I think that he cares, and he seems content. I've been budgeting carefully, too, and we've been eating almost as cheaply as one. I've started roaming the neighbourhoods sometimes during the day after he's had breakfast and is caught up in vacuuming. A large old house five streets away is for sale. Although there's a housing order on it, I went in. It has eight rooms. The agent said he would look at mine to tell me what he thinks it's worth.

The Child

Nene Gare

OUTSIDE the sky was a brilliant hard blue; the shadows of the buildings were black and accurate and bare feet burned on the hot beach. The holiday town was ready for the holiday weekend. Even the air was expectant. City sophisticates showed residents how to stay cool and relaxed even if they happened to be walking the main business street and, more modestly, the people from the reserve at the end of the town gathered in tittering groups about their favourite corners or shopped delicately in the big new centres.

It was Saturday morning and summer far enough advanced for everyone to have become blasé about the endless unfolding of hot and perfect days.

Inside the gaol the air was hot and fuggy and smelled of Hannah's sweating body. But it was dark and quiet and she could lie there on the bed with her arms over her face and stop thinking, almost stop breathing. If she could truly stop breathing she could stop living but there was no way. Though she scarcely moved on the blanket-covered bed, air passed through and was pushed out again between her heavy parted lips. Her eyes were closed under protecting arms. She had kept them closed even after the footsteps had receded. She did not want to go on being. She wanted agonisingly to stop—get off—go away somewhere where there was nobody. Except Mum! At the thought moisture seeped from between Hannah's closed lids and ran into the declivity between arm and cheek. After a little while she had to wipe the wet from her face with her forearms.

24

She wished she had never had to leave Mum and go to school. She should have stayed up there on the station instead of going into the town to live at the hostel. Except for the basketball she hadn't really liked it. Mum had liked that, her being picked to play with the team. 'You stay here and learn reading and writing', Mum had said. 'Get good job somewhere. Not like me.'

School was boring. She had hated it. Too much sitting down—hours and hours of it. Teachers never liked her either. Only liked the smart ones that did everything right. Only time she got a nice look was basketball practice and that was because she was big and strong and she could stop the goalies from getting the ball. Running was all right. Once she got a prize for running. No good job but, when she left school. Same job as Mum only not so good people. Soon got out of that place. Three different jobs now and the last one the best. Should have stayed with those people but her and Betty saved up a bit of money and the two of them had gone off to the nearest town for a bit of a holiday. Had some fun too, the both of them. No harm in that. Might as well have a bit before—the fear hit her again suddenly. What was going to happen to her? Why wasn't Mum here? If Mum was here she'd know what to do. And she'd tell these people to go away and stop their questions and after, she and Mum could go back to the station together where Hannah's mother worked and Hannah would stay there too.

'How old is she?' the magistrate had asked. Impatiently! Frowning! After all, it was a holiday weekend.

'Can't get a thing out of her', the sergeant had answered, shrugging. 'Frightened, I suppose.'

The magistrate's humour was as heavy as his frowning brows. 'Thinks we might use it in evidence against her.'

'Maybe she doesn't know.'

'She doesn't look very old.' Hard blue eyes appraised Hannah as she stood there in the dock, overweight, slommicky in her shapeless dress, her sullen face scarcely emerged from child-hood. 'Not much more than twelve or so.'

'Think she'd be a bit more than that, sir.'

'Shouldn't be in gaol anyway. Isn't there some other place I can send her?'

'I tried the convent. They're full up—not a room to spare.'

'That woman up on the hill—what's her name?'

'Mrs Gentle? Tried her too. All her folks down for the Show this weekend.'

'We'll have to think of something.'

'Nobody in the women's quarters sir, not yet anyway. She'd at least have the place to herself.'

The magistrate, not a bad chap if only it had not been a holiday weekend, snorted. 'You really think that's a good idea—for this child to spend the time in gaol—alone.'

The sergeant did not speak.

'You mean to tell me that in this whole town there isn't a soul who'd take this child. In custody, of course.'

The sergeant stayed stolidly silent, his gaze polite. The frown grew darker. 'All right then. Over in the women's quarters for the weekend. After that we'll have to see what we can do about her.' The magistrate, with a further exasperated look at Hannah, went off to his holiday weekend. The sergeant led Hannah off to hers.

The Department peope had another go at finding out just why Hannah was a neglected child.

She was fourteen and she was pregnant, but Hannah was not going to tell anybody that. Let them find out for them-selves.

A different someone came to see her. It was not a police officer and it was not someone from the Department. Hannah's tears rolled again when she felt her hair pushed gently back from her hot sweaty face. But no, it wasn't Mum. Just a woman. She talked nice but. Not impatient or quick. Nothing to be fright-ened of anyway. Smoked too. Looked a bit surprised when Hannah asked her for one but handed over the packet and lit up for her. That was better. Hannah sat up to enjoy her smoke.

Tilted her head and watched the smoke float in the shaft of light from the doorway. Good, that was.

The woman had a game. Hannah had never seen such a game. First the woman made a word then it was her turn and she made one. They scored and sometimes she beat the woman. When the woman left she gave Hannah the rest of the cigarettes to smoke.

Hannah had two and a half days to spend in the gaol before the weekend was over. The nights were terrible, long and lonely and full of dark creeping shadows but the days were bearable because she and the woman played The Game and there were always the cigarettes. She and the woman took the grey blankets off the bed and spread them on the cement outside. For minutes at a time Hannah felt almost happy.

On the Tuesday the doctor came down to the gaol and examined Hannah and asked her some questions and found out what she herself had known for a long time. In another four or five months, the doctor said, her baby would be born. Another four or five months on to the other seemed like time without end to Hannah. The weight in her stomach became the actual weight of her frustration. A frenzy of impatience was succeeded by such heaviness of the heart as Hannah had never in her life known. As soon as they let her out she would go home. Would Mum say anything to her about the baby? Give her a beating maybe? Or would she just laugh? If she laughed everything would be all right and they would sit down and wait for the baby to come. To be home again! After this weekend in a gaol, to be home again with Mum. Hannah felt like crying with happiness and relief.

'Thought she was a bit older than twelve', the sergeant said. 'Not that I haven't seen some even at twelve, poor little devils.'

The magistrate had another good long look at her and Hannah felt her belly grow hot. This was the man who had stuck her in gaol for nothing. She hated and despised him but better not be cheeky or he might do something even worse. While the magistrate coughed and cleared his throat Hannah looked steadfastly at her feet and kept her hate to herself.

'Everything fixed now?' he asked the sergeant.

'She'll be okay.' The sergeant said to Hannah, 'You'll be okay now.'

Someone from the Department came and had a talk with her. She wasn't going home right away. The Department man had spoken with her mother over the telephone and they had both agreed that Hannah had better wait at this place down south until she was ready to have the baby. Had she made up her mind yet what she wanted done about her baby?

'Done?' Hannah looked fully at the Department man, lip jutting. The question had halted the wave of sorrow that had risen inside her. What DID girls do with babies? 'Givim ta mum I spose. Mum look after im.' Had she thought of adoption—giving up the baby for adoption? She was very young for the responsibility of a baby. He and Mum had discussed adoption and Mum had thought that might be the best thing.

Hannah shrugged. But she felt happier suddenly. It was as if Mum had reached with love and care from all those miles away. She knew Hannah was in trouble and she knew what to do about it.

'I like go home now but', Hannah said, mainly into her chest. 'Before, I help Mum round house. Mum got lotta work. She like me help her.'

At this place down south, she could go to school and learn a bit more while she was waiting. It was a very nice place. Hannah would like it. And she would find folk there that she knew. Quite a lot of the boys and girls had come from her own district.

Hannah did not care about that. Again there came the frightening feeling of helplessness, of being caught. She did not properly know how she had stepped on to this new path, nor where it would take her. Would she ever get safely back to Mum?

All that she had to do, the Department man reassured, was to go down there and wait until she had had her baby, then she could go home, back to the station and Mum. He did not seem to understand how scarey was the thought of having it without Mum there. Hannah wanted to fight but there was only this quiet man who was no stronger than the sergeant had been.

Behind them, Hannah sensed forces much stronger than either of them. Forces too big for a fourteen-year-old girl to shift. Her last thought was that she would run away from this place they were taking her to. Somehow get back to the station. Mum might be worried then but, her doing two bad things. Might be she would just have to go—and stay.

It was a training centre, the place down south. Hannah had spent more than a month there now. It was all right. The food was all right. She didn't like those other kids much. She might have, if they had liked her, but they didn't. At night in her bed she cried because she wanted Mum. The kids teased her because she was fat and having a baby. She felt different from them because of the baby. Sometimes she even felt superior. They didn't know as much as they thought they did, those girls. On the verge sometimes of telling them a few of the things she and her girlfriend had done she always hesitated. Had she been clever, or just stupid? It was stupid not to be able to play basketball. Basketball was a good game. She had been a good goal keep.

Mum wrote sometimes. The woman with the Scrabble wrote too. One day a new Scrabble game had arrived for Hannah. A gift from her friend, the Woman. Hannah had proudly shown some of the girls how to play. They had all wanted to play but Hannah was boss because it was her game and she had picked out only those of the girls who had been a little bit nice to her. Nothing was fair in this world though. Before the day was out a half-dozen of the girls knew how to play the game better than she did. Back where she started, with the exception that it was still up to her to lend her Scrabble. It was hers, wasn't it? She hid the box under the mattress. If they were all so smart they could find their own Scrabble game to play.

The boss of this place had had a talk with her. He had repeated what the other bloke had told her. Stay here until the baby came, have the baby adopted, then go home to Mum. She could forget everything. She wouldn't even see the baby. She could go back to being what she had been before—a kid having fun.

29

'I wish I had some fun now', Hannah said sadly. 'Them others don't like me.'

They made her feel different because she wasn't in a proper class and didn't have to attend at school unless she felt like it. Hannah showed them she could write as well as they could. Read, too. But they still laughed at her. Hannah knew it was her stomach and she hated her belly that would not sit down but kept always growing bigger and bigger.

It grew so hard and big she had to walk leaning back to balance it. If waiting had been weary though, much worse was to follow. Hannah had had no idea there was such wracking pain. She was shocked and humiliated. If the people about her could allow this to happen to her it showed they didn't care if she lived or died. While she howled with agony they stood and watched her. The pain proved finally that Hannah was nothing and that nobody cared. Mum might have, if she had been there. Mum! Another thing Hannah had not known about when she was having fun was the tears. She had shed so many in these last months. She did not see the baby. She saw other people's babies and liked them but she did not see her son. She did not even know where he had gone and she didn't like to ask. This was the way they had told her it would be.

But at least the baby was over. Eagerly now she waited the promised reward. Mum, up on the station! She was going home to Mum at last. The end of this terrible world and the beginning of another beautiful one.

The Woman wrote: 'Why don't you go back to the Training Centre, Hannah, and stay there for a year or so? You could learn to make pretty dresses, or take a Commercial course and become a typist. Wouldn't you like that? And you could play games again now the baby's over—you could join in with the others.'

Even the Woman didn't understand. Hannah gushed with hatred and fright. She felt the forces closing about her again and knew she had to do something, quick, to stop them. She wrote a letter. But though she addressed it to the Woman it was really to Everyone—to all of those who had taken her and made her do things. A thrill of fear warned her to be polite, not cheeky, but

the most important thing was to make Everyone understand.
She wrote:

Dear Missus, I got you most welcome letter today. I thought
that I would have my baby on the 14th but I had it on the 9th
of this month, it was a little boy and also very fat, it wade 8 lbs.
6 ozs. I was very glad you hear some news for you and your
family. I don't like the way you told me to stay at the training
place for one more year, because it is going to be a long time
away from seeing mum, I don't get lonely when I am out in
the station with mum and I won't be silly to ask her to pay a
fair to where ever I wont to go, and also she is not well, she
might look well but she is not, I know what the matter with
her she told me all about her sickness when we were in Three
Springs, if she get sick out on the station who will look after
her nobody, she will afto maneg herself, that why I wont to
go up to her, nobody will care for her if her get sick nobody
but only my brothers and sisters will care for her nobody will
care fore her if she get sick nobody nobody she will be way up
in the station and I will be stuck at the training place for all of
my life, I can't go to see her at all. Do you no what I like you
do to myself missus, killing myself because I am put here just
like I got no feeling for my mother, why don't that man try
and let me go up to Mum they got a constant job up their I
would like to go up their I would like to up to them. It was
very hot down here I know how it is up that way how hot it
is. I will promise I won't get in the state again to go through
all the pains, the boys can go to hell for my liking. I am
closing now write backe please, missus. Give my love to your
little family my very best love God–Bless you all for now
Goodbye,

> From Your Sincerely
> Hannah

Three Happy Japanese

Helen W. Asher

*T*HREE happy Japanese came to a brothel and it was like a scene from an *Ozu* film. Or almost. We didn't have the dubbing. The three little Japanese smiled perpetually and chattered incessantly, with guttural sounds popping and curdling like chewing gum noises. It seemed—and since reality was subdued—it must almost have been to them as if they had come to a geisha house after having consumed enough *sake* somewhere else.

The girls joined in their giggles. It was all so pleasant, and their wantonness contagious. The foreign language was discarded as soon as each of the doors closed behind them.

The girls, by all means, could be compared to geishas if appearance was ignored, which was not hard to do at all.

Melissa's Japanese, in the happiest of moods, kept humming and giggling and talking Japanese to himself to stay awake and retain his elevated state. Melissa was delighted. He was extremely cute. A pearl he was, amongst the rough-edged rubble.

Nothing can ever be perfect for longer than seconds. In the relaxing, soft-lighted atmosphere his vigour left the happy Japanese when it should have poured out of him like an artesian well. He began to giggle again, and though not heavy he lay upon her like a stone, puffing into her ear so that it tickled.

'My goodness', she said, 'you are drunk, aren't you?' And since shuffling about made no impact she began to direct him, pumping her arm and ordering him around in the ever-so-effective tone of voice of a petty officer. 'Up', she said.

He obeyed.

'That's a good boy', she praised him. 'And now down. Up and down and up and down—that's the boy. Now now, don't fall asleep again, not on top of me.'

He giggled. She just *had* to giggle along with him. 'Up you go—and down again.'

He was so funny. Eventually he stopped giggling, as laughing doesn't help, and this is a serious matter, to be executed in a rather solemn frame of mind for its successful completion.

He completed. Then he giggled again and fumbled himself back into his stone-grey business suit, talking Japanese to himself and garbled English to her.

'You are cute', she said. He nodded. Even his nod was cute.

She asked him where he came from and what he was doing in Sydney, but he was not much good to have a conversation with.

He met with his friends again in the corridor, which had roses strewn all over the wallpaper. One wanted a shower, then decided to have it at the hotel. They left the house of happiness, talking rapidly, churning up guttural sounds like frothy air bubbles.

Perhaps they talked about business all the time? Or did they compare this place to a genuine geisha house? Who knows?

Fifty-Eight Cents

Jennifer Paynter

GWEN Searle had been a tea lady in the Fine Arts Department for fourteen years and some of the staff still forgot her name. They called her Glad or Grace. 'Sometimes I'd like to murder the lot of them', she told her niece. 'Sometimes I wonder what my life is worth.' Her niece said, 'They're a bunch of wankers. Why don't you poison them? Put cyanide in their tea.'

Gwen liked some of the Fine Arts staff better than others. She had favourites. Professor Silk was a favourite. He was tiny with chapped cheeks and hair like a dandelion seedhead. He had four fork prong marks on the end of his nose. When he was a baby his sister had tried to mash his face, he told her. He wore cravats and turned up his shirt collars as if he were about to walk into a head-wind. She put aside Monte Carlos for him in a special jar, *Professor Silk's Assortment*. 'Our little secret, Gwenny', he said. '*O noctes cenaeque deum!*'

Dr Margot Tripp was another favourite. Gwen loved to watch her. 'She flies,' she told her niece, 'and life is an adventure.' When Dr Margot Tripp was a young girl she must have had long hair, Gwen thought, long fair hair flying and a lovely little smile peeping out. And people must have loved her, men. She would have collected men with her smile peeping out, flying, and the men would have flown with her, riding on her hair, hanging to the hem of her petticoat. When Dr Margot Tripp flew into the Fine Arts common room, Gwen dropped everything. Two or three men usually touched down with her,

VIPs. 'Coffee for me, Gwen, and Roger takes his black. Keith?' And they would taxi off, carrying their cups, and sometimes more men would orbit and be airborne, 'Gordon. Russel. Good to see you. You know Roger. Keith?' Oh it was lovely, Gwen thought. 'Margot Tripp is a fascist dickhead', said her niece.

But she did not like Professor Truscott. It was his eyes. They turned round the corners of his head like Holden Commodore headlights, big blue blowfly eyes. And he never talked to her. He never said good morning. When he came into the common room everyone stopped talking, and he never flew with Dr Margot Tripp; he sat down and pulled her back to earth and talked about cricket and looked at the typists' legs. 'I'd like to smear a cockroach with Vaseline and shove it up his bum', she told her niece. Her niece said, 'Why bother with the Vaseline?' One morning she had got to work late and the typists had made the tea. Professor Truscott was talking; he hadn't known she was there. 'I could make a better cup of tea than Gwen', she heard him say. 'Any day.' She decided to write him an anonymous letter. 'You are just a wanker', she wrote. 'You think you know so much but you don't.' She had changed her mind after she had written it, but her niece had grabbed it and posted it. For a week she had been very frightened. 'He'll know it was me. I'll get the sack.' She trembled when he walked into the common room. 'What'll I say if he asks if it was me?' She asked him, 'Would you like an Iced Vo Vo, Professor Truscott, sir?' Her voice had cracked, offering him the biscuit plate. She dared not look at him and when she had looked up, he was gone; he was sitting at the coffee table drinking his tea. 'He didn't hear you, love', said one of the typists.

'What's your life worth, Gwen Searle?' said Peter Mooyaart one Friday afternoon. Peter Mooyaart guarded the Fine Arts building and carried heavy things for the staff. He had just carried a carton of crockery for her up to the common room.

'Peanuts', said Gwen. She was still worried about Professor Truscott.

'Fifty-eight cents', said Peter Mooyaart. 'That's what it costs to buy a bullet, 58 cents.'

35

'If we survive the bomb', said Gwen, 'and have to start from scratch again, that'll be the real test. No books or films or anything arty, just common sense.'

She filled the urn and lit up a Winfield. Peter Mooyaart hitched his khaki shorts and sat on her kitchen bench-top. He patted his gun holster. She could see he wanted to talk about Vietnam. He had taught men how to kill with their bare hands in Vietnam.

'This lot would've been completely useless in Vietnam', said Mooyaart. 'Imagine Silk on a Search and Destroy.' Mooyaart still wore his dog tags, his identity discs. 'When you're dead, they take these off you. They pop one in your mouth and take the other back for the records. Once I found this helmet with just a bit of brain in it. Everything else was burnt up. Imagine Truscott piloting a chopper.'

'They don't have any common sense', said Gwen.

'They worry about everything', said Mooyaart. 'They worry about their bloody health. That Joshua Meek, he worries that the ceilings are asbestos. He worries that the fluorescent bloody lights might hurt his little eyes. Pete, he says to me the other day. He calls me Pete. Pete, he says, should I wear a leather apron when I'm photocopying?'

'You wouldn't read about it would you', said Gwen.

'All they talk about is bloody food', said Mooyaart. 'Vanessa Badgery was photocopying this recipe yesterday. For an emu egg soufflé. You wouldn't catch me eating an emu egg soufflé, I told her. She gave me a dirty look. Emu eggs are protected, I said. That bloody shut her up.'

'Neil Fitt is writing a book about meals in the movies', said Gwen. 'He's calling it *I'll Never Be Hungry Again*. He's a lovely fellow, Neil Fitt.'

'Bloody fat Gwenny. Bloody unfit.' Mooyaart roared with laughter and slapped his khaki thigh, 'Neil Unfit'.

'I'd better get cracking, Petey, or I'll be out on my ear.' Gwen had half a mind to tell Mooyaart about her anonymous letter.

Mooyaart patted his holster again. 'Remember, Gwenny. Fifty-eight cents.'

'Let's get a lottery ticket and call it that, well', said Gwen.

After Mooyaart left, Gwen lit another Winfield and waited. She only set out ten cups on Friday afternoons and she didn't bother to arrange the biscuits in wheel-spokes. Hardly anyone came in on Friday afternoons. She switched the urn to medium and started singing 'When They Sound the Last All Clear'. Suddenly the common room door swung open and the staff, all 23 of them, walked in and began queuing for their tea. They had been in a meeting. Gwen raced to the cupboard for thirteen more cups. She would have to water the milk. Professor Truscott was at the head of the queue. She felt him watching her and her hands shook. He thinks I'm too old, she thought, he thinks I'm past it. Professor Silk had slunk into her kitchen, looking for his jar of Monte Carlos. 'Here you are. Take it.' She had never been rude to him before. 'The urn seems to be boiling over', said Dr Margot Tripp. 'Would you like me to turn it off for you?' 'Yes. No. I don't know', said Gwen. She had slopped some milk and now she wouldn't have enough for all of them. Professor Truscott was inspecting the rim of his cup. 'Lipstick', he said and smiled, holding it up for her to see, for everyone to see. 'Whose cigarette is this, for God's sake?' Vanessa Badgery was stubbing out Gwen's Winfield. 'Do you *have* to smoke in here, Grace?' Gwen had begun to breathe very fast. Fifty-eight cents, she thought, multiplied by 23.

She told her niece about it later. Her niece worked at the CSIRO and always wore overalls. She bracketed her hair with pink plastic buttercups, one on either side of her small-featured furious face. Gwen was afraid of her and told her everything. Her niece began to talk about cyanide again but afterwards Gwen had a good laugh about it. Thank goodness I haven't lost my sense of humour, she thought.

But on Monday morning one of the lecturers, Stephen Jefferson, came up to her in his safari suit and sandals and said, 'Why does Silk have this oh-so-secret cache of cream biscuits, Glad? It is most unfair and I intend writing a memorandum to the administrative assistant.' Wanker, thought Gwen and lit up a Winfield. She couldn't be bothered wheel-spoking the biscuits. Nobody noticed or cared. What's my life worth? she thought.

Jennifer Paynter

When she came back from flushing the tea-leaves down the lav, Truscott was talking to Stephen Jefferson. 'The typists could easily do it', he was saying. 'They just sit round all day reading *New Idea*.'

'I'm going to be retrenched', thought Gwen. 'I'm going to be rationalised.'

'Gwenny!' It was Professor Silk. She had been weeping into the washing–up water and he had come up behind her. 'No more biccies, Gwenny. No more Monte Carlos. It was naughty of you to spoil me and I can't allow it to continue. *Consummatum est.*'

Her niece danced with rage when Gwen told her. 'I'll get some cyanide tomorrow and you must mix it with their milk.' Gwen sat down to write a list of the people she would spare. She would spare the typists and Peter Mooyaart and Neil Fitt. She wept, writing it, and added more names: Dr Margot Tripp, Joshua Meek, Vanessa Badgery and then Silk and finally even Stephen Jefferson and Truscott. She would spare them all. Her niece heard her crying and pounced on the list. 'It's my hit list', Gwen told her. She would have to go through with it now.

On Tuesday Gwen brought in two Christmas cakes and cut each one into twelve pieces. She would let Neil Fitt have two pieces. 'Poor things', she thought. 'Their last Christmas cake.'

That night she quarrelled with her niece about sparing the typists. 'I can't poison them. They're lovely girls. If you don't let me spare them, I won't do it at all.' Her niece had grabbed a bible then and made her swear on it but Gwen kept her fingers crossed behind her back. She had worked out how she was going to do it. She would mix up the cyanide milk in the jug with the university crest and put aside some good milk for the typists in the green glass jug. She wasn't sure yet whether she would drink the cyanide milk herself. Life with her niece wasn't worth living. She decided to make them some mince pies. 'It's the least I can do', she thought.

On Wednesday morning she dressed carefully. She put on her good underwear and her cerise suit with the scalloped lapels.

She wanted to look her best. Her niece was going to drive her to work, right into the university grounds. Gwen was beginning to feel excited. 'It'll be bigger than Bogle/Chandler', she thought. She put a photo of herself in her handbag. It had been taken in 1941 when she had sung and danced at the Tiv. 'For the newspapers', she told her niece.

When she walked into the common room, Peter Mooyaart was up a ladder, hanging Christmas decorations. 'You look bloody wonderful, Gwenny!' Gwen opened her handbag to take out the cyanide. She felt as if she were eighteen again. Outside, the cicadas were singing. Mooyaart tossed her a tinsel streamer, 'Wrap it round the teapot, love.' Gwen laughed and fastened it round her head instead. She sang 'I'm a little teapot, short and stout. This is my handle. This is my spout.' Mooyaart jumped off the ladder and capered on the coffee table. Gwen sang as she mixed the milk in the jug with the university crest. 'We've all got to go sometime', she thought.

After she had wheel-spoked the mince pies, she got out the photo of herself to show Mooyaart. 'Taken when I was young and gay, Petey.' Professor Truscott loomed over Mooyaart's shoulder. He had come up early for his tea. He took the photo, 'Is this you, Gwen?'

'Yes sir. Taken when I was young and gay.'

'Did you wear stockings during the war', said Truscott, 'or did you paint your legs?'

Dr Margot Tripp flew in, 'You were a fine-looking girl then, Gwen'. She touched the tinsel on Gwen's hair, 'Very festive'. Professor Silk crept up behind her. He was holding a box of Red Tulip liqueurs. 'To make up for all the trouble I've caused you, Gwenny. *Mea culpa.*'

Gwen started to cry. The typists had arrived, and Neil Fitt, and after them Vanessa Badgery and Stephen Jefferson and little Joshua Meek. They were all waiting for their tea. I can't do it, she thought, I just can't do it. The tinsel had fallen over her left eye and Professor Truscott reached out and adjusted it. She seized the green glass jug. She would tell her niece to go to hell. Vanessa Badgery helped herself to a mince pie. 'God bless us, every one', said Joshua Meek. 'Amen', said Gwen.

When she was coming back from flushing the tea-leaves down the lav, she saw her niece in the corridor. 'Well?' said her niece. 'Well what?' said Gwen. Her niece hadn't gone to the CSIRO; she had gone to the markets instead and bought a whole lot of roses. Now she was tearing them up, 'For strewing.' Gwen said, 'Go to hell. They're not dead. I changed my mind.' Her niece kept on tearing and said, 'I knew you'd chicken out so I didn't give you cyanide, I gave you glucose, but I put cyanide in the mince pies and they're dead all right. Take a look.'

Gwen raced to the common room. Dr Margot Tripp had crash-landed by the door. Two or three VIPs were spreadeagled beside her. Peter Mooyaart hung head-down from the ladder, his face red as a pay-phone. The others were dead in their chairs. Professor Silk still held a fragment of mince pie in his little lifeless hand. Gwen knelt on the floor and keened. Already her niece had started strewing and singing, 'Where have all the wankers gone? Long time passing.'

Peter Mooyaart's revolver had fallen onto the common room floor. Gwen stared at it through a flurry of rose petals. 'When will they ever learn?' her niece sang, strewing. 'When will they ever learn?'

There was only one bullet in the revolver. Gwen let her niece have it right between the pink plastic buttercups.

Coral Dance

Glenda Adams

*T*HE Captain was infatuated with Donna Bird from her first day on board. He had tried to have the bright overhead light moved for her although he made no effort to have the schedule of stuffed green peppers changed for Lark, who could never eat the sodden khaki lumps. Donna Bird made the Captain forget he believed that women on board brought bad luck.

Like all things on the *Avis Maris*, the overhead light was firmly anchored to its fixture, and it had to stay where it was. And Donna Bird had to continue wearing her sun visor to dinner. She insisted she was allergic to all light, natural and artificial.

One night, soon after they had left Samoa, they came in to dinner to find the Captain on a chair tying some kind of paper shade over the ceiling light.

'We all want to see your pretty faces as much as possible', he said, looking down at Donna and Lark, but clearly addressing Donna.

'Oh, you shouldn't, you're so kind?' Donna whispered in that murmuring voice of hers that turned every statement into a question.

Then Mr Fischer, the first mate and engineer, who had not forgotten that women on board tended to bring bad luck, told the Captain that the paper shade was a fire hazard. The Captain, happily entranced, was losing his nautical judgement.

'I'm so sorry?' Donna whispered. 'I'm so sorry to be so

allergic? Please don't bother on my account?' In order to hear her the men had to place their ears close to her mouth, nodding and answering, 'Yes, yes,' to her questions. She spoke beseechingly, submissively, commanding a response. 'Please don't bother on my account?' murmured Donna, while the Captain fiddled with the paper shade.

'Of course we bother, yes, yes, *nicht*?' said the Captain.

'*Ja, ja*, naturally', said Mr Blut, the second mate.

When Lark had first seen Donna Bird creeping up the gangplank she had disliked her, in her grey slacks, grey socks with silver threads, brown leather sandals, a grey turtle-neck sweater, sunglasses, long gold earrings and straw sun visor. Donna had also been wearing one of her scarves, the brown and grey imitation snakeskin chiffon, wrapped around her thin neck and hanging limply. She could have looked interesting, even stylish, but the effect was contrived, peculiar. She braided her wiry red hair in original ways, and kept touching it as she spoke, fingering it, tossing it around and stroking it, looking at it in the glass of the bookcase or the portholes. Sometimes she let her hair loose so that it formed a rough cloud around her head.

Lark had boarded first and had been delighted to learn that there would be another passenger on the little freighter for the 21 days at sea, someone besides the three German officers. And then Donna Bird had crept on board, and Lark had stepped forward and shaken her hand.

At lunch that first day, as they were pulling away from the coast and passing through the coral reefs heading into the Pacific, Donna, in her visor and sunglasses and her contrived dull grey outfit, said to the German officers, '*Zauber*', and then, '*Zauberei*'. She carried a fan decorated with a woman's face, which she used both to keep cool and to protect her face from the sun.

The Captain guffawed. 'Good, good. You know German. *Zauberflöte*, one of our best operas.' Then he turned to Lark sitting there stonily and said, 'Magic, Magic Flute.'

'It's funny what one picks up?' said Donna. 'One is absorbing, picking things up, information, all the time. These things

42

surface and are very useful much, much later, I assure you?'
'And she will teach us English on this voyage?' said Mr Blut.

The twenty or so sailors who slept and worked below were rarely evident. Occasionally they could be seen checking the ropes around the cargo of aluminium rods stacked on the deck and swabbing the parts of the deck that were not covered by the rods. Occasionally Lark saw mice, which she had to admit were probably rats, nipping in and out of the rods.

Lark went to the bridge and watched the Captain and the two officers doing their navigating. The Captain was charting the rest of the voyage, to Tacoma then through the Panama Canal to New York. They had sailed due east from Australia, clearing the Great Barrier Reef and other coastal formations, then northeast to Samoa. The Captain was checking the readings. He took a ruler, Lark saw him do this, and ruled a line straight up through the Pacific, past hundreds of little islands, across the equator, passing south of Hawaii, to Puget Sound.

'Once we owned most of this', he said.

They had no scheduled stop until Tacoma.

'Garibaldi was wrecked in the Bass Strait.' It was the dreaded Donna, who had crept up behind them and was watching the charting procedure. She put her finger on the path of water between the Australian mainland and Tasmania. 'And a boatload of lambs headed for the Middle East went up in flames there, too', she said. '*Quel* barbecue.'

The Captain had taken out a length of rope and was tying the wheel into a fixed position. For the next three weeks they were to sail along that ruled line, the wheel tied into position, with no helmsman holding it steady, just an officer checking the bearings now and then, or a sailor standing nearby.

There were coral reefs at various spots on the chart. They showed light brown in the light blue of the water. The reefs brought forth from Donna anecdotes about coral.

'There is a poisonous coral, pinkish, that has a fatal sting?' she contributed. 'If you step on it, there's no hope?'

The Captain said that later on, out in the Pacific, he was going to stop the ship, if they made good time, so that Lark and

Donna could walk on one of the reefs and observe the coral and reef life closely.

Donna clapped her hands. 'Standing in the middle of the ocean? Like walking on water?'

'Are you allowed to do that?' asked Lark. It seemed highly out of order for a freighter to come to a halt in the middle of an ocean for such a frivolous undertaking, and she was scornful once again of the Captain. 'I'm not walking on any coral', she said.

'We will go faster than we expect', the Captain said. He gave a tolerant smile. 'It is an opportunity to test equipment and for passengers to enjoy. Like on the Kew-Ee-Two, ha, ha.'

'Queen Elizabeth the Second', Donna explained.

'I know that', said Lark.

Then to the Captain Donna said, 'Please don't bother about stopping the ship on my account? It's too much trouble?'

'Of course we bother', said the Captain. 'Is it not boring on this ship for beautiful ladies? You will walk on coral.'

'We'll need sneakers?' Donna stated.

'I'm not walking on coral', said Lark.

'Mine are pink', Donna went on. 'In fact, I bought them especially for reef walking. On the Great Barrier Reef. Once I was there', she put her hand to her lips and lowered her voice, 'on holiday?' And she told the intricate story of paying twelve dollars for a pair of sneakers and of choosing pink, rather than turquoise or yellow.

As Donna told her tedious story she was watching the Captain, bent over his charts searching for a reef for the coral walk.

'Ha, ha', he said, and marked a spot.

'That's in the middle of nothing', said Lark. 'There's no land. I'm not walking on any coral.'

'I'll show them to you', said Donna, and she ran or rather sidled out to get her pink sneakers and bring them back, holding up their soles and pointing to the cuts and lacerations made by the coral. 'As you can see, the damage wasn't too great. I still wear them. But you can see what coral could do to your feet. Like glass?'

At dinner the Captain started on his jokes, beginning with, 'Why does the Statue of Liberty on Liberty Island stand?' and answering it himself, 'Because she cannot sit down'.

'They tried to blow it up once, not so long ago', said Donna. 'They were bringing the explosives down from Canada?' She was wearing her formal grey and beige, a long skirt and a blouse, unbuttoned for evening, with her straw sun visor plus earrings and a brooch of little grapes pinned to the side of the visor. And there was the fan, which she waved back and forth, queen of the *Avis Maris*.

'Our lady passengers will now give English lessons, ha', yelled the Captain. Donna's inaudible voice seemed to make everyone else shout.

The fan paused in its scan across Donna Bird's face. 'Yes? Certainly, yes.'

'Where the queens of England are crowned?' asked Mr Blut, pronouncing it crown-ed, two syllables, as if he were reciting a sonnet, and he looked at Donna, a big smile on his face, pleased with his offering. 'In the head', he answered.

Donna smiled.

'*Kopf, Kopf*', he explained to the unsmiling Mr Fischer, tapping his own head. '*Kopf*, ha.'

'On the head? On, on the head?' Donna suggested.

'On on on the head', sang Mr Blut.

'So', said the Captain, turning to Donna, not to be outdone. 'I remember at the opera once, and Brünnhilde sings to Wotan. She must sing, "*weiche, Wotan, weiche*", which in English means', and he searched for the word.

'Surrender', Donna said, nodding encouragement. 'Surrender, Wotan, surrender.'

'This clever lady knows so much', said the Captain, shaking his head. 'Surrender. And also it means "soft" in German. So, before Brünnhilde takes her big breath to sing "*weiche, Wotan, weiche*", whispers Wotan to her, *sotto voce*, so that only Brünnhilde hears, "How do you like your boiled eggs in the morning?" and she must sing loud, for all to hear, "soft, Wotan, soft," without laughing. You understand?'

Lark thought he looked like a soft-boiled egg himself, that

45

Captain, with his smooth round head, wider and pudgier at the cheekbones than at the forehead and chin, and a smile that was a perfect arc, painted on by a child.

Donna laughed a little. She had got the Captain's joke. Then she started with her own story. 'I love practical jokes. But they can be so dangerous. Sometimes you can get killed with a joke, just laughing, against your will?' The Captain looked hurt, and Donna placed her hand on his arm.

The three men were leaning forward and staring at her lips, following her.

'Killed, laughing? How so?' asked Mr Blut, making little haiku fragments.

Dessert, a coconut thing, had been placed before them. Donna took a deep breath. 'Man killed by lamington', she said, observing the coconut-covered cake.

'Yes, yes, yes.' The men were eager for their lesson.

'A lamington is an Australian cake, sponge cake, cut into little cubes, and each cube is rolled in chocolate icing and then coconut. Lam-ing-ton.'

'Such lamington killed?' prompted Mr Blut.

'It was meant to be a wonderful joke', said Donna. 'The jokers at this party had covered a piece of sponge rubber with chocolate and coconut and given it to the guest of honour. He ate it, tried to, and it stuck in his throat. He was dead in a matter of minutes. It plugged his throat?'

'Stuck dead, plug throat?' said Mr Blut.

'I think he is going to make us do it,' said Donna.

'I'm not going coral walking,' said Lark. 'He can't be serious.'

Donna looked down at Lark's feet. 'Of course you, Lark, will be less vulnerable than I, with those feet and that skin.'

Donna had spent the days inside, away from the sunlight, usually in her cabin or in the dining-room, which became a library and lounge-room between meals, where she sat, pale and soft.

Lark, keeping her distance, had gone around the ship bare-footed. The soles of her feet were becoming rough and hard, her skin was turning brown and tough, her hair blonder and coarser.

'Walking on coral must surely be against the law of the sea,' said Lark.

Donna tucked her arm into Lark's. 'If you don't go, I won't go.'

The *Avis Maris* came to a stop. The shuddering of the engines, then the absolute silence frightened Lark. This was so stupid.

'I can't see any coral reef,' she said.

'It is good to test equipment, and we make very good time so far.' The Captain was rubbing his hands together as he ordered one of the boats to be uncovered and the winches started up. 'Go now', he said to Donna. 'Get in the *boot*.'

He put his arm around Donna's shoulder and started to lead her to the boat. His grip was firm. Donna, her hat crammed low on her forehead, her scarf muffling the lower half of her face and her khaki trousers rolled up with the lolly-pink sneakers at the ends of her white legs, held on to Lark's arm. And the three of them stumbled across the deck, as if they were chained together.

'You'll get burnt?' said Donna, looking at Lark who was wearing shorts and suntop and espadrilles, with no hat or shirt, and she took off one of her several layers, a T-shirt she was wearing under her long-sleeved sweatshirt, and made Lark put it on.

'You're all mad', said Lark. She still believed the Captain was joking.

Half a dozen crew members were standing beside the un-covered lifeboat and helped the two women in.

'Don't push me', Lark yelled, refusing to climb up.

The men lifted her off the deck and placed her in the boat. Donna got in on her own. The men climbed in after them. Then Mr Fischer got in, carrying two large glass salad bowls. The boat was lowered down the side of the ship, something Lark had seen only in the movies, in an emergency, as when the Titanic hit the iceberg. The boat hit the water, the sailors started pulling away from the ship, Mr Fischer sat in the bow giving orders. The sailors were silent, no joking among themselves. But as they rowed they studied these two women sitting in the stern facing them, the two passengers they knew were on board yet rarely saw, just the glimpse of a scarf here and there, or a bare brown leg disappearing up a ladder.

'But why did he make us do this?' Lark asked Donna. 'Men are so stupid.'

Donna laughed. 'We shall learn something new, perhaps?'

'That foolish man is in love with you. The whole thing is the centrepiece of this voyage.'

Mr Fischer ordered the men to stop rowing. They were now a mile or so from the ship.

'Get out now', he said.

'There's nothing here', shrieked Lark. 'We're in the middle of the ocean.'

'Now you get out', said Mr Fischer, pointing over the side. 'Out get. Legs up, over, so', and he demonstrated how they were to swing their legs over the edge of the boat.

'Don't do it', said Lark.

But Donna, having peered over the side of the boat, slipped off her trousers, under which she wore a bathing suit, and swung her legs over, twisting her body and lowering herself into the water.

The ship seemed far off. The ocean surrounded them—there was no land, no break in the ocean surface—and there Donna stood, up to her armpits in water, next to the boat, still holding on with one hand.

'This is wonderful, Lark. You'll never get a chance like this again.'

Donna let go of the boat and started to wade away from it, her body slowly emerging, until the water was at her waist then, about 17 metres away, at her knees. 'It's wonderful.'

Lark was holding on to her seat in the stern of the lifeboat. Then, knowing she should not panic and scream and lose control, she squinted at the sea taking it all in, turning her head 180 degrees from the ship behind them scanning the water until her eyes found Donna, standing knee-deep in water, and continuing to scan the full circle, a further 180 degrees back to the ship floating in the deep. Where Donna stood the sea was slightly choppy, with little points of miniature waves, little disturbances, different from the broader swells behind them. This subtle change in the texture of the sea marked the reef. As she peered at the water at Donna's knees and tried to see through it, she discerned the brownish surface of the coral and the white of Donna's legs.

'Now you go', said Mr Fischer. He signalled one of the sailors to help Lark over the side.

Donna was frolicking now, jumping up and down.

'I'm not going.' Lark was shrieking again. She pushed at the sailor who was trying to get her legs over the side of the boat.

'*Komm, komm*', he said, encouraging her.

'This is an adventure', Donna called. 'Once-in-a-lifetime.' She was standing on one leg like a flamingo, one hand on her hip, one at her eyebrows, peering over the water. 'You must take whatever chance you can get to do something you would never do under normal circumstances.'

'Get away from me', said Lark, pushing the sailor so hard that he fell back onto the floor of the boat.

The tide was moving fast. Parts of the coral reef were beginning to be exposed and the water was almost down to Donna's ankles. She started to walk about, fossicking on the reef, bending down to examine the coral shapes and colours, and at one point she squatted right down and put her face into the water, then lifted it out again, laughing and brushing the water from her face.

Mr Fischer suddenly remembered the glass bowls. 'You take these', he said to Lark. He nodded at a second sailor, the first one having picked himself up, and the two, together, picked Lark up and lowered her over the side. She was yelling at them, kicking her legs. They almost threw her over. Then, when she saw she would not prevail, she stopped screaming and again concentrated on not panicking. She found her footing and clung to the edge of the boat.

'Take', said Mr Fischer, holding out the two glass bowls.

'Take them, Lark. We can view the coral better.' Donna had wrapped her scarf around her face again.

Lark found herself clasping two glass salad bowls to her chest with one arm, clutching at the bobbing life boat with the other, trying to find her footing in waist-deep water on the uneven coral. She would not let go of the boat. One of the sailors pried her fingers loose, causing her to lose her balance and stagger in the water.

'Don't drop the bowls', called Donna. 'Don't fall. You'll cut your legs on the coral. And I happen to know that coral cuts take weeks and weeks to heal. When I was little we were told that coral cuts and oyster cuts never healed, never, never?'

And again, Lark concentrated on not panicking and not losing balance. She did not want to cut herself, and she also remembered the treacherous pink poisonous type that Donna had mentioned.

The boat had now drifted off a little. Donna was beside her, taking the bowls and offering her hand, which Lark gladly took, allowing Donna to lead her to the exposed part of the reef.

'They're thugs', said Lark. 'Why are they doing this to us?'

Donna laughed. 'They think they are the QEII.' She had taken one of the bowls and walked off a little so that the water was up to her thighs. Lark followed her. Donna pressed the bowl into the water, just far enough for the water to come half way up the outside of the bowl. She bent over and peered into the bowl. 'Oh, Lark, you must do this. Now you can see the brilliant colours. And there are fish.' She was using the bowl as if it were a glass-bottomed boat. 'How thoughtful of the Captain to give us each one.'

Lark was standing transfixed. She had let her bowl go and it was floating off, bobbing away with the current. She was watching the lifeboat drifting and the ship in the distance. Then, as she watched, the men in the lifeboat lowered their oars and began rowing back toward the ship. And Lark stood in the middle of the Pacific Ocean and sobbed. Donna looked up from her bowl and saw that the boat had left them. She rested her hand on Lark's arm.

'They can't leave us here? They'll be back?' Lark cried.

Donna bent down to fossick at Lark's feet, picking up little bits of coral that had broken off. 'Here, Lark', she said, holding up a little branched piece, light coloured. 'Take this back? A souvenir?'

Lark was looking at the lifeboat growing smaller. Donna slipped the coral into the pocket of Lark's shorts. 'You've let your dish go. That's a pity. But come, you can look through mine. We'll share.'

She placed the bowl in Lark's hands and then made her hands place it in the water. 'Look into it, silly. You'll never see anything like this again.' She placed both her hands on either side of Lark's head and pushed it down, so that Lark was looking through the glass at the coral, which, under water, was as colourful as a garden of flowers.

'That pink coral is there', gasped Lark. 'That poisonous one.' She looked up, imploring, at Donna. 'What'll we do now?'

Donna took the bowl. 'Where is it?'

Lark pointed, and Donna guided the bowl close to herself and peered down. Then she burst out laughing. 'Oh, Lark, that's my sneaker. Look', and she wiggled her foot around under the bowl. Lark started to cry again, silently, the tears running down her cheeks and dropping into the ocean.

The lifeboat was back at the ship. The tide was nearly as low as it would go and would soon turn. Several hundred metres of the reef were exposed.

'We might as well sit and rest our legs while we can', said Donna, perching gingerly on the coral, her knees drawn up to her chin, sitting very still so that the coral would not cut through her bathing suit. She bent her body over her knees and lowered her swathed head, so that the sun struck no part of her.

'I wish I had a camera?' said Donna, her voice muffled by her scarf.

Lark stopped crying and subsided beside her. The tears were still wet on her cheeks, her eyes were fixed on the ship. 'They're going to leave us behind.'

'I'd reckon we have about two hours until the reef is covered and we can't stand any more?' said Donna. As she spoke, the water was lapping again at their toes and soon was covering their feet.

'Like those galloping tides in England?' said Donna chattily.

51

'The shore is so flat that the sea just rushes in at high tide, like a train. People are always drowning, trying to run away from it. You have to somehow not fight it, but go with it, go with whatever is pushing at you, in order to master it.'

They stood up and picked their way to what appeared to be the highest part of the reef. Donna had now let her glass bowl go and was leading Lark. Even at the highest point the water was at their ankles, rising steadily.

'It's hard to believe, isn't it, that this solid wall of coral is alive. It's not that the coral is built by living creatures. It is the living creature itself.' Donna stamped her foot in the water. 'We are actually standing on living creatures?'

The water was at their calves. It was getting more difficult to stand as the currents of the deepening water began to push at them.

The two women were standing thigh–deep in water. One was upright, in shorts and a T-shirt, no hat, her short hair close to her head, like a bathing cap. The sun struck her face, rendering it round, flat, almost the colour of her hair, without definition. The other was crouched over, her bathing suit just visible below her long-sleeved sweatshirt. Her sunhat and a long scarf, which anchored the hat and wrapped around her chin and neck, obscured her face. They stood braced, their arms outstretched for balance, their legs apart and vaguely outlined beneath the water. The horizon, dividing blue water from blue sky, crossed behind them. They looked into the distance, expectantly, urgently. As the water swelled and pressed against them they were forced to take little steps, first this way, then that, in unison, two women dancing on coral.

'Look!' cried Lark. 'They're lowering the lifeboat again.'

The boat hit the water, and the oars began to dip in and out. When the boat reached them the water was at their waists. It was Mr Blut who now sat in the bow. He brought the boat around so that its broadside was next to Lark and Donna, who both grabbed at it. Mr Blut lifted their fingers off.

'One first, the other then', he reprimanded.

The sailors hauled Lark in, then Donna. Both sat in the stern, shivering in the wind.

'Ha, ha', said the Captain with his Humpty Dumpty smile as they clambered onto the deck. 'You see coral, we check the *boot*. All is in good order.'

Lark stood for a moment, then walked up to him and kicked his shins and punched his chest. He took her wrists in one hand and held her at arm's length.

'You tried to kill us', she yelled.

His eyebrows went up, as he kept on smiling. 'It was a yoke, a practical yoke', he said, 'for crossing the equator'.

'Practical jokes can kill people', Lark yelled.

'But you must go in the water at the equator', the Captain laughed. 'It's tradition, and it is the time for yokes. Bad luck if no yoke.' He looked at each of them in turn. 'Two very clever ladies who know so much should know about the equator.'

Donna stood adjusting her scarf, pulling on her trousers. 'I love practical jokes', she murmured.

The Captain put his arm around Donna. 'Did I fright you?' he asked.

Lark flounced off to her cabin.

Lark stayed in her cabin for dinner, and for breakfast and lunch. She placed the piece of coral from her pocket on the ledge beside her bed and next to it her espadrilles with the rope soles that were now torn and ragged.

When she went in to dinner the next night, she wore high-heeled sandals and a long skirt. The others were already sitting at the table, laughing. It was stuffed peppers again.

'So sexy tonight?' the Captain said to Lark. 'Such fine shoes? I shall buy some for my lady friend when I am next in New York.' He winked at Donna.

Lark sat down without speaking.

'Lark, he is right about the equator and the tradition of playing practical jokes. That had completely slipped my mind as a possibility', said Donna. 'Such fun.'

Everyone laughed. 'Equator such fun', said Mr Blut. 'King Neptune is a kind one.'

'It was a good yoke', said the Captain.

'Joke?' said Donna. She paused. 'We've done something no

one else in the world has done. Thank you, Captain, so much?'

'And tomorrow', said the Captain, lifting his glass to Lark, 'we have no tomorrow, ha'.

Donna chuckled.

'Tomorrow we have no tomorrow', the Captain repeated.

And finally, when Lark refused to play his game and ask why, he said, 'Tomorrow it will be today again. We cross the dateline, and when we go east, we have the same day twice. We live a day longer. When we go west we lose a day in our life. Sad.'

'Better than losing your life in a day?' said Lark.

'A yoke, a yoke!' said the Captain. 'The afraid lady is yoking. She is better again.'

'Joke?' said Donna kindly, putting her hand on the Captain's sleeve. 'Please, jay, jay, joke.'

'Jay, jay, joke?' said the Captain.

And life on board returned to normal.

Brass on the Cannons

Robin Sheiner

*T*HEY were selling off the cannons. No one wanted them spoiling the nice lawn opposite where the three rocking-horses were in the park. Besides, trees were being planted, sugar gums in commemoration, and there was the war memorial, too, in the best position, on the point, casting its long shadow down the hill and out across the river, inscribed with the new lists of the dead. It was enough. The cannons were an eyesore. They had to go.

'Who'd want them?' they asked.

'Reffos. They're buying up all the scraps. Bits of iron: gates, wheels, any old junk. Should see their backyards. A disgrace.'

'Take a lump of dynamite to move the buggers. Whoever buys them's not all there.'

Below the park the river shone, polished silver. Standing on the hill it was possible to see for kilometres in all directions; the city buildings, decorated with plaster whirls and stucco, clustered on the left, and wherever you looked the silver river was edged with reeds, with birds sunning themselves on banks of sand. There was so much space and so much of the blue, unclouded sky it was difficult to know what the limits were.

'What am I offered?' the auctioneer called to the crowd assembled on the lawn.

My father and Uncle Solly counted up their shillings.

'A pound', Uncle Solly shouted, then became embarrassed, everyone looking his way as though he had a Star of David hung upon his back.

'A pound. I'm offered a pound. An insult on these fine cannons. Who'll offer me two? Condition of sale, buyer takes away the lot', the auctioneer shouted but no one else seemed to want the cannons until a man wearing a panama put up a finger. 'To decorate the porch', he told his lady friend, who sniggered.

Over at the rocking-horses children ran about while they waited for a turn. There were three sizes of horse: one small and dappled grey, one middle-sized and brown, and one very large and black which the big boys always fought to ride. 'Let's gallop across to the cannons and slice the dagos' heads off', one boy called, his arm raised for a bayonet charge. He rocked the black horse back and forth. A small girl, trying to keep up, fell off the dappled horse, and grazed her knees on the buffalo grass.

'Chaimy, you want the cannons or don't you want the cannons?' Uncle Solly asked. 'I'm telling you something. Brass is brass. It's not every day you get brass like that. We take the brass off the cannons and we sell it. We make our money sing.'

'Two pounds 10 shillings', my father called.

'I'm offered two a half', the auctioneer said, looking towards the man wearing the panama to see if he would make another bid, but he was walking away. 'A joke, poppet', he was saying to his lady friend.

'Going, going, gone, to the two gentlemen in the corner there.' The auctioneer sounded displeased. Everyone turned to stare. My father and Uncle Solly were in their working clothes. They tried to look Australian but there was something about them that made them different, perhaps because there was no parting to their hair, perhaps the way their belts were buckled high upon their stomachs.

'What do they want with cannons? New Australians, look at them. They knife each other in James Street. And now cannons. They'll probably blow us all up.'

'You're kiddin'. Them cannons haven't been used for years. They're after the brass. Shrewd as a barrel-load of monkeys. It's the brass, I'm tellin' yer. But wouldn't like to be them tryin' to move them cannons. Bet yer 10 shillings to a quid they don't make it. Them cannons'll stay there till they rot.'

Uncle Solly and my father sat on the cannons. 'They're ours, Chaim', Uncle Solly said.

'You're telling me?' my father replied.

What are we going to do with them?' Uncle Solly asked.

'You tell me to buy the cannons, then you ask me what we're going to do with them? What we're going to do with them is this. We take off the brass and we sell it. We get ten pounds for the brass, we pay for the cannons and still we have 7 pounds 10 shillings. We set ourselves up in business.'

'You're right, Chaimy. You're right. But tell me. How're we going to move them? God himself couldn't move these cannons.'

'You think I would buy cannons I can't move? You think that? Let me tell you something. These cannons are on wheels.'

'So we wheel them down the Terrace, just like that. A pair of madmen wheeling cannons down the Terrace.'

'There's alternatives, Solly. Believe me, there's alternatives.'

The children had left the rocking-horses and were gathered about the cannons. They skipped around them, and one boy held his fingers to his nose. 'You pong', he said, and all the children started up in chorus then. 'They pong, they pong, they pong.'

'Come over here', my father called the children closer. 'Ever seen a cannon fire?'

'Nup, bet ya can't fire it', the children said.

'You think we'd buy a cannon that doesn't fire? These cannons can shoot right to the other side of the world, all the way to Sevastopol. Who wants to be a corporal? Who wants to stand here and guard the cannons?'

'Bags me, bags me', they all cried, pushing one another.

My father picked out the largest boy, the one who had held his fingers to his nose. 'Now I know a corporal when I see one and you're a corporal or no one is. Stand there, my boy, guard the cannon well. If you see anyone suspicious creeping over the hill, shout, and we'll be back with the cannon fodder. If you don't guard it well you might make cannon fodder yourselves.'

The boy stood proudly beside the cannon and his friends stood around in admiration. My father and Uncle Solly went off and climbed into their old truck. It had to be cranked to get it started and then it rolled down the Terrace open to the sky, bags of fowl manure that they sold door-to-door fastened with rope upon the back.

'Chaimy, we can't leave the cannons like that. We paid 2 pounds 10 for the cannon.'

'We come back for them. We come back. We take the brass off. Then we bury them.'

'Bury them?'

'Solly, you don't want we should wheel them down the Terrace? So, Solly, we bury them. First, we take off the brass. Then we bury them. If we leave them there, the police ring us. 'You the owners of the cannon?' they ask. 'Then remove them from the park or you get a fine', they say. Alternatives, Solly, alternatives. We take off the brass. We bury them. The police don't know anything.'

'What ideas he's got. I'm telling you, Chaimy, you've got ideas.'

'You want to be quiet, Solly, while I tell you? We come back. We have a picnic. We dance a little. Ima packs the blintzes, the strudel. The kids play on the horses. Everyone is happy. Then, Solly, we take the brass off the cannons and we bury the cannons.'

They laughed together as they rolled along the street and the Australians all stared at them because no one would drive a truck laden with fowl manure along the Terrace laughing, except New Australians.

'They'll stop at nothing', one man said.

'Take the bread out of our mouths', said another.

'And the manure out of our chook yards', a woman added.

'Good on ya, mates', two men cried, raising thumbs in the direction of the truck.

My father and Uncle Solly smiled back at them. 'Nice people', Uncle Solly said.

'Some nice and some not so nice', said my father. They passed the army disposal store run by my father's youngest brother, Abe. 'Now there's luck for you', Uncle Solly said. 'He buys up cheap. The war over. Who wants army gear? He sells it to the

workers. Good working boots, oilskins, rucksacks. He sells
them cheap. He buys bigger—tents, cookers. He sells them
cheap. All good stuff. He opens another shop. That's what I call
lucky.'

'That's what you call lucky? That's what I call smart. Find out
what people need and sell it to them but sell it honest. A man
who cheats, Solly, I tell you, is a fool.'

'So we sell Abe our cannons?'

'Abe doesn't need cannons. We sell Abe the brass.'

On the day of the picnic everyone got dressed in their best
clothes. We were all scrubbed, and Johnnie wore the new
two-piece suit our auntie had made. The pants hung down over
his bony knees. 'We'll ride the horse, Ellie', he told me. I was
dressed up, too, in a lace dress our auntie had made from
curtains.

My mother was talking in Yiddish to our auntie like she
always did when we weren't supposed to hear. It sounded like:
'Who buys cannons, I ask you? He buys cannons then he says
"Pack a picnic, Ima, and, please God, we'll bury them". Such a
head I've got without his ideas. "Your ideas, Chaim", I tell
him. What's he want with ideas, Bertha? Tell me that?' Then
she saw Johnnie and spoke in English like she did when she was
cross. 'And where's your shoes, Johnnie? Isn't it enough I
should have to put up with your father and his ideas?'

'I'm not wearing no shoes.'

'Bertha, listen, the boy says he's not wearing shoes.'

'That's what comes of coming to a country like this', Auntie
Bertha said.

My mother flung herself across the settee in our tiny,
immaculate two-bedroom home, and I brought a fan over for
her. She began fanning her face rapidly. 'Did I or did I not pack
a picnic with all his favourite things, chopped liver and sour
cream blintzes, I ask you?' She leapt from the sofa suddenly.
'Don't talk shoes to me, Johnnie. You talk shoes to your father.
First it's cannons now it's shoes, you tell me, is this family going
mad or not? Next thing Ellie will be riding the horses in her best
dress.' She grabbed a brush and began flattening Johnnie's hair
with it. 'Do you want to look like an Australian?' she asked.

'Your hair all sticking up?' Then she brushed my curls until they rose about my head. 'They make me proud, Bertha. Look at them. They make me proud.' She began to cry. 'Where's the camera?'

By the time we had all assembled there were twelve of us. When there was a picnic on all the family came (except my rich Uncle Abe who was too busy) and brought enough food to last a week. My family could make food from nothing—offal; sour cream; windfall apples; baby cucumbers, pickled, which grew by the hundreds along the back fence. 'Sure we've got enough food?' my father always joked. 'Wouldn't want to starve, now, would we?' he said as he put his arm around my mother, squeezing her.

All the children were loaded onto the back of the truck with the picnic basket and the adults somehow managed to slide into the front, except Uncle Solly who rode on the bumper so he could watch us—clinging on—though it made Aunt Bertha scream. 'If they fall off, don't say I didn't tell you so', she said.

The hardest part was going up the hill to the park. My uncles had to get off and push the truck from behind to help it up. They sang all the time—Russian folk songs they had learned as children in Odessa and Sevastopol. We huddled on the ledge of the truck hoping not to be seen.

'Why do they have to sing?' I asked. 'Everyone's staring.'

Johnnie said nothing. He was removing his shoes and socks and tying them by the laces to dangle from the truck.

'Wait till you see the cannon', Uncle Solly was telling us all, as he stood upon the bumper, hanging on with one arm. It was a bright, clear day and above us was so much blue sky we felt dizzy. The rugs, chair and tables were set up on the lawn, opposite the horses, close to the cannons which pointed out across the river. 'Where's your shoes, Johnnie?' my mother called, but he was already over on the big black horse, riding off into the blue sky and I was after him, climbing onto the medium brown, my lace dress tucked into my bloomers.

It was Uncle Solly who saw what was painted on the cannons first. 'Dagos go home', was printed in large white letters.

My father said nothing at first. Then he called, 'Where's the food, Ima?' and my mother quietly spread the food out upon the table. A crowd of children gathered round to stare and point. 'Yuk', they said. 'Dago food', and ran off licking icecreams. My mother covered the food with a net embroidered with stars and Aunt Bertha stood guard with a swat against the flies. Then my father started to sing as loudly as he could, and my Uncle Solly began to dance. Uncle Solly clicked his heels and squatted down kicking out his legs, strong as a buffalo while my mother and aunties clapped.

We rocked hard on our horses, pretending we did not know the silly people who sang and danced, but soon we rode no hands, clapping too—Uncle Solly was so strong he twirled upon his heels. Our mother was smiling at the crowd that had gathered. She offered round the blintzes and everyone took one, except the children with their icecreams and a man who said, 'Who do you think you are? You'd think you owned the park, the way you're carrying on.' But my mother only smiled, then lifted her skirt slightly and swung in circles.

When my father and Uncle Solly had finished dancing, sweat dripping down their cheeks, they took their screwdrivers and a rucksack borrowed from Uncle Abe and went over to their cannons. 'Come here', they called, and we went over with our cousins who had been sitting in a line upon the rug. 'We'll show you something. See this', my father slapped a cannon on its side. 'A cannon is only a cannon', he said. 'But brass fittings, now they are something else.'

'What are they doing?' people in the crowd were asking each other, getting bored. The children with icecreams ran over to the horses, and leapt upon them whooping.

'They're stealing the brass. Coming to our country and stealing the brass off our very own cannons.'

'Cannons that we fought a war with. The Great War.'

'Me Uncle died. Next they'll be throwing paint on the memorial and pulling up the sugar gums. Bloody foreigners.'

'Eh, leave them cannon alone.'

'We bought them', my father said politely. 'We own the cannon.'

'That's a laugh. They say they own the cannon. The old

61

soldiers own the cannon, that's who. They fought a bloody war with those cannon.' Men gathered around, belligerent. But Uncle Solly was very strong; a Cossack dancer had to be. He was a wrestler, too, in the pubs for pocket-money, and when they came closer the men didn't like the look of his thick arms bulging. His teeth were big and strong enough to lift chairs, and he didn't stop smiling, even when he was mad. My father, as always, was ready to debate. 'You want some cannons. You buy them', my father said. 'But not these cannons. They're not for sale. Now, if you're looking for some brass, then we might be able to do a deal.' However, it was Uncle Solly smiling at them with his big white teeth who made the men retreat.

As they began to drift away my mother cleared up. All the food was gone. Our plump cousins lay motionless upon the rug in the sun while Johnnie and I ran about, then rolled like sausages down the slope. 'She'll burst her new lace dress', Aunt Bertha said. 'And Johnnie should be taken to a doctor, legs like chickens.'

Our father and Uncle Solly worked hard to remove the brass but it took them longer than they expected. By the time they were finished the sun was nearly going down behind the river, and everyone was tired. Most of the people had left the park. 'Just as well', Aunt Bertha said. 'Dancing is one thing, burying cannon is another. Enough is enough.'

Our father and Uncle Solly found a place a little down the hill, towards the river, where the earth was not so hard and the lawn had not begun to grow. There were kangaroo paws and spider orchids, wild. Uncle Solly did most of the digging and in no time he had two holes like graves dug in the side of the hill. By this time it was getting dark. Our mother lit a kerosene lamp and put it on the rug so we could huddle around it making shadows and playing 'star light, star bright'. Then, when the men were ready, we had to go over and help to push the cannons down into the holes. We all heaved and pushed, even our mother and Aunt Bertha, and soon the cannon began to roll, down the hill and in. 'Hooray, hooray', we all shouted, kissing each other as the cannons sank, and Uncle Solly began to shovel sand back over them, blotting out the words painted on their side, leaving the kangaroo paws and spider orchids in clumps behind.

'Soon they will be covered in wildflowers and no one'll even know the cannons are there', my father said.

When my father saw a notice in the newspaper asking if anyone knew the whereabouts of the two cannons he rang Uncle Solly. The article said the cannons had been missing for years but were wanted now, as testimony to the Great War, like the sugar gums and the memorial. West Australians needed reminding, to make them proud, the article said, and no one knew what had happened to the cannons that used to be opposite the rocking-horses in the park.

Uncle Solly came and my father showed him the article. Then they rang the newspaper and said that they knew where the cannons were. The photographers and reporters all followed them to the park. My father, who had gone into partnership with Uncle Abe, was driving a big car with a roll-back roof. Uncle Solly and my father posed in smart suits for their photographs as the gardeners in the park assembled to dig, on the side of the hill near to where clumps of kangaroo paws and spider orchids grew.

When the cannons were revealed everyone wanted to know what had happened to the brass. My father said it had been turned into liquid assets, but didn't say how much. Then he offered, as a special gesture towards his new country, to have the cannons restored for the people as a gift.

The cannons were wheeled back up the hill. My father insisted that, before they were restored, the words painted on their side should be scrubbed off. After this was done, though no brass was found to replace that which my father had sold to Uncle Abe, the cannons were decorated with metal strips, and polished until they shone.

When my children come to the park on a picnic with us it is hard for them to decide which they would prefer to play on, the rocking-horses, or the cannons. However, when their grand-father sings and their Great-uncle Solly does his Cossack dancing they forget about everything else, even the Whippy icecream van, and gather round with all our family to clap their hands, while their grandmother unpacks the strudel and blint-zes, passing them around. As we twirl and clap in time to Uncle Solly's clicking heels, the blue sky makes me dizzy, sparks fly across the river, and the cannons gleam with brass again.

The Dowry

Penelope Nelson

*T*HERE is a Saturday morning rush at the Northern Suburbs Crematorium. Our funeral—my mother's funeral—is running late. We mourners are trampling over the poppies and rosebushes outside the chapel as we wait our turn. My husband and elder son are both wearing ties. Excluding school ties, there proved, when we ransacked the house this morning, to be a choice of three: one plain, dark red wool (London, designer unknown, circa 1955); one blue and green, Florentine-patterned silk (Pucci, circa 1969), one fawn silk with burnt orange stripes (Pierre Cardin, circa 1978). They are wearing the silk ones. My son's legs have grown so much in 12 months that he has had to wear black cord jeans under his brown corduroy jacket because the trousers that matched the jacket revealed a band of hairy calf.

My uncle comes up to greet me. He has not spoken to me since the 1975 election but he advances cordially today. He calls me by my mother's name.

My younger son is handing out copies of the readings for the service. Kate, an elegant woman in her late sixties, says to me: 'Your darling boy has offered me a copy of the service but my eyes are hopeless. I don't read any more; I'm reduced to listening.'

'It must be terrible', I reply, 'but we'll all be peering at this tiny print.'

'It's unspeakable, ducky', Kate says. 'I can see outlines, though', she adds. 'A little further off I see a bit. I can tell you, for instance, that your mother would have adored your suit.'

'Do you think so?' I can feel decades of parental disapproval evaporating. I am with a hundred people who thought John Kerr was right but, for today at least, I can accept them. If they cared for my mother, they are all right by me.

'Think so?' Kate says. 'I know it.' My suit is a black and white check (Trent Nathan,end–of–season sale, 1982) and I also wear dark glasses, prescription lenses, 1979. A man in a black suit approaches my husband and offers to relieve him of the bunch of roses he is holding. I look daggers through the glasses.

'Thank you', he says. 'I think my wife prefers me to take these in myself.'

I kiss people. I try to comment coherently on my mother's last days. There are friends of my parents from the 1950s here today, although there has been no notice in the papers. Unhesitatingly, I remember their names. I feel as if I could recall whole slabs of the Walter de la Mare, Norman Lindsay and Robert Louis Stevenson that my mother used to read to me at Palm Beach in the years after the war when she was a young woman with long hair like Rita Hayworth's. However, I don't have to do that. All I have to do is read the beatitudes without bawling. Blessed are they that mourn. My younger son and I have a pact: If I look as if I am going to cry when it is my turn to read, he is going to make faces. But I know now that he won't have to. Blessed are they that mourn, for they shall be comforted.

'You're very lucky you've had your mother for this long', a secretary at work tells me. 'You've known her and your boys have, too. My mother died when I was three; I scarcely even remember her. And my son has never had a grandmother.'

'Yes', I say. 'You're quite right—we've been very lucky.'

Kate and I speak on the telephone a couple of times. I am sitting at my typewriter one day, using Bob Marley for rhythm as I type. She rings. I can scarcely hear her. 'National Trust', she says. 'Darling Point ... diary exhibition.'

'But I'm fascinated by diaries', I shout. 'I'm writing a novel set in 1897 and diaries are just about the best source. Just a moment; I'll turn this down.' Marley fades a little, the Wailers wail; his backing musicians repeat the only reggae chords they know in a minor key. I can hear Kate now.

'Dowries', she is saying. 'Dowries from 1880 onward. Some of it is very witty. On loan from the costume museum.'

'Oh', I say, disappointed. Dowry, not diary. Pity. 'I love costume exhibitions.' There is some truth in this. I get high in fabric shops. I don't know the name for the proneness to sexual fantasy inspired by layers of filmy, floating cloth—soft and sensuous on the skin—but these phrases would not have been stolen by the cosmetics copywriters if my fetish were not widespread. Silky, satiny, gossamer, sheer. 'I'll go, of course', I tell Kate. She explains how to find Lindesay, the National Trust house.

It is bitterly cold on the day I go. Winds scud across the little park at the end of Darling Point Road, leaves pile up against the security fences.

Inside the white building, volunteers from the Trust's ladies committee are waiting in vain for anyone to buy their teatowels, pot-pourris and place mats.

I enter the first room. There are handsome dresses, all from different periods, all expensive. If the conjunction is witty, as Kate has assured me it is, I am slow to get the joke.

As I go from room to room, I begin paying more attention to the custodians than to the exhibits. Trust ladies are wearing fairly standard Sloane Ranger gear: navy blue suits, tartan skirts with plain blazers, the obligatory silk scarf, pearl earrings. Many of them are even talking valiantly to each other about the items on display. This is frustrating to me. I would prefer to overhear some good gossip. The words that recur in their conversation today are 'the lace'. 'Have you seen the divine lace?' they are asking. Out of this world.

It may be my mother's fault that lace does nothing for me: She never had a lace tablecloth or a lace runner or a decent pair of lace drawers; she did not bequeath me any antique embroidery, she had no time for any of that stuff. She did struggle with Viyella children's clothes for a few months when my brother was small but she wisely abandoned the effort and headed for David Jones, instead. No, what she bequeathed to me was altogether different.

My mother read me verses that scanned. She taught me not

to split infinitives. When other children learned catechisms, I recited after her 'Different **from**, opposite **to**, contrasted **with**.' Thanks to her, I twitch every time someone says 'between you and I'. This is my dowry, in that other sense of natural endowment. She taught me my mother tongue.

'Have you seen the lace? You must see the lace before you go.' The committee ladies are most insistent. The lace is on display in an area designated the Marble Hall. I never dreamed that I dwelt anywhere so decorous. Black satin, violet chiffon—those are the fabrics that move me. Here everything is white and creamy and delicate. 'Crochet collars, handmade pillows, set of 9 circular extremely finely knitted cream lace round mats 13cm diameter.'

Suddenly, in the middle of all this, I do see a joke.

Is it the one Kate meant?

Propped in the marble hall is a photograph of Les A. Murray. The Australian poet, the Trust ladies have labelled him. The boy from Bunyah, the peasant mandarin, grins from one of his XOS handknit jumpers. I read the catalogue entry.

95 Christening Dress & Coat, of the Australian poet Les Murray. 'Hand-worked silk crepe made by Mrs Miriam Murray (nee Arnall) Bunyah, NSW 1938. Miriam Pauline Murray was born in Kurri Kurri, NSW in 1915 & died in Taree, NSW in April 1951, just a month short of her 36th birthday. Daughter of a Cornish coal mine manager who died when she was a child, Mrs Murray grew up in Newcastle & was a nursing sister there before her marriage, in 1937, to Cecil Allan Murray, dairy farmer of Bunyah, a district on the lower north coast, south of Taree. The christening ensemble which she made for her son Leslie Allan, born 17th October 1938, was used for his christening in the free Presbyterian church at Bunyah; kept by her widowed husband for many years after her death, it was passed on to Leslie in time for the baptism of his son Alexander Cecil in 1978.' Quote Les Murray. Contemporary photograph of poet.

Suddenly, I am not at all indifferent to lace. The handworked cream garments bring re-readings of his poems flooding to my mind. 'The Widower In The Country', 'Evening Alone At Bunyah', 'Cowyard Gates'—none of them will be the same for me now. I have had glimmerings before. 'The great unstated subject in Les's poems', I said once to a professor of English, 'is his mother'. I picked a reticent and upright man to say this to and he replied: 'It would be a bit tasteless to pursue that, wouldn't it?'

Ignoring that warning, I once concluded a study of ritual in Murray's poems with this observation: 'The major loss in Murray's life and his father's life is also mentioned in this poem ('Cowyard Gates')

> my mother placing and placing
> a tin ring on some dough, telling
> me about French.
> The first weeks of her absence.'

'It is significant', I wrote, 'that, in her one overt appearance in Murray's work so far, his mother is glimpsed performing a ritual act.'

Certainly I have found a joke—the mountainous poet dwarfing his own christening robes. A current poem of his refers to the aristocracy of the fat. It is dedicated to Robert Morley.

But there is another message here, too: hope, tenderness, a mother's gift. A dowry.

When I get home, I telephone Les Murray. 'I know what you've seen', he says. 'In fact, we got some sort of notice that the exhibition is on. Yes, she had a great ability for that type of handwork, didn't she?'

'Come off it, Les', I say. 'It's a poem; you know it is.'

The Life of Art

Helen Garner

MY friend and I went walking the dog in the cemetery. It was a Melbourne autumn: mild breezes, soft air, gentle sun. The dog trotted in front of us between the graves. I had a pair of scissors in my pocket in case we came across a rose bush on a forgotten tomb.

'I don't like roses', said my friend. 'I despise them for having thorns.'

The dog entered a patch of ivy and posed there. We pranced past the Elvis Presley memorial.

'What would you like to have written on your grave', said my friend, 'as a tribute?'

I thought for a long time. Then I said, '*Owner of two hundred pairs of boots*'.

When we had recovered, my friend pointed out a headstone which said, *She lived only for others*. 'Poor thing', said my friend. 'On *my* grave I want you to write, *She lived only for herself.*'

We went stumbling along the overgrown paths.

My friend and I had known each other for twenty years, but we had never lived in the same house. She came back from Europe at the perfect moment to take over a room in the house I rented. It became empty because the man—but that's another story.

My friend has certain beliefs which I have always secretly categorised as *batty*. Sometimes I have thought, 'My friend is what used to be called 'a dizzy dame'. My friend believes in

70

reincarnation: not that this in itself is unacceptable to me. Sometimes she would write me long letters from wherever she was in the world, letters in her lovely, graceful, sweeping hand, full of tales from one or other of her previous lives, tales to explain her psychological make-up and behaviour in her present incarnation. My eye would fly along the lines, sped by embarrassment.

My friend is a painter.

When I first met my friend she was engaged. She was wearing an antique sapphire ring and Italian boots. Next time I saw her, in Myers, her hand was bare. I never asked. We were students then. We went dancing in a club in South Yarra. The boys in the band were students too. We fancied them, but at 22 we felt ourselves to be older women, already fading, almost predatory. We read *The Roman Spring of Mrs Stone*. This was in 1965; before feminism.

My friend came off the plane with her suitcase. 'Have you ever noticed', she said, 'how Australian men, even in their forties, dress like small boys? They wear shorts and thongs and little stripey T-shirts.'

A cat was asleep under a bush in our back yard each morning when we opened the door. We took him in. My friend and I fought over whose lap he would lie in while we watched TV.

My friend is tone deaf. But she once sang *Blue Moon*, verses and chorus, in a talking, tuneless voice in the back of a car going up the Punt Road hill and down again and over the river, travelling north; and she did not care.

My friend lived as a student in a house near the university. Her bed was right under the window in the front room downstairs. One afternoon her father came to visit. He tapped on the door. When no one answered he looked through the window. What he saw caused him to stagger back into the fence. It was a kind of heart attack, my friend said.

71

My friend went walking in the afternoons near our house. She came out of lanes behind armfuls of greenery. She found vases in my dusty cupboards. The arrangements she made with the leaves were stylish and generous-handed.

Before either of us married, I went to my friend's house to help her paint the bathroom. The paint was orange, and so was the cotton dress I was wearing. She laughed because all she could see of me when I stood in the bathroom were my limbs and my head. Later, when it got dark, we sat at her kitchen table and she rolled a joint. It was the first dope I had ever seen or smoked. I was afraid that a detective might look through the kitchen window. I could not understand why my friend did not pull the curtain across. We walked up to Genevieve in the warm night and ate two bowls of spaghetti. It seemed to me that I could feel every strand.

My friend's father died when she was in a distant country.
   'So now', she said to me, 'I know what grief is.'
   'What is it?' I said.
   'Sometimes', said my friend, 'it is what you expect. And sometimes it is nothing more than bad temper.'
   When my friend's father died, his affairs were not in order and he had no money.

My friend was the first person I ever saw break the taboo against wearing striped and floral patterns together. She stood on the steps of the Shrine of Remembrance and held a black umbrella over her head. This was in the 1960s.

My friend came back from Europe and found a job. On the days when she was not painting theatre sets for money she went to her cold and dirty studio in the city and painted for the other thing, whatever that is. She wore cheap shoes and pinned her hair into a roll on her neck.

My friend babysat, as a student, for a well-known woman in her forties who worked at night.

'What is she like?' I said.

'She took me upstairs', said my friend, 'and showed me her bedroom. It was full of flowers. We stood at the door looking in. She said, "Sex is not a problem for me".'

When the person ... the man whose room my friend had taken came to dinner, my friend and he would talk for hours after everyone else had left the table about different modes of perception and understanding. My friend spoke slowly, in long and convoluted sentences and mixed metaphors, and often laughed. The man, a scientist, spoke in a light, rapid voice, but he sat still. They seemed to listen to each other.

'I don't mean a god in the Christian sense', said my friend.

'It is egotism', said the man, 'that makes people want their lives to have meaning beyond themselves'.

My friend and I worked one summer in the men's underwear department of a big store in Footscray. We wore our little cotton dresses, our blue sandals. We were happy there, selling, wrapping, running up and down the ladder, dinging the register, going to the park for lunch with the boys from the shop. *I* was happy. The youngest boy looked at us and sighed and said, 'I don't know which of youse I love the most'. One day my friend was serving a thin-faced woman at the specials box. There was a cry. I looked up. My friend was dashing for the door. She was sobbing. We all stood still, in attitudes of drama. The woman spread her hands. She spoke to the frozen shop at large.

'I never said a thing', she said. 'It's got nothing to do with *me*.'

I left my customer and ran after my friend. She was halfway down the street, looking in a shop window. She had stopped crying. She began to tell me about ... but it doesn't matter now. This was in the 1960s; before feminism.

My friend came home from her studio some nights in a calm bliss. 'What we need', she said, 'are those moments of abandon, when the real stuff runs down our arm without obstruction.'

My friend cut lemons into chunks and dropped them into the water jug when there was no money for wine.

My friend came out of the surgery. I ran to take her arm but she pushed past me and bent over the gutter. I gave her my hanky. Through the open sides of the tram the summer wind blew freely. We stood up and held on to the leather straps. 'I can't sit down', said my friend. 'He put a great bolt of gauze up me.' This was in the 1960s; before feminism. The tram rolled past the deep gardens. My friend was smiling.

My friend and her husband came to visit me and my husband. We heard their car and looked out the upstairs window. We could hear his voice haranguing her, and hers raised in sobs and wails. I ran down to open the door. They were standing on the mat, looking ordinary. We went to Royal Park and flew a kite that her husband had made. The nickname he had for her was one he had picked up from her father. They both loved her, of course. This was in the 1960s.

My friend was lonely.

My friend sold some of her paintings. I went to look at them in her studio before they were taken away. The smell of the oil paint was a shock to me: a smell I would have thought of as masculine. This was in the 1980s; after feminism. The paintings were big. I did not 'understand' them; but perhaps I did, for they made me feel like fainting, her weird plants and creatures streaming back towards a source of irresistible yellow light.

'When happiness comes', said my friend, 'it's so thick and smooth and uneventful, it's like nothing at all.'

My friend picked up a fresh chicken at the market. 'Oh', she said. 'Feel this.' I took it from her. Its flesh was pimpled and tender, and moved on its bones like the flesh of a very young baby.

I went into my friend's room while she was out. On the wall was stuck a sheet of paper on which she had written: 'Henry James to a friend in trouble: "throw yourself on the *alternative* life ... which is what I mean by the life of art, and which religiously invoked and handsomely understood, je vous le garantis, never fails the sincere invoker—sees him through everything, and reveals to him the secrets of and for doing so".'

I was sick. My friend served me pretty snacks at sensitive intervals. I sat up on my pillows and strummed softly the five chords I had learnt on my ukulele. My friend sat on the edge of a chair, with her bony hands folded round a cup, and talked. She uttered great streams of words. Her gaze skimmed my shoulder and vanished into the clouds outside the window. She was like a machine made to talk on and on forever. She talked about how much money she would have to spend on paint and stretchers, about the lightness, the optimism, the femaleness of her work, about what she was going to paint next, about how much bigger and more violent her pictures would have to be in order to attract proper attention from critics, about what the men in her field were doing now, about how she must find this out before she began her next lot of pictures.

'Listen', I said. 'You don't have to think about any of that. Your work is *terrific*.'

'My work is terrific', said my friend on a high note, 'but *I'm not*.' Her mouth fell down her chin and opened and sobs came out. 'I'm forty', said my friend, 'and I've got *no money*.'

I played the chords G, A and C.

'I'm lonely', said my friend. Tears were running down her cheeks. Her mouth was too low in her face. 'I want a man.'

'You could have one', I said.

'I don't want just any man', said my friend. 'And I don't want a boy. I want a man who's not going to think my ideas are crazy. I want a man who'll see the part of me that no one ever sees. I want a man who'll look after me and love me. I want a grown-up.'

I thought, 'If I could play better, I could turn what she has just said into a song.'

'Women like us', I said to my friend, 'don't have men like that. Why should *you* expect to find a man like that?'

'Why shouldn't I?' said my friend.

'Because men won't do those things for women like us. We've done something to ourselves so that men won't do it. Well—there are men who will. But we despise them.'

My friend stopped crying.

I played the ukulele. My friend drank from the cup.

Nothing Happened

Margaret Coombs

*I*T is seventeen years ago. I am waiting at the bus stop just up the road from our house. Our house is the big one on the corner of Beresford Road, the one with the funny-looking staircase out the front and the ornamental arch between the chimneys. I am waiting for the bus.

Today I am going to the beach with Anne. I am meeting Anne at Double Bay and from there we will catch the 365 to Bondi Beach. We'll make our way to the end of the beach right away from the baths and the lifesaving club, and find a spot under the Lost Children sign where everyone meets. All the Scots and Cranbrook boys and all the Ascham and Kambala girls who belong to a sort of a *set* come here to sit, all the ones who learn dancing at Miss Cay's and go skiing in the May holidays and hang around the VJ yacht club all summer and in winter watch the GPS football, or play it, and who always have the right clothes to wear and all that. I guess the vital thing they all have in common is that they all have the right kinds of *bodies* as well as the right kinds of clothes. I don't. If I were by myself, I'd go out of my way to avoid this part of the beach. One of the girls who comes here is a model for the *Teenagers' Weekly*, and another has actually been in a film on TV! The film star girl is thirteen like me. Her name is Janey Wynne-Williams. She goes to Ascham. She is also a friend of Anne's.

Anne is neither a model nor a film star but I'm sure she could be if she liked. She's fourteen. She and I go to Kambala. She's the nicest girl in our class. She's not the cleverest, not the

77

richest, not even the most fashionable; but she's kind-hearted and happy, and everybody likes her, even I do. She can afford to be my friend even though I am neither nice nor happy. I am not rich or fashionable either, and if I am clever (I think I am) it does not always show in my marks.

I am neither a model nor a film star and I know I never could be. I have no boyfriends, not even friends of the family or cousins. My family has no 'family friends' and I have no cousins of a suitable age, or none that I've met. What if I did? My nickname is Pud. What boy would be caught dead with a girlfriend called Pud?

I have read the collected works of Havelock Ellis, all seven volumes. But so what? I am not a social asset.

I am not fat, I am just *called* Pud from when I was a kid. I used to tell myself it didn't matter, it gave me distinction, it proved I was tough, things like that. *A rose by any other name would smell as sweet*, I used to chant to myself. A lie, that is! I hate everybody calling me Pud. Everybody does, even the fat ones, the ones much fatter than me. I know they can't help feeling they must be better than me because I let them call me Pud. I don't know why I do. I can't help it. I can't protest, not with my voice.

Anyway, the fact is that though I am not fat, I am not as slim as Anne. And if Anne were fat, she would just look voluptuous. So would Janey Wynne-Williams. If I were fat, I would just look fat.

I think of what it must be like to be Anne . . . a girl so certain she is loved that she can go with me, Pud, to Bondi Beach to sit under the Lost Children sign and chatter to people like Janey Wynne-Williams and not even try to pretend she's not with me—with the body in which I am. She's not like me! When I'm at the beach, I try to pretend this body has nothing to do with me, I would like to be able to disown it completely. I lie leadenly there on my stomach, sweaty and dazed, my sunglasses on, pretending to read while Anne darts about like a little bird and chatters and dashes off into the surf and swims. I never go in. I hate to expose myself, hate the crowd, the stares, the freezing water, the waves that threaten to knock me down. Surfing is sport and I am no good at sport, I don't like it. Only the pretty, popular girls go in. I stay with my face hidden in a book. I am waiting. I am hoping for something to happen to me.

What is it that I'm always hoping will happen? I try to think: what, exactly, am I waiting for?

I am waiting for the bus.

The bus sure is taking a long time to come! I gaze vacantly at the oncoming cars.

A taxi pulls up at the kerb just in front of me. It startles me. I look round to see who has hailed it. There is no one there.

'Where are you going, pet?' the driver asks.

I realise he is speaking to me. He is old, with grey hair. He looks older than my father. He looks kind. I take all this in at a glance.

'To Double Bay', I reply automatically. 'But I'm just waiting for the bus. I haven't got enough money for a cab.'

I wish I did! I wish I could just open the door and step into the cab and say, 'Double Bay, thank you, driver', and pretend I'd intended to catch the cab all along, pretend I'd hailed it. I didn't hail the cab, I didn't even blink. Did I? But he'll say I did. He'll accuse me of having waved him down, tell me by rights I should pay him the flag fall, drive off angry at me, thinking I'm a bloody nuisance and a liar. It's not fair! How can I make him believe he's made a mistake, stop him from hating me?

'Hop in. I'm going that way. I'll give you a lift', he says.

I look blank. Then I look puzzled. I keep thinking: *I haven't got enough money for a cab*. I turn around to make sure again that nobody else is there.

'Come on , pet, I'll give you a lift', he repeats. 'I'm going that way.'

By now he has opened the front door of the cab. He gestures for me to get in. He smiles. He has a lovely smile, friendly and kind. I like his smile.

'But I haven't got any money', I say. 'Not enough for a cab.'

'That doesn't matter', he answers. 'I'm going that way anyway. I'll give you a lift. Hop in.'

I hesitate.

'For nothing', he emphasises. He grins at me.

I should run away. I should run home. Mummy says I must never accept lifts from strangers, she's told me this again and again. I should say firmly to this man, 'No thank you, my mother doesn't allow me to accept lifts from strangers', and then I should run straight home. I rehearse all this in my head.

But if I don't go with him, the driver will be insulted, I know he will. He'll think to himself that he was only trying to do me a *favour* for goodness sake, and be disgusted that this is how I repay him. And anyway Dave, my brother, *he* accepts lifts. He's over 21 so no one can stop him, he hitchhikes everywhere, it nearly drives Mum berserk. *He* says Mum's bloody paranoid, says the main reason she thinks it's wrong to accept lifts from strangers is that 'It isn't the Done Thing'. He pipes 'It isn't the Done Thing' in a funny voice, mocking my mother. She becomes furious, calls him a smart aleck and a lout, seethes with hatred for him. She says you just *cannot* trust everybody. He says that *her* trouble is she's never trusted a soul in her life. He always walks out at that point. Slams the door. My mother always turns on *me*, tells *me* if I ever accept a lift from a stranger she'll kill me, *kill* me.

But taxi drivers aren't strangers. Are bus drivers strangers? I know taxi drivers aren't strangers because once when I was a little girl, eight, I got lost at Kings Cross and it was a taxi driver who found me and brought me home safe. That was when we'd just arrived in Sydney from the country and were living in a flat at Elizabeth Bay. One day I went for a walk by myself and got lost and couldn't find a policeman so I asked a taxi driver the way and he gave me a lift home. For nothing. He didn't even wait to be thanked. Mum and Dad kept saying what a decent chap he must have been and what a pity they didn't know who he was and wishing there was some way of rewarding him. I remember all this without even thinking of it.

'Are you coming?' the taxi driver asks.

Well, why not? I *can't* go home. Anne is waiting for me at Double Bay. We are going to the beach. My mother doesn't like me going to the beach, she doesn't understand that everybody goes to the beach, everybody who isn't a droob. She'll make a dreadful fuss if I run home. She'll grill me endlessly about what has happened. *Nothing* has happened. An old man has offered me a lift, that's all. She will suspect . . . . I don't know exactly what she'll suspect, but she'll suspect me of *some* unmentionable crime. She'll blame Anne. She'll blame going to the beach. I'll never be allowed to go to the beach again.

I am going to the beach with Anne.

I climb in.

The driver leans across and locks the door. He looks respectable. I don't dare look at him, but the blurred impression he makes on my brain tells me he looks respectable—what my mother would call respectable: neat and clean and suitably dressed. There is nothing odd about him, nothing unusual. *Of course* there isn't! I am limp with relief.

Now I am quite proud of myself for having climbed in, for not having been such a child as to refuse this lift, be afraid, go running blindly home to Mumsy-Wumsy. I think of Dave. I am on his side against Mum, glad that I've used my common sense and realised it was quite all right to accept this particular lift, behaved like an adult. *I'm* not afraid to trust people or do what's 'Not the Done Thing'. *I'm* not like my mother. Stupid old bitch!

The taxi is turning.

My eyes confirm the fact that the taxi is turning.

The taxi is doing a U-turn across New South Head Road. My brain reels. Something collapses inside me. I am dizzy. I am sick with dizziness. Is the cab turning or am I just dizzy?

The cab is turning. I watch the world outside the window turn back to front. Everything seems upside down. I feel sick with terror, my heart contracts with terror. I feel as if all the blood has gone out of my head. All the blood has fallen down out of my head.

'Isn't Double Bay the other way?' my voice asks meekly. I *know* Double Bay is the other way. I know the only *possible* way to Double Bay is the other way. 'The bus goes the other way', I explain, lest he think it presumptuous of me to question him.

'Oh yes', says the driver. He seems perfectly calm. 'I just thought we'd park over here for a little while and look at the view. You'd like to do that, wouldn't you?'

I can't think how to say no.

'OK', I say.

So he parks in the parking bay just down from the pier. He switches the engine off. Something inside me switches off. My heart sinks. Suddenly it seems very quiet. My heart is thumping inside me in a way that is making it difficult for me to breathe.

'Pretty, isn't it?' he says, gesturing towards the water.

I agree. 'Yes.' Well, it's true. It is! I smile to show I am not afraid. I think of Dave. It's silly of me to be so frightened. All the same, I am stiff as a doll and fuddled with fear. I stare at the view seeing nothing. I concentrate on hiding my feelings. The taxi driver must not know how I feel, must not guess what I'm thinking. He must not guess that I'm the slightest bit afraid.

'Do you live near here?' he asks casually.

'Yes.'

'Where?'

I am terrified. This man must not find out where I live. My mother will murder me if she ever finds out about this old man. If this man ever finds out where I live, my mother will find out about this man, and then she will murder me. I am almost panting with fear. I control my breathing carefully. As long as this man beside me does not find out where I live, I will be all right, I'll survive whatever it is that is happening to me now, it will never happen again. But if he does find out, I'm done for, finished.

And yet I can't lie. 'Over there', I say.

'Where?' he asks again.

Perhaps he already knows where I live. Perhaps he's just testing me to make sure I trust him. He'll know if I tell a lie, and he'll despise me for it.

'Over there', I say. I nod vaguely towards the other side of the road. For the first time I notice we're parked right opposite my house. That shocks me. If my mother comes out on the balcony with the binoculars, she will ... What will she do? Kill me? Save me?

The driver looks.

'Which house?' he asks. He sounds as if he's just curious, just wondering.

I feel it must be *obvious* which house. I'd hardly live in a shack on a building site and the other place is so plainly a private hotel.

'Oh, over that way', I say with a shrug. I pretend I'm simply not very interested in where I live. I turn back to peer intently at the view: boats, pier, sea.

'What, in a flat or a house?' he asks.

He might still be just curious. Dave would say he was just curious.

'In a house', I find myself saying. I feel cornered, helpless.

'Do you? Which one?' he casually insists.

What does he mean *which one*? There *is* only one!

Unless he thinks I mean up Beresford Road somewhere.

'Oh, just over there', I shrug again, doing my best to sound bored. I pretend to yawn. I stare hard at the sea. I am terrified this man will find out how frightened I am of him. What right have I to be frightened? What has he done to me? Nothing. *Nothing!* It's not fair of me to be frightened like this.

There is a silence. Somebody toots in the distance. The traffic hums by.

'What's your name, pet?' he asks.

I freeze.

'Just your first name,' he says. 'I don't want to know your second name. Just your first name.'

That makes it worse. But I tell him. 'Rosalind.' I don't tell him everyone calls me Pud.

'Rosalind? That's a lovely name', he says warmly. 'Rosalind. Lovely.'

He *makes* it sound lovely, pronounces it in three distinct syllables, Roz-a-lind. I like the way he says Rosalind but I am terrified almost out of my wits. I am finding it almost impossible to think. His eyes are studying me. I can feel them. He is really noticing me, really paying attention to me. I look down and stare into my lap. My fingers are busy unravelling the fringe of my beach towel. My beach towel is bright pink and has a black fringe. I sewed it on myself.

'A lovely name for a lovely young lady', he adds.

That's a bit corny. But, 'Thank you', I mumble.

I notice there is ink on one of my fingers.

'And how old are you, Rosalind?' he asks.

'Almost fourteen.' I am thirteen years and ten months.

'Do you like being fourteen?' he asks. 'Do you like being a woman?'

I should run away.

'Yes', I say.

Silence again.

I pull a thread out of the towel and knead it into a little ball.

'Your parents must be pretty mean—not giving you much money', he says. 'Don't they give you much pocket money?'

Oh Christ! Does he want me to pay him after all?

'Not much', I say.

'Your parents are mean to you, are they?'

His voice is full of the promise of sympathy. I am petrified. My mother would murder me if she knew I were here.

'Oh no, they're OK really', I manage to lie, brushing nonexistent hair out of my eyes.

I'm sure he doesn't believe me. He *knows* what my parents are like.

'How much do they give you a week?' he asks.

'Ten shillings', I say. I know that's what Anne gets. I don't get pocket money as such. I'm not supposed to be interested in money.

'Gosh, that's not much! I'd give you much more than that if you were *my* daughter', he says. 'I'd give you twice that if you were *my* daughter!'

I don't comment. I flick the pellet of thread onto the floor.

'I haven't got any daughters, you know, Rosalind', he says—and adds wistfully, 'I'd love to have a daughter. I've always wanted a daughter.'

Silence. I pick at the fringe.

'Rosalind . . .?' he says. His voice is soft, intimate. My breathing ceases. I am stiff with apprehension. I say nothing.

'Rosalind . . .?'

He takes my hand. My heart lurches. The blood rushing up to my heart turns to ice. 'I like you, Rosalind', he says. *My mother will murder me.* I should scream, run away.

I don't move a muscle. I stay riveted to the seat.

84

Gently he puts my hand palm-down on the bulge between his legs, cups it over the bulge between his legs. He cups his own hand down over mine. My hand is like ice. His hand on mine is heavy and warm.

'You don't mind if I do that, do you, Rosalind?' he asks me languidly.

My mind is a blur.

'No', I murmer, polite as ever. I glance sideways to where the end of my arm disappears under his hand. Does that arm belong to me? I look away.

'What did you say? Mmm?' he asks, leaning forward attentively.

'No', I say, 'I don't mind.'

Yes, those *are* the words I speak.

Something in my head explains to me that I'm not supposed to know enough to mind, I'm not supposed to have the faintest idea what this man is doing. All I should know is: NEVER ACCEPT LIFTS FROM STRANGERS. I am a nicely-brought-up thirteen-year-old girl and I oughtn't to understand so well the gist of what this man is doing. I'm not supposed to have read Havelock Ellis *et cetera*, I'm not supposed to know about men and all that. My mother would murder me if she ever found out how curious I am about all that, if she found out a fraction of the things I know. As far as I'm supposed to know, there's nothing wrong, nothing wrong at all: an old man with grey hair and neat clothes and a young girl in green bermuda shorts are sitting on the front seat of a taxi parked on the esplanade at Rose Bay admiring the view, and the old man just happens to be holding the young girl's hand cupped over the bulge between his legs. It *is* a funny place for him to put her hand and the girl might very well be puzzled, but she should explain to herself that he's put it there absent-mindedly, it just *happens* to be there, the old man would be disgusted, utterly scornful, very indignant if the young girl let on he was frightening her. He wouldn't think of hurting her, she must be mad if she thinks he'd do her any harm—he's only trying to be kind to her, trying to help her. Hasn't he offered to drive her to Double Bay? For nothing?

I don't want to seem rude and ungrateful to a man who has offered to drive me to Double Bay. For nothing.

I don't want anyone to think *I'm* obsessed by sex, that *I'm* mad.

I smile. I try to look innocent and calm. I try to look indifferent.

He presses my hand down harder on the bulge. He begins to stroke my wrist with his thumb. I am close to delirious. I cannot think.

'I'm so glad you don't mind', he says softly. 'You're not embarrassed, are you, Rosalind?' His question sounds concerned, not bullying. I have only to say, and he'll take my hand away. He's not forcing me to keep my hand there.

'No, of course I'm not embarrassed', I answer with a nonchalant toss of my head.

'I'm glad you're not', I hear him telling me. I'm so frightened that I hardly know what is happening any more, hardly know what I'm doing. I am drunk with fear. I go on pretending to be rapt in the view.

He squeezes my hand on the bulge between his legs.

'Don't you think it's wonderful how God's made men different from women', he says.

Oh Christ! I don't know what to say. Is it *disappointment* I suddenly feel? I'm an atheist. I don't believe in God, despise droobs who believe in God. The man's a droob!

'You know how God has made men different from women, don't you, Rosalind?' he asks. 'Don't you think it's wonderful?'

Is he trying to talk down to me? I'm not a child! I glance sideways at him again. He is looking solemnly down at his hand on my hand on the bulge between his legs. Silly old fool! I realise he actually means what he says, that he's being quite serious. It scares me more to think that he must be some kind of crackpot, some kind of nut. How can I explain to him that I'm an atheist? Hasn't he ever heard of Darwin and Freud?

I'm too frightened of him to explain. I am too polite. 'Yes', I gush, 'yes, it *is* wonderful.' My voice is peculiar, though. It sounds guilty and false as well as childlike and terrified. I can tell just from my voice that I'm trying to humour him.

He can't. Or won't. Or doesn't care. He goes on talking about God. All the time he is speaking, he is gently pressing down on the bulge beneath his trousers with my hand. I try to seem not to notice. I try to seem totally absorbed in what he has to say and in the view, but it's like trying to pay no attention if my hand were being held down on a lump of burning coal. A voice is rambling on in the distance about God and our bodies and love and forgiveness and sin. He is murmuring on and on about there being more joy in heaven over one sinner who repenteth than over ninety and nine just persons or something, but all I am really thinking of is that bulge. There must be a ridge of cloth where the zipper is, and I can't feel anything definite, just a lump: it doesn't feel much like the thing in the diagrams in books. My mother would murder me if she knew I were here, she would never forgive me for this. The old man keeps pressing my trapped hand down on the firm lumpy bulge and talking of God.

He lifts my hand slightly. He sort of adjusts the lump thing sideways a bit. He closes my fingers around the firm lump thing through the cloth. My heart stops.

'Does that feel nice?' he asks me softly.

I stare at the dashboard.

'Does that feel nice, Rosalind?' he asks again.

I mumble yes. I am dizzy, scared rigid. The inside of my body is in turmoil, the outside as stiff as a china doll's. I am like a china doll whose hollow body is filled with a tumult of feelings. I stare straight ahead of me at the meter, my eyes like a doll's eyes—painted on. I concentrate on the words *FLAG FALL* on the dial. *FLAG FALL*. I *am* those words.

'You feel it, Rosalind', he offers, he pleads, squeezing the firm lump with my stiff hand. My brain reels again. I can hardly breathe. He tells me how wonderful it is that God has made this part of a man to fit inside a woman to give her babies, that it's all part of His Design. I hear. This is not real. This is not really part of my life. He asks me gently if I'd mind if he undid the zipper of his trousers and got me to put my hand inside so I could feel this part of him properly, hold it in my hand, feel for myself what a man is really like. He doesn't want to hurt me, he says.

87

He just wants to show me how different from a woman God has made a man, he just wants to show me the work of God. There's nothing wrong with looking upon the work of God, he says. There's nothing to be ashamed of about the way we've been made by God. 'Will you do that for me, Rosalind?' he asks. 'Will you do that for *me*?'

I'm so frightened I think I will die. *My mother will murder me.* I am shocked. I am dazed with shock, panic and shock. How will I stop myself saying yes? How will I stop myself?

'Oh, well, I haven't time really', is what I say.

I can sense how crestfallen he is.

'I think I should really be going now', I add.

'Do you?' he asks.

'Yes, I think I'd really better go.'

'Why?' There's resentment in his voice. Oh God, let him not be angry with me! He'll say I led him on. Oh God!

'Oh, well, you see, I've got to meet my friend at Double Bay. She'll be waiting for me, you see. She's expecting me. I really do think I ought to go.'

'Who's your friend?'

'Oh, she's my friend from school. I really should be going.'

'Are you sure?'

'Yes, I really do think I should.'

There is a silence. My heart pounds. I listen to my own breathing.

'Well, if you really have to . . . ?' he says petulantly.

'Yes I do, I really do, my friend'll be waiting for me.'

'What time do you have to meet her?' he asks.

I tell him the truth. 'Eleven o'clock.'

He looks at his watch. I can't see what it says. I don't dare look at mine.

Silence. Cars toot. Seagulls screech. Traffic hums.

'All right then, pet,' he says at last.

But still he doesn't release my hand.

I don't dare try to drag it away. I sit there helplessly. He says nothing. He is gazing out at the bay.

I decide to try again.

'I don't mind getting out and catching a bus if you're not

going that way right now after all', I offer, desperate to appease. 'Buses come pretty frequently along here, it would be no trouble.'

He snaps out of his trance. 'No, no, I'll drive you, I said I'd drive you, pet', he says, affronted. He puts my hand back in my lap. Just like that. It is just a thing, of no further interest to him. He discards it the way my father discards a book he's been looking through but has found doesn't tell him what he wants to know after all; in the way you discard what has now become an encumbrance.

He leans forward to switch on the ignition.

'To Double Bay then, eh?' he says, entirely matter-of-fact.

'Yes thanks', I say.

He does a U-turn back across New South Head Road and begins to drive towards Double Bay.

He doesn't say anything else at all. Nor do I. I watch the scenery go by.

I glance sideways at him as we go down the hill past Cranbrook. He is concentrating on driving. I realise that he has completely lost interest in me, he has forgotten me. I am just a young girl in green bermuda shorts with a pink beach towel on her lap whom he is driving to Double Bay. That's all I am.

When I turn round to look at him again, he is craning to see beyond the car in front of him, intent on passing. He is a respectable-looking elderly taxi driver carefully driving a young girl in green bermuda shorts to Double Bay. There is nothing odd about him. He has grey hair. He is just a man.

I am just a girl, thirteen, taking a taxi to Double Bay to meet her friend, Anne.

I think of telling Anne about what is happening to me. How will I tell her? I think of crying on Anne's shoulder, pouring the whole story out to her: her big blue eyes will be wide with amazement, alarm. She will make a fuss of me, comfort me, *admire* me, almost, for having had such a strange thing happen to me. Something exciting and dreadful has happened to me! I think of how interested she'll be, how kind, how concerned. I can't wait to tell her about it. It will be our secret. I can't wait to tell Anne.

All the time I am thinking this, I'm aware of the taxi driver beside me, driving. I shouldn't be sitting in the front, I realise. Mummy says never to sit in the front of taxis. Never mind. We're almost there, almost at Double Bay.

I see Anne see me coming in the cab. Her face lights up. She darts forward smiling as I get out. The taxi driver shouts goodbye, good-naturedly, just as if nothing had happened. I thank him, smiling. My face is twitching, but I am smiling.

Anne doesn't notice that I don't pay my fare. She doesn't seem to notice that I am trembling, that my face is ashen. Am I flushed or ashen? It doesn't seem to surprise her at all that I've arrived late in a cab, she takes lateness and cabs for granted. She doesn't notice how close I am to tears. I can't wait to tell her what has happened to me, can't wait for her to pity me.

The taxi is held up at the lights. I'm afraid to stop smiling until it has driven away. As soon as it's out of sight I will break down and cry, will tell Anne all that has happened to me. But there are dozens of people around. I wish there weren't so many people around. They'll stare when I begin to cry.

The lights change. I'm aware that the taxi drives off. Anne is still talking about the divine bikini she has seen in the window of The Squire Shop while she's been waiting. I can't think of how to butt in, how to begin what I have to say.

I can't think what I have to say. What is there to say?

I realise: Anne will not understand. Nice Anne. She won't understand what happened to me. Did anything happen? It would make a better story if he *had* made me look at his penis or tried to rape me or something like that. Now I wish he had! I feel obscurely cheated. It is terrible to have felt so much terror and yet not be able to explain what caused it. I *couldn't* have been more frightened no matter what he'd done, but Anne can't be expected to understand that. Anne can't be expected to believe I felt in such dreadful danger, so afraid, when really almost nothing happened to me: what happened to me was all my own fault or all in my head. It's not fair, this! I want to cry, I long for someone to understand how I feel and to pity me. How can I explain to Anne what was in my head? She'll ask why on earth I didn't take my hand away, why I didn't just jump out of the cab and run away. 'The taxi was *stopped*, wasn't it?' she'll say, baffled. It will be beyond her comprehension why I didn't run away, why I didn't run home and tell my mother, why I let this man do what he did with me. Did he *force* me to do anything against my will? No, nothing at all. I acquiesced to everything. Anne will be horrified, she'll think I'm quite depraved. Why didn't I scream, she will say. She won't understand at all why I didn't scream. She won't understand why I don't ring my parents now, straight away, and tell them every detail of what happened. How can I explain?

How can I explain to Anne what I don't myself understand? *There is nothing to say. Nothing happened.*

When Anne stops talking, all I tell her is that the bikini sounds really terrific. I go on smiling. Together we walk across the road and catch the 365 almost straight away. She chatters brightly to me all the way to Bondi Beach. All the way to Bondi Beach I chatter back. We talk about the kids at school. I feel myself grow calm.

I forget what has happened to me. Nothing happened.

We make our way to the end of the beach right away from the baths and the lifesaving club. All the Scots and Cranbrook boys and all the Ascham and Kambala girls who have come to the beach to meet each other are here, clustered beneath the Lost Children sign, rubbing oil on each other's backs, laughing and talking, flirting.

Anne sits with me under the Lost Children sign and chatters to people like Janey Wynne-Williams and introduces me as her friend and is surprised, really *surprised*, when we haven't actually met before, when it turns out that I've only *heard* of them. The people like Janey Wynne-Williams aren't surprised. I can see they can see I'm a waste of their time.

I lie there leadenly on my stomach on the hot sand, sweaty and dazed, my sunglasses on, pretending to read while Anne darts about like a little bird and chatters and dashes off into the surf and swims. I don't go in. I stay with my face hidden in a book. I am waiting.

I am waiting for something to happen to me.

The Holiday House

Gwen Kelly

ABOUT midday, the coast. Having spent or maybe mis-spent a morning on the road. Your chin juts purposefully beneath your partially open mouth. There is a glimpse of your death mask. Your sinuses are swollen with dust or maybe the pollens of the conservationists' Utopia, the rain forest. Later your nose will bleed. My knee aches. Whinge. My shoulder is stiff. Grizzle. Countless irritations. Why have we survived over 30 years of the marital tour while our daughter is deserted in little more than a decade. Not a matter of moral worth surely. We are just as selfish, just as petulant, just as intolerant. Maybe simply more resilient, conditioned to the traps from childhood; aware of the pitfalls in the dark, lonely world outside. Probably time ticked slower then, time to weigh the alternatives. A generation lost in the twin furnaces of Depression and War. The three children sit in the back seat. Endurance for 130 miles in near silence. The coming divorce is subduing them.

We look for the agent. We want a holiday house. You, my ageing spouse, favour the old-fashioned: rooms tacked on to an open veranda. But up-to-date facilities, please. No oil lamps, fuel stoves, down-the-yard dunnies. Our granddaughters go for a swimming pool. Groovy! A coloured TV. What on earth would we do at night?; a tennis court. Can't miss out on practice, our coach says ... Cease to listen.

Perhaps Dick would have preferred sons. Maybe he is ex-hausted by tuition fees. Ballet, music, tennis. Not likely. Boys play tennis too. And pianos for that matter. Real reason not as complex. Sexual. New girl, younger, more appreciative. Pneumatic. A Huxley word. The firm, rubbery flexibility of prime grade youth.

The money angle? Think it over while you park against the gutter. As usual the boot sticks out, a metal bum obstructing the traffic; if there were any, but there isn't. An ageing billboard above the shops says, 'HOLIDAY HOUSES FOR RENT' W.S. DOAK. but W.S. Doak is not there, Merely Mrs Doak. Ageing, grey hair topping a putty face, cheeks bulging like a Toby mug, six whiskers on the chin, face astute. With a glance, she almost but not quite dismisses us. 'Have kids have you? No cottages to let' (the billboard lies). 'You're lucky though. There is a flat.' 'Maybe we could look at it', you say. The hesitation shows in your voice. Even in bed your tone conveys reluctance. She smiles but not quite. She almost says, 'Why bother?' but changes her mind. 'There are tenants in it at the moment. You can look at the outside.' You take the key. She inquires about numbers; mutters 'No pets' then writes the address on a card.

The eldest granddaughter, Anna says, 'We can keep Sheba at our place. Daddy is upset but Marilyn hates Sheba. I took her to Daddy's flat and Marilyn screamed, "Get that bloody dog out of here." She told Daddy she was sick of his animals and his brats. I suppose she meant us.'

'Possibly', I said. 'You were probably naughty. She's only eighteen.'

Mrs Doak leans back in her chair and stares at the street. Petra, the middle girl, says, 'Daddy had to take Tamara to the park when we stayed there last time.' Tamara is four. 'She wet the floor. An accident because she was nervous. Marilyn was cranky because the carpet is new but Dad put his arms round us and said, "Let's walk in the park until Marilyn finishes the housework. The grass is already damp there." Why does he stay, Grandma? Our house is nicer.'

Nod, smile. What else can I do? Mrs Doak's eyelids droop. O to be an estate agent rather than a wife or mother. To harvest the good earth into building blocks kerbed and guttered, to garner endless units from free-as-air cottages, all mod. cons., cheek by jowl, earning six rents or even twelve. Her earthenware body

93

spreads across the desk and her eyes lift as we pass into the street. The board still reads HOLIDAY HOUSES FOR RENT. Vacation. The annual pilgrimage to permanent houses for permanent families. No longer. New temporary dwellings for temporary relationships. Mum and Dad and the kids. Mum and kids and no Dad. Dad and kids and no Mum. Dad and the new missus and the old kids; Dad and the new missus and the new kids; Mum and . . . Stop! the permutations are endless and only half of them work. Dick is not pneumatic. Not now. There is a jelly-wobble, an undulation as yet barely perceptible beneath his shirt. What is there for Marilyn? A new Daddy resurrected in the image of childhood's Daddy, one her Mummy can't have. In no time Anna will be as old as Marilyn. Have all men a secret desire to ravish their daughters? I look at you dangling the key from your fingers, lines of anxiety creasing your face. I am sure the thought has never entered your head. You are not a ravishing man. Maybe you should have been.

'Just like home', Mrs Doak says lifting her lids from the droop of slumber. 'You wouldn't know the difference.' I fear she is right.

You, my ancient of days, drive round the block with the same apparent lack of interest that propelled you down the corkscrew mountain road, through the rain forest, where you were pushed almost into the precipice by the harvest-the-trees timber jinkers. You have a crick in the neck from your attempt to peer round Australian Meats packed in silver foil riding in a spacious white van that swayed across the double yellow lines a few feet from your windscreen. Australian Meats now stands parked in front of Ocean View pub. Pass it triumphantly, horn blowing. Better late than never. You halt soon in front of red-brick oblongs, built facing a side paling fence, instead of the ocean, to increase the number of units, the number of tenants, patios, balconies, glass doors. Each identical with its neighbour. Could be anywhere. Coffs, Ballina, Sawtell, Nambucca, even Terrigal. The brick veneered Australian dream with garage at the back, barbie in communal yard. All with a view if you can bear to leave the shelter and stand on the front lawn.

You shrug off your coat. Sun-warm shoulders. The kids spill

94

on to the road. 'Gosh, there's a tiny beach down there.' 'There's a slide in the park.' 'There's swings.' They speed across the road to the grass, not looking at the unit. The river glints in the sunlight as beautiful as ever. The lazy Bellinger. First glimpsed 40 years ago from the veranda of the almost-new-then Ocean View pub. Honeymoon. Look at his bearding face. Does he remember, hands clasped looking at the river? Bodies entwined in the dark night with the music of surf beyond the breakwater in our ears. 'That was wonderful', you said. Grunt. Not quite as wonderful as hoped but nothing said. It will improve with repetition. Hours later the same surf drums beyond the morning sunlight on the bed. A threnody. The first repetition. Bodies swayed in sea rhythms. So many repetitions since that morning. Most of them forgotten, momentary sensations, past and gone. But that early repetition stains my consciousness with a kind of remembered joy. Feel now automatically for your fingers. An ageing wife, hair grey, dyed fawn. Fat. Medical term 'obese'. Your lean young Chips–Rafferty figure is now stringy. Your firm chin above the crinkling neck juts, beaded with beard. But your hand presses back. You remember. Drowned in nostalgia, decide to take the unit. Call the children. Return to Mrs Doak who is not surprised.

'Will we go to the unit in August?' Petra asks.

'That's right.'

'Who?' says Anna.

'Grandad and me and all of you and Mummy.'

'Not Daddy?' asks Petra.

'No.'

'Not even for the weekend?'

'Of course not, silly', says Anna. 'Daddy has his own holidays with Marilyn.'

'We can go with Daddy', says Petra. 'Two holidays instead of one.'

'I won't go', says Anna. 'Not even if they ask me.'

Tamara says, 'Daddy will take me. I'm the youngest.'

'No, he won't', says Anna. 'You're the biggest nuisance.'

Tamara stamps her foot. 'I'm not. I'm not.' She begins to cry.

I frown at the older children and put my arm round Tamara.

You are busy with Mrs Doak who grunts, 'A week's rent.'
'Bankcard?' you ask.

She takes it and flexes it in her fingers with contempt for all
credit in her eyes. But she fills in the form like an expert. Think.
Plastic cards for veneered units. Australian vacation. 1980s style.
She passes the receipt. You put it in your wallet. You go
through the door. The children follow you. Mrs Doak is again
muttering 'no pets'. Wonder if she would like to add 'no
children'.

Time to eat sandwiches in the park with the children. Drink
hot coffee from a thermos or coloured fluids from tins. Time to
turn back. Yet another vacation packed ready to be delivered in
spring, like all those other vacations. But not like. Veneer, not
timber. TV not 500. Stove not primus. Electricity not oil lamps.
Washing machine (twin tub) not an enamel basin. The century is
limping to its close. Who wants to fish from a row boat? Why
surf? There's a tiled pool. Next year, maybe, you can spend
your dollars at the Lido. Vacation villages are booming. The
century is rushing to its close. And countless marriages rush
with it.

'I like Marilyn', says Tamara. 'She let me climb into bed with
her and Daddy.'

There is a loud hiss. Anna and Petra stand, necks extended
like geese, towards Tamara. They hiss again, a long sibilant
angry crescendo of hate.

The Saddest Pleasure

Inez Baranay

POSTCARD
RAFFLES HOTEL

Dear . . . . .
As you see we are at the famous Raffles Hotel
sipping a Singapore Gin Sling on the palm
fringed veranda.
I have been told that this drink was created
by barman Ngiam Tong Boon in the Long Bar
sometime in 1915. Here is the recipe:
2/4 Tanqueray Gin
1/4 Peter Heering Cherry Brandy
Drops of Benedictine and Cointreau
1/4 Orange, Pineapple and Lime juice
Angostura Bitters
Decorated with Pineapple and Cherry
Topped with a little secret

Love,

ANOTHER POSTCARD
This 'resort' is my first few days in Penang, Pearl of the Orient;
moving on soon. Meanwhile I sit on this palmfringed terrace
over a palmfringed sea eating papaya and surrounded by group
tours of German nuclear families in their batik sundresses and
palmfringed T-shirts: we exchange horrified stares while non-
stop speakers play Asian cover versions of disco hits. . . .

At sunset in Penang the Muslims are called to prayer on one side, the Chinese light joss-sticks on the other, the fishing boats are pulled high up on the beach, the village people stroll and look at the sea, I have moved from the fabulous to the mythical. The spectacular colours leave behind shadows of greys, blues and black in the melting sky then white-lit clouds of pearl appear and I remember that pearly white glow, that I missed for years then forgot, which you see here at twilight in the sky and stamping along wet sand and in the spray from a boat on the sea. Mr Fu is a Chinese opium devotee who looks like a legendary ancient sage. So lively for an old man, he swims energetically, goes off to the O-den, hangs around all the hippies (this now includes us I fear), works a few late hours at the Resort up the beach and loves to give advice mainly about taking it easy and getting into opium. His tiny bony face crinkles as he laughs, his eyes disappear. I find out he is 36 years old. Michael takes me to the O-den. An old man makes the pipes, I have eight, I didn't know if this is more than usual the first time. Afterwards Michael becomes amorous. His skin is like silk but so is everything else. Don't hassle me Michael I say. OK he promises readily but insists on giving me a photo. I rejoin David on the beach, the night swells. Sometimes there is movement, once I realise an old Malay fisherman is lying near me, once an African arrives saying it's 3 a.m. and he's just reached Penang penniless but he has a pink and gold scarf 'like the moon' so he sells it to me, I pay, I don't say a word, he goes, we continue, we lie never sleeping dreaming for hours as if floating on those shimmering waves or on clouds of scented silk.

I was used to having multiple lives and it began in Penang.

I was a RAAF daughter and had a way of checking out men in uniform. I played mah-jong, learned Japanese flower arranging and English cooking and had a lot of manicures. I helped out at the radio station and collected requests from the base hospital. It was suddenly full of boys who'd had limbs blown off in Vietnam. What did I know about Vietnam, something about a threat to Australian beaches, Vietnam seemed even further away from here, what questions could have occurred? I was a bridesmaid, learned to waltz, loved gin and tonic and the Officers' Mess, read Françoise Sagan, wore white and pink.

This milkbar was frequented by soldiers and Asians and such. I wore boy's jeans and someone told me that the guy was jumping like that by the jukebox because of something he did smoke. I bought a little packet. One night I took my father's pipe and the packet down to the beach. You know those tropical nights, drive you crazy. The silkiness, the lights in the sea and wet sand, the blue lights playing lightning flashes all over your skin and each hair. Memory links with a grateful appreciation of the herb. There must have been some time I noticed the first weird-looking travellers but never heard of the trail.

I lived in my bedroom, my palace, my cage, and lived deeper in my unquiet heart. I knew what existentialism meant, wrote verses, and wept suddenly at things no one else noticed. I was mystifyingly tortured by intimate aliens, my unrelated family. I constructed arguments for androgeneity and a perfect world, I would rather burn than marry and howled at the moon.

The French girls would bring their governess, she was only nineteen and beautiful with mascara layered thickly like a doll's. The English girls had bellbottom pants and the soundtrack. To the Mersey sound we tried lots of different kinds of drinks. I nearly went all the way oh so many times, never quite. The Commanders' sons took us for motorbike races on the airstrip. Charlotte tried to cut my hair in her mod style; she knew Soho well. We had her house all weekend, I smoked menthols and had my first memory loss as a compensation of alcohol.

Thirteen years later, in Penang again. There's a big white house on a hill and I knew I'd be going back there, just to walk by or drive and I'd look at it, just because I'd lived there and it was a certain time and seemed to have a lot to do with a certain part of me. And when you travel you must have certain allegorical journeys too, and I'd go and look straight and long into the face of the past and it would be like a pilgrimage and maybe a moment of sublime understanding and a corner of the house would be waiting to release a precious and important memory.

I knew every bit of the steep road up, and you could see

passing by below that it hadn't changed, you pass the two Chinese hairdressers and the Indian general store with its odd and colourful range . . . around the bend up to the house, large and square, a sullen young girl pouting at a camera from a deck chair, an extravagant view of palms and the brilliant sea.

It would have been easy to go there, I just wanted to pass it, I could have told the taxi to detour on the way from the airport, and the hill wasn't far from where you changed buses between the fishing village and Georgetown. There is a row of Chinese hotels and, between buses, you could sit out the back of them by the sea wall and feast on fish and crabs. At the bus stop I'd always buy a slice of papaya and they would put it in a little plastic bag. I accepted, bemused, a couple of times, and didn't throw the little pink plastic sacks on the ground with the others, but then I'd always buy the papaya and refuse the plastic: my protest against corruption by Coca-Cola culture. It wasn't the multinational beach resorts up the coast, but those scraps of pink plastic lying around that made me agree that really Penang is now Fucked Up. Still we had nice lunches at Tanjong Bungah between buses and David would agree that one day soon we'd hire a car and see the whole coast and the monkeys and the temples and the railway up Penang Hill, and then I'd drive up the hill just behind us but not yet because there was the village and all that food and dope and hypnotic sea and narcotic sun, and the boys who lent me their motorbikes. I rode up the coast and then down again, and near the bus stop there was a nightclub, the same one from which I used to hear the thrilling thin wail of song from my room up on the hill and there was the night I wandered out, late, careless of shame, to sit hidden on the beach down there closer to that music, teased by that tantalising music.

At the waterfall Mac turned up and pranced for the camera, we all pose, here we are, colourful and tan and framed in foliage. Then Mr Fu led us back to the hangout and Fu and Michael screamed at each other in Chinese, it was wonderful. I think they were fighting over us. Michael said Fu was stupid and Mr Fu told us Michael is crazy. The Malay boys massage each other to relieve the ordeal of Ramadan fasting. The hippie men sit around strumming a guitar and growing their beards while their girlfriends do the washing. A Cosmo girl or debutante could pick up a few tips on how to keep your man from a hippie chick. A hippie chick follows her man waits on him lets him do the talking placidly takes a load of bullshit and never rocks his boat. And she's always so feminine in that faded-sarong and ankle-bells look, that spaced-out glaze. (So laid back she's half dead.) They're all into Asia because it gets you away from Western materialism and it's so cheap. The trouble is finding somewhere you can eat yoghurt. And more trouble, in India they don't eat brown rice. But you can get good jaffles here. They exchange names of where the hash is cheapest and really amazing. They tighten the barricades around their couples in the face of an onslaught of Asians all threatening to Rip Them Off. He looks after the big hassles like telling her where they're going next and scoring the dope. The chick packs up the washing.

You don't have to explain why you came back to Australia, everyone comes back. It's a good life. The clairvoyant said we choose Australia, it's a hard country to live in, it's a test, it's something we have to learn. As we choose our parents, we choose Australia. It's a good life in a hard country. Of course you came home broke. Australia is where you make money. Your friends are here. The weather. You've got used to it. You can save up and go away for holidays. Where else are there beaches right in the city. Opportunity. And things are changing, look at all the restaurants, Lebanese, Vietnamese, Korean. Elsewhere in the world they have bloody bitter wars, here in Australia we get better restaurants. The one place in the world you're not too late for its best times. We're getting international trends, all-night bars.

There's something else. In Australia your distant heart is full of unknown things, secrets, possibilities. In Australia your dry vast centre is unseen, unknown, anciently loved.

The first stage of love is love. It lasts for hours or months or any time at all but not long. The second stage of love is nostalgia for the first stage. It is called love. It recreates love in the search for the love that was. Do you agree?

101

Croup

Kate Llewellyn

A lasso whips round your chest as you wake and can't gasp. A sound of a kettle the moment before it whistles whines and keens in the back of your throat, frightens the cat and brings your father walking in his sleep, saying: 'I'll just get over this rope'. He thinks he's in his little boat. The rope's round my chest and he knows what to do. He strokes my head and turns to get the metho. The old one two three.

He poured it onto a damp cloth, splashed on some vinegar and wrapped it round my throat, fastening it with a big safety pin. The smell would cut a rope of any thickness. He took my 'Ebb and Flo' book from a shelf in the wardrobe, pulled up a chair and began to read to me. Ebb and Flo were black people with several children with very curly hair who had adventures I knew by heart. He'd drone on until the choked neigh in the back of my throat got fainter and fainter like a horse disappearing over a hill and finally faded away. Sometimes he'd keep on, not noticing I was getting better and I'd say: 'That's enough now, Daddy. I'll go to sleep now.' He closed the book and turned off the light, saying: 'Sleep well, Princess.'

In the morning the almost dry cloth round my neck were croup's night gifts. Old Santa Claus croup. My mother came in and said: 'Don't go to school today'. My father brought in my breakfast tray, saying: 'Not too good, Dooley Pegs?'

The doctor arrives with an old black bag, saying: 'Now let me see'.

His voice is soft and winning. The voice people use to speak to a very sick animal they love. It is rather fussy too, an anxiety to be helpful makes it slightly nervous. My mother loves him. He rescues her from fright. He helps her by being available from the old black phone with a handle she turns to ring. I think she thinks she's ringing God. This is better than prayers because he will arrive at the door. She puts down the phone, saying proudly: 'Dr Wilberforce is coming!' As if she was announcing the war was over. She runs quickly to empty the chamber pot.

Dr Wilberforce lends me his daughter's 'Amelia Jane' books because she had little brothers as I have. Amelia Jane stole cakes from a party for her brothers at home, put them in her umbrella and forgot them when she put it up in the rain as she left the party. I never stopped being horrified with embarrassment for her.

He sits on the side of my bed and turns to ask my mother a question. I pull up my nightie and he places the cold coin of the stethoscope on my chest, then pokes the second black question mark into his other ear. He presses the stethoscope over my chest and asks me to sit forward and presses on my back with the now slightly warm coin. He places his cool, pink, very clean fingers round my jaw and gives me a quiet summing-up look. It is impossible to imagine those hands not being clean. His dignity and white hair have the consolation of a cool change after a long heatwave. He speaks a few words to my mother in the passage, pops his head round the door and says something about soon being better and leaves. I know he treats and calms us both in these visits.

My father comes home at lunchtime and the smell of roast mutton is filling the house. I can tell from the scraping of the pan that the gravy is being made. He walks in and gives me a packet of Columbine caramels: a long, thin blue box covered with dancing fairies which I found out later were ballerinas. There is also a packet of Butter Menthols in an orange packet with a medicinal design.

'Feeling any better, Dooley?'

I nod and smile and ask him to read me some Amelia Jane before he goes back to work. He sits down and reads some before lunch and puts the book down as my mother brings in the tray. She is wearing a green apron made from old kitchen curtains. It has a frill patterned with red berries over the shoulders.

A whine. A cat fighting. A chook the moment before the axe falls. A kettle the moment before it whistles. I tumble out of bed and wake as I walk through the door. It's croup. It's my daughter.

'It's the old croup, Angel.'

I pick her up with her creaking throat. Her hair is wet and her eyes are wide, fighting that rope. I take her to the kitchen, get a cloth, bend under the sink, holding her in one arm and get out the vinegar and metho, talking to her all the time: 'I won't be a moment, darling.' Turning on the hot tap, wetting the cloth, I squeeze it out with one hand and pour on some vinegar. I don't think the vinegar helps, but do it anyway, just in case. I drench the cloth with metho. She jerks her head back as I put the cloth near her face.

'Breathe it in, Angel, breathe it in.'

I lie on my bed and put her across my stomach and breathe with her trying to warm and calm her. Help her get her breath. My bellows, my body, her lungs. It helps, but not enough. We breathe together for half an hour, enveloped by the smell of the spirit and its moisture. Finally I say: 'We'll have to go to hospital, babe, is that OK?' She nods and I reach over and call a taxi. He arrives and drives as if I'm having a baby in the car. He could hear her in the street, he says, and he thinks she's dying.

'Slow down a bit', I tell him, 'she's only got croup.' He's never heard of it.

She's admitted and put into a tent cot. It's covered with a plastic lid and is hot and moist inside and makes her hotter. She hates it, but goes in, resigned. It makes her sweat more and more and I'm scared she'll have a convulsion.

'You can go home now, Mummy.'

In the morning I take her the tiny woollen gloves my Mother sent on the train when she heard the news.

'Look what Muttee sent you.'

There's fever in her face. She says: 'Glubs'. I pass them to her

under the tent and out fall all the five cent pieces her Grandmother filled them with.

'Don't you like them, darling?'

'Yes, but I'm sorry, Mummy, I can't smile.'

She was always like that, wanting to please.

Just as she is now, getting me a cup of tea in bed and calling me
Mrs Travers. I call her Warner and she stands with her hands at
her sides and bows as she imagines a maid might do. We're from
Katherine Mansfield's story 'Such a Sweet Old Lady'. I told her
I'd like the big white cup on the Chinese red lacquer tray.

'Do you want the white lace cloth on it?'

'No thank you, Warner, I don't want to give Cook the
trouble of sending it to the laundry.'

I can hear the clink of the cup as she comes in and I see she
hasn't brought the tray and the tea is too strong. I tell her this,
and she laughs and gives my jaw a gentle slap and I say: 'Warner!
Have you lost your senses?'

Lady Weare and the Bodhisattva

Kylie Tennant

O N any flight between Sydney and Melbourne there would be at least one Australian woman exactly like Lady Weare. She was half a stone overweight, and her knitted woollen suit, which she wore because she expected Melbourne to be cold, did nothing for her figure. Her hair was going grey and she couldn't waste time at the hairdresser's. Her husband and children loved her anyway. Her immovable face, which made her look like Queen Victoria, was more haughty than usual because her new shoes were giving her hell. She had bought them yesterday especially for this trip and they were too tight. She would continue to wear them because they were expensive and elegant. They exactly matched her off-white handbag. She also carried a shabby briefcase full of papers which she needed for her speech at the conference in Melbourne, and other papers for the committee meeting in Adelaide.

The briefcase didn't match anything except Lady Weare who was worn with a lifetime of work. It was as much part of her personality as the glasses she wore when she was reading, something indispensable which must not be mislaid.

The passengers tramped aboard the plane into an atmosphere something like plunging into a warm feather pillow. They looked about them as their ancestors must have done when transported, a look of bravado mixed with caution and the dreadful knowledge that they would be sitting next to strangers and might be expected to speak to them. Lady Weare took her seat and gave her companion an icy glance which crossed one even more icy. The man buried himself in his paper. Lady Weare took out a clip of statistics from her briefcase and bent her head over them. Shutting her eyes as the plane prepared to take off she ran through her accustomed prayers. She had been on so many flights she couldn't remember them all and this was only a bus run. But she prayed nevertheless that if anything happened someone would look after Jim and the children. She then went on to pray from force of habit for the long list of friends, connections and some undesirable characters who needed help. They would have been very surprised to know this praying was going on. Others she prayed for from old affection's sake. Lady Weare prayed the way other women knitted. She filled in odd moments and kept herself busy. She did not pray for herself because that might have been undignified.

She merely hoped that whatever hellish thing Melbourne had in store she might meet it without failing. She never refused to go to Melbourne, but it was her hoodoo city, a black jinx. Every time she went there something appalling happened, some bad luck, some disaster. She had gone to work in Melbourne when she was eighteen and suffered every humiliation and misery imaginable for someone young and poor. Now that she was old and rich Melbourne still lay in wait for her like a trap. On one visit, a year ago, she had stayed there for a week and congratulated herself that nothing had happened. But she reached the airport to come home to find that fog prevented her plane from leaving. The scene at the airport became more and more crazy—thickened with noise, crying children, crowds milling desperately as planes piled up. Lady Weare was there for 6 hours trying to get away and being met by rudeness; at last like a refugee refusing to struggle, sitting in despair, then listening to the unintelligible roar of the loudspeaker, realising finally that she was being called.

And what about the time she had been lost in a strange suburb after midnight and all the houses were dark; there was no one to tell her the way? And the other time when the hotel made a mistake in her booking and she could not even find any of her friends and was given a couch in a stranger's living room? Other people might find Melbourne charming. To Lady Weare it was

107

Kylie Tennant

a disaster city. But she never refused to go there; that would be to admit a failure of nerve.

She eased her feet out of the tight shoes. The man next to her stirred and turned his flinty, suspicious face towards her. 'Excuse me', he said. 'Aren't you Jill Weare? We met at the Amorys'. Did you ever find out what happened to Ernest?'

His face split into a smile so friendly that Lady Weare immediately stopped looking like Queen Victoria and became Jill Weare. They talked warmly and almost excitedly all the way to Melbourne because they were interested in the same committees. Lady Weare forgot she was going to her hoodoo city until she came down from the plane into the middle of a heatwave wearing a wollen suit.

'Lovely weather it's been for the Festival.' The driver of the government car thought he might as well be nice to the old bag, because she might be important if a car was sent to meet her. 'The whole fortnight it's been like this, sunshiny and glad to be alive.'

Lady Weare said, 'I am willing to place a small bet that tomorrow it will be raining heavily'.

'Ah, don't say that.' The driver was of a cheerfulness to match the weather. 'Why would that be, then?'

'*I* am here', Lady Weare said sardonically. 'It never fails.'

'From Sydney then?' The driver nodded understandingly. He knew about Sydney people.

The house where Lady Weare was to stay for the two nights of her visit was old and had a friendly garden. The sunlight came through windows as though into a Dutch painting. Apples in baskets, pears in baskets, were lying on the marble table by the back door. The terrace had a grapevine just losing its leaves. Her host and hostess, when she had changed into summer clothing, introduced her to friends who came fluttering in; the wine cellar and the Western Australian native plants; and the children of the doctor who lived next door. There was a Persian cat and an old mastiff. When evening came and they all drove into the city in the bigger of the two cars, Lady Weare's host even found a place to park outside the restaurant where they dined before the conference.

The evening was a great success and on the way home, in the warm caressing night with the lights velvety and flowerlike, they laughed as though they were young and careless. As they sat in the kitchen having a last drink together Lady Weare's hostess exclaimed that it was raining.

In the morning, the Melbourne Lady Weare had known, the Melbourne of misery and wretchedness, was weeping with the grey skies that wept as though the rain was a loss to them. Lady Weare spent the morning transacting business for her husband. She felt gay—relieved—what could happen? She was to lunch with a professor at the University, who brought two friends to meet her. They asked what she was doing that afternoon. She told them she would be leaving early next morning for Adelaide, but that afternoon was for enjoyment. 'I thought I would seize the chance to go to the Art Centre. My daughter will be quite disgusted if I don't see it.' She assured them that she was quite capable of finding her way by tram across the city, and they drove her to a tramstop.

The rain was now being discharged as a vicious barrage, missing nothing. Lady Weare felt quite cheerful in her raincoat and knitted suit. Her feet were hurting her, the rain splattered into the tramcar. Well, if this was all there was to Melbourne this time, it was quite bearable. The Art Centre amused her with its neo-Aztec heaviness. There was nothing pleasanter than walking—even with aching feet—around an art gallery by yourself. You could stop to examine something you liked and were not hurried on to look at something you didn't want to see.

Lady Weare decided she would look at the Eastern art. You couldn't look at everything. She had never appreciated the Hindu convention—as simple really as comic-strip balloons—whereby gods with as many arms as a spider sat in the middle of this halo of limbs. It reminded her of the Italian picture of a man walking his dog and the dog had a whole blur of legs. What was the word?—'gimmicky'.

She strolled from one magnificent scroll painting to the next. They were old, faded, brown, with intimate details of houses appearing when you looked closely. And strolling thus, dignified and not thinking about anything in particular except the pain in her feet, Lady Weare with her catalogue and her handbag, her cream-coloured raincoat, her glasses—for looking at the details closely—her sensible cloth turban—for rain, Melbourne rain—came upon the Bodhisattva.

She had noticed a number of these female Bodhisattva figures in the Asiatic paintings she had been studying. What these spirit-women were doing besides being decorative she had not the slightest idea. They posed around the edges of whatever heavenly or religious action was going on, representing some principle, perhaps. She would never know. But Lady Weare's Bodhisattva was quite different. A bronze statue about life-size, she came writhing up like a flame of goddess, dancing-girl, narrow-waisted, all dark energy.

Lady Weare peered at the Bodhisattva's face under its curved headdress. The eyelids were tilted, the narrow curved mouth was tilted in a smile at once menacing and unearthly. Perhaps she was representing some principle, but the hands that were holding a hammer and gong looked like just a beautiful woman's hands. Lady Weare felt drawn towards the Bodhisattva. Here was the embodiment, she felt, of all that she was not. This Bodhisattva had never sat on a committee or chaired one. She would not be worried or elated or try too hard.

Lady Weare admired the Bodhisattva a little wistfully and walked away. She walked back. She gazed intently at the figure of the spiritual being. Something was trying to get through to her. She looked again more closely. The clenched hand of the figure showed a worn place where people had touched it on the bronze knuckles. There were notices asking people not to touch anything. Nevertheless Lady Weare cautiously put out her ungloved hand and touched the hand of the Bodhisattva. She felt that the Bodhisattva would like that. It might make her feel,

Note: Bodhisattva: a spiritual being conceived by Buddhism who has by his morality and meditation reached the status of full enlightenment, but who refuses to abandon all other beings in their suffering. From compassion he stays in the world to help.

Philip Rawson, *The Art of Southeast Asia*

in this strange place, that she was receiving the deference to which she was accustomed.

Touching that worn bronze was like touching one of those electric machines in a penny arcade. A current of force prickled through Lady Weare so astonishingly that she touched the hand again to make sure. Then she hurried away—rather shaken. She found herself gazing at some Papuan deathmasks. Upstairs, the day darkened around her as she looked at a Raising of Lazarus and then a Vision of Hell. Even the portraits looked very dead. I must go, she thought desperately, beginning to be afraid. But she hesitated, stumbled on with those painful feet more excruciating now, until at last, exhausted, she found herself outside in the rain.

Opposite the Art Centre, beyond three streams of traffic, trams were arriving and departing almost empty at a strip of grass, while outside the Art Centre a group of people waited to run across to the trams, looking for a break in the line of cars.

If I were not so faint-hearted, Lady Weare thought, I would take a chance—dash across. The woman beside her took a break in the traffic and darted forward, and Lady Weare hesitated, almost went with her. The woman was about her age, had the same cream-coloured raincoat. Her grey hair was showing under just such a head covering as Lady Weare wore. If *she* could do it, Lady Weare thought, looking up the rushing traffic for the next break, can't I?

There was an exclamation from someone in the group and a thud. Lady Weare turned back to see the woman's handbag—so exactly like her own—lying in the wet roadway. The woman herself—where was she? Lady Weare looked in the wrong place because the woman had been flung forward by the car that had hit her such a long way beyond her handbag. Lady Weare felt a dreadful sinking. The traffic was still flashing past. No one stopped. She could not get across the road. Finally she managed to struggle over and ran towards the woman who was lying in the rain and the dirt.

'Don't touch her!' a man ordered. He was standing sternly, saying nothing, with a group forming a kind of defensive ring. They had their lips tight shut, they had sent someone for an

111

ambulance, they were waiting for the police, they were keeping off inquisitive people, doing 'the right things'.

The woman had her hand flung out, her fingers were clenched. Lady Weare wanted very much to take that hand in her own. Where the woman's face had scraped the road it was dirty and broken. As Lady Weare stooped down, the man said again, 'Don't touch her', quite threateningly. The outflung hand shivered a little like the wing of a frightened bird. Then the fingers opened, stiffened, lay limp.

Lady Weare, under the hostility of the men from the car that had smashed into the woman, turned away. When she sat in the train going home the hand of the woman kept quivering and then lying still. Around Lady Weare the kind of squalor that Melbourne provided especially for her darkened the dirty carriage. People with faces that are only seen in nightmares, mowed and leered at each other, read newspapers and smoked filthy stubs of tobacco. The floor was littered with repulsive garbage. An empty beer can clattered across the carriage. The colours ranged from deep soot to mid–mud. The landscape outside the windows could have been limbo.

The charming house, her warm friends, welcomed her. 'I saw an accident', was all she told her hostess. 'It gave me rather a shock.' That night her host walked into the sharp corner of a wardrobe and was knocked unconscious. He was not badly hurt, but he lay on the floor with his hand flung out.

Next morning as she walked towards the plane for Adelaide, her rather chilly face set in its Queen Victoria repose, her feet hurt her worse than ever. The sun was shining in a cloudless sky and it was going to be a glorious day in Melbourne.

Arriving at the hotel in Adelaide she felt that even if it made her late for her meeting she would have a bath and change all her clothes. There was a Viennese maid of about her own age flicking about the bedroom. 'My shoes hurt me', Lady Weare observed to the maid. 'If I had any sense I wouldn't wear them.'

'But, madame, they are so elegant!' The woman had a bright, sparkling look. 'Oh how I know the shoes that are elegant and hurt one's feet! When I come to this country I think: "One will not get good things there," and I buy *for forty dollars* a pair of crocodile-skin shoes. Think of it! And they hurt me so I can hardly walk onto the boat. They hurt me for years. They never wear out. At last I throw them away.'

Lady Weare sat down on the side of the bed. She regarded her elegant buckled shoes attentively while another maid came in and engaged in an animated exchange with the Viennese. I wonder if I am punishing myself, she thought. If so, I wonder what for?

Was it that if the shoes hurt her this might propitiate whatever provided the bad luck in Melbourne? That they would realise she didn't need more suffering? Ridiculous! Then she thought, I wonder if they mistook that woman for me? Ridiculous! She wondered what would happen next time she went to Melbourne, and shrugged. Then, with the icy expression which indicated her feet were hurting she took up her briefcase and set out, exactly on time for her committee meeting.

In three months' time, she knew, she would again be going to Melbourne.

Licorice lozenges. french safety pins. and jelly snakes.

Bronwyn Sweeney

*I*T'S may now. and pearl goes to school. for a month. she can feel the weather getting colder   a chill in the air jack frost on the ground when she and eric leave at eight o'clock. the sun shines and the adults talk of rain. she'd like to dawdle and the trees are empty cutting the sun and the sky into pieces. she says so to eric but he walks fast and talks about half an apple and half again of an apple pie. pearl looks through the empty trees   and they end up being late.

   it's may now. and pearl mutters the last month of autumn   under her breath. she learns it at school and tells her mother. margaret edwards nods and shells the peas and tells pearl that her grandmother always said it was the middle of spring. pearl nods and shells peas. she learns this at school too.

   it's may now. and pearl's been going to school for a month. and the teacher remembers her name. mr mills. he calls her out the front. she does simple addition and subtraction. she chews her finger. she sucks a strand of hair. she looks at her feet. she usually gets the answers right. while the whole class watches her. except eric   rushes off at three thirty yelling goodbye to his friends and he's got work to do to pearl: pa said. eric always seems to have work to do. so does pearl's father. so does pearl. that's why he hadn't wanted her to go to school. when mr mills came and said pearl was eleven and should be getting an education and they were breaking the law according to the act of eighteen   . pa couldn't remember the date and then he decided it didn't matter no daughter of his was going to school:

pa said. pearl's mother put her hand on his arm. she thought maybe it was a good idea. and pearl might even end up being a schoolteacher she was a bright little thing. and anyway they couldn't afford to break the law. and pearl's mother took her hand off his arm and when she put his dinner down in front of him. he wanted a piece of bread   and when she had cut a slice and buttered it and handed it to him   . he stirred two sugars into his tea   and said allright. but only until she's thirteen. pearl is glad. she's tired to shelling peas. and she likes the idea of becoming a schoolteacher. pearl's mother is glad. as well. although she hates shelling peas. as well. and is in the habit of saying twice the hands half the work   when pearl gets in from school.

for the defence:
it is about a mile and three quarters from canley vale school to where pearl edwards resides; she should have reached home by four o'clock if she had not stopped on the way; accused and his brother are hard-working boys.

margaret edwards stands at the back door for an hour to look at the view. the few acres that her husband owns   he's out there somewhere   wanting his lunch already. and she ignores the glint of metal and sweat from that corner of the east paddock. he's clearing more land more plans more money and debts he'll tell her about when he comes in.

she stares at the grey and brown. she can't understand her husband's passion. she wants penny postcards of an english garden. a french coast. a german castle. she wishes the rain would come. she likes the colour green. she knows they'll then talk about the new machinery and the new regulations and the man from the dairying board. she likes the man from the dairying board and pours the top off the cream into his cup. he licks the cream from his upper lip and touches his neat black moustache with the tip of his tongue. she smiles. she says she likes them. she can't take her eyes off his mouth just under the neat black moustache. she sings 'will you love me in december as you do in may' and her voice is thin and lonely in the air. she

115

counts her regrets on her fingers and her fingers are green from shelling peas. she looks at the view and her husband is walking through the east paddock. she puts the kettle on to boil and the bread and dripping on the table. she reminds herself to scold her daughter pearl when she gets in from school. three buttons off her dress and grass stains all over the back of it. even a small rip in the hem. and margaret edwards jabs the knife into her hand when she thinks about how long she stood at the wash tub that morning trying to get it clean. an accident. and when the blood doesn't come she puts her hand under running water and thinks how much she wishes pearl had been a boy. like eric. climbing trees. how much she wishes pearl hadn't been born. and margaret edwards reminds herself to scold her daughter pearl when she gets in from school.

for the defence:
i did not see accused's face when he was running away; his side and back were towards me as he was going home; he was about fifty yards from me when i first noticed him, and he never came nearer; accused had grey trousers and a white hat; i am sure it was accused; i saw accused and pearl edwards both at the one time; i saw no one else in the clear.

every mother knows the folly of delay where sickness among her children is concerned. the invention of peps is believed to have brought a valuable medicine within the reach of the most modest home, and by always having a box handy in this cold and changeful weather, parents may save themselves time, worry and expense.
sarah sherer reads the label as the little tablet lies on her tongue. dissolving quietly. she knows she shouldn't but she can't help herself. she eats them like lollies. like they're going out of fashion. the breath on her face and down her breasts in to her legs. she swells and stretches on her bed. turning her eyes suddenly languid and soft as jelly. this licorice of pleasure teeth and tongue turning black but she can't help herself. this soothing sucking fume back into her throat her lungs she knows she shouldn't. watch him. over his shoulder and in the mirror.

let him. let the sugar. is burning and boiling over thick crystals
sharp as glass on the floorboards to break her teeth on but he'll
get her more blackberries more blueberries red currants. a new
stove. another kitchen if she wants. she wants

for the defence:
i never saw pearl edwards that day.
i did not see pearl edwards on that date.
i had my dinner about twelve o'clock.
i went to work with my brother arthur on my father's ground
until about four forty five.
—i know the time because the train leaving liverpool at four
thirty passed.
i went up to the house.
i saw my mother and brother there.
i did not leave the premises between lunch time and dark.
i was not in spicer's clear that day.
i saw eric edwards pass our place that day.
i did not see pearl edwards pass our place that day.
i never saw pearl edwards that day.
i never saw pearl edwards.
and i never had a quarrel with anyone.

margaret edwards asks pearl about the buttons and the stains.
pearl goes into hysterics. margaret edwards slaps her daughter
on the face. pearl cries and sits in the corner.

the sun stops in the sky at four thirty. the shadows won't crawl
to meet each other won't cover the ground. while the buttons
break down her back break her back so step on a crack dark
things in the bushes. a twig. snap. and have yellow eyes.
whisper ginger. red hair and the sun stops. red hair and under
pants of clean cotton. no dirt in finger nails. but snakes slither in
the grass. in the winter sunshine stopped. in spicer's clear. in the
middle of a cold snap. snakes. behind the bushes   in the
clear   in the middle of winter   the end of autumn   in
the middle of spring.

117

margaret edwards tells her husband. john. john forster edwards reckons that's what happens to girls who go to school. margaret edwards says don't be a fool. john forster edwards reckons its all her   the mother's   fault. margaret edwards says don't be a fool. john forster edwards goes off in search of constable mckinley pulling george sherer by the ear after him.
margaret goes to bed.

for the defence:
the accused is my brother; i was home on the tenth instant and had lunch about twelve fifteen; after lunch i went to work with my brother; the five o'clock whistle at granville sounded about five minutes after we knocked off work; during the afternoon neither my brother nor i left the premises; i saw eric edwards and barbara schiffler pass between four and five o'clock.

for the defence:
— what's this pearly has been saying about me?
— nothing particular as i know.
— didn't she tell you i tore the dress off her back.
— no she told me you were messing her about.
— my mother and i are coming over to see you about it on sunday afternoon.
— i'll find out all the particulars when i go home.

for the defence:
i am a married woman and reside with my husband at landsdowne; the accused is my son; i was at home on the tenth instant making jam; accused and his brother were at work that day on the premises, about one hundred yards from the house; accused came up to the house about four forty five p m; the boys were not out of my sight for five minutes at any time, and were not off the premises from noon till eight p m that day.

they wait there. they whisper ginger and shift their weight amongst the bushes. they warm their old grey skins in an old grey sun. every afternoon. at four thirty. as pearl comes from school. pearl runs to catch up with eric. pearl has work to do peas to shell a mother to scold a father to check the buttons down her back. regularly.

and babs and lucy don't believe pearl when she tells them in the toilet during the dinner hour. about the snakes at spicer's clear. and eric wants to catch one to keep as a pet. and pearl's father doesn't understand. and pearl's mother does. for there are black moths in her dreams. fluttering between the sheets and her toes at the bottom of her bed. and rosetta knight. who saw it all and pulls pearl against her sagging apron and lets pearl cry when she tells pearl that they don't just bask in the sun at spicer's clear.

The Young Priestess from the West House

Nadia Wheatley

I am holding a postcard of a woman holding a smile. On the back, among other things, is written: *Thera (Santorini). The Young Priestess From The West House (about 1500 B.C.)* On the front, there is this woman.

She is, I suppose, quite beautiful, though perhaps not every man would love her sleek pile of aqua hair, topped with a large black ornament of a snake, or a real snake. Her nose is long and slopes straight down from her brow. Her lips are thick, prominent; or maybe it is just that they are pushed forward into a pout? She wears a lot of blood-red lipstick. Her face is turned sideways, so I can only see one eye; that eye is big, oval, brown-gold, vacant, and above it leaps a dolphin of an eye-brow. Her ear is a red question mark, thick, like her lips, and from it there hangs a heavy gold ring. Her skin is whitish grey, the same colour as the background wall, and her dress matches her eye, except for the sleeves, which mimic her hair. A wide blue choker encloses her throat.

She is a striking woman. Yet you barely notice because of the extraordinary thing which she holds in her two hands. It is hard to describe. It is a smile.

It is as wide as her face, though only half as tall. At the top there are three dark red, roundish bumps: like three rubies, or three scoops of raspberry jelly, or an upper lip. Beneath this there stretches what I can only see as a double row of big white teeth. Under the teeth is another line of red lip, and beneath that a strip of aqua. I'm afraid I haven't explained this properly, I'm not at my best just now. The teeth are much taller than the lips, are set, bared. Yet the impression of the smile is not ferocious, but rather . . . forced. It is meant to look like a genuine, happy smile, but the smiler is sad, distracted perhaps, and so she makes her smile especially wide. She exaggerates it into a banner of joy so that no one will notice that she is greyish white and a little shaky today.

This man I know who's an archaeologist, well, he would call the smile a casket, 'A casket of ritual fire'. He would point to the reddish smear (which I neglected to mention) above the three top lumps and say that this was a sacred flame that the priestess was carrying to, or from, the altar. He would say, 'Look, her right hand is touching the top of this red, she is clearly tending the flame!' He would say that the teeth were a grilled brazier or something, to hold the fire, and would declare that the red lumps, the lower red line, and the pale blue strip at the bottom were jewelled ornaments: rubies of course (even I saw the similarity) and probably lapis lazuli; symbolic; or just because as we all know these Minoans were a bright people.

But I would not believe him because those teeth are *teeth*! How do I account, then, for the 'flame'? Easily: her lipstick has smudged. It tends to, on days when one is distraught. Everything goes wrong. She put a lot of lipstick on today to cover her sadness, to increase her smile, and it has splodged. The blue strip is her choker, which has ridden right up to her chin because tears are swelling inside her neck. She touches her mouth to see if her lipstick is smudged, and smudges it more. Her lover has left her. He'll never return. And the snake that arches on her head can't comfort her; it might even be real.

The sleeves of the Young Priestess's dress are patterned with white, x-shaped flowers. Inside her earring is another cross. A blue bracelet clasps each wrist. The snake's eye is tiny. The wall is probably limestone. In about 1500 B.C. the civilisation of Thera mysteriously exploded. Some archaeologists believe the island holds the secret of Atlantis. There is nothing left to say about the picture.

I turn the postcard over, and read it again. *Thera (Santorini). The Young Priestess From The West House (about 1500 B.C.)* say

121

some of the words. Others say: 'Dearest, Arrived Thera a couple of days ago after one hellish trip (boat v. crowded). Still, sun came out and I joined the others at the site. I'm afraid it's all so fascinating that I've decided to stay on indefinitely ... ' Then cross-kisses that can't comfort, they're not even real.

A woman drops a postcard that splashes at her feet like a tear. She licks her mouth to see if her lipstick is smudged, and smudges it more. Yet you barely notice because of the extra-ordinary thing which she is suddenly holding. It is hard to describe. It is a smile.

In the Conservatory

Carmel Bird

ONCE upon a time, there was a lady. She wore surgical boots. She lived in a house with a conservatory, and the floor of the conservatory was made of marble. Paved with squares of black and white marble. The lady walked on the marble floor of the conservatory with her surgical boots. Clop, stump she went on the black and white check floor of the conservatory. Marble. She carried a brass can, a little tiny watering can. She carried it into the conservatory and sprinkled water on the plants. Clop, stump, pitter, patter. She went surgical booting around the conservatory and poured fine rain from her watering can onto the soil. Onto the leaves. Pitter.

The sex life of the plants in the conservatory is such that it does not require bees. Bees, those messengers from the under-world, are not needed here. There are no bees in the conserva-tory. Life here is all a matter of the water and the spores. Ferns and light and dark and the water, pitter patter and the spores.

Yes, once upon a time there was a lady, and she wore surgical boots. Now this lady had two sisters. The sisters were called Sissy and Mags. Sissy was short for Cecilia, and Mags was Margaret. The original sister, the one in the conservatory watering the ferns, fish fern, maidenhair, was Alexandra. Named after the queen, the beautiful one. So Ally was in the conservatory, watering. Sissy was tall and she was dusting the piano. One of her eyes was glass. Sissy had a little glass eye. Is that hard to take, after the news about Ally's surgical boots?

Well, it is true. And what is also true, but *very* difficult to believe, in the face of Ally's boots and Sissy's eye, is that Sissy also wore surgical boots, and so did Mags. There was something fundamentally wrong with the family's feet. Apparently.

When Ally was in the conservatory, and Sissy was in the parlour dusting the piano, Mags was in the kitchen. She was cooking. What was she cooking, then? Mags was making cauliflower cheese. You could smell it all over the house. Practically. Cauliflower cheese to go with the Sunday roast. Mags was in the kitchen in her beret, cooking. She always wore the beret. Did she wear it to bed? Probably not. But she wore it up to the shop, and always in the kitchen, and in the garden, she was the weeder. Mags was the weeder. She could be seen in the afternoons on her knees on the gravel path, weeding the shrubbery and the flower beds. Her old head in her old beret, bent in concentration over the weeds. The beret was burgundy. Dark burgundy. Mags wore a dark burgundy beret.

Out in the garden, there were bees. No bees, you remember, in the conservatory. Yet out in the garden, there were bees. Yes, humming furry messengers from the underworld. Messengers with fine glassy wings veined with mysterious designs, honeycombed with fine dark veins. Veins like the stems of the maidenhair fern. Fragile, glassy wings of maidenhair on bees. The pattern on their wings is the same as the pattern in the glass on the roof of the conservatory. The bees love this garden because it is full of lavender. If the old ladies don't want the bees, they had better get rid of the lavender. But they don't know that. Bees love blue flowers.

This garden is full of lavender and delphiniums and jacaranda and wistaria. Amongst all the flowers in this garden, the blue ones are the main attraction for the bees.

You will notice that we have slid into the present tense. The blue flowers are the main attraction for the bees.

The aunts are wearing their boots. Ally, Sissy, and Mags. Great aunts in great boots, black boots. Laces crisscrossed on old ankles. There are three great aunts. Ally, Sissy, and Mags, and they have little crippled ankles, all of them. What, all of them? Yes, all of them. Little crippled ankles in little leather bootie boots, little black leather boots, crinkled on their ankles, little boots.

Ally carries a brass watering can. She waters the ferns in the conservatory where there is a black and white marble floor. Sissy has a duster and a pot of polish. Lavender and beeswax. True. She is polishing the piano in the parlour. The piano is an upright Steinway in dark wood. Behind the fretwork there is pleated satin. The satin behind the fretwork is red. Dark red. Sissy, with her one glass eye and her surgical boots, is polishing the piano. It has a lovely tone. It is an upright Steinway. Mags is in the kitchen cooking cauliflower cheese. She is wearing her beret (burgundy) and she is making the cauliflower cheese to go with the wing rib and the tomato pie and the mint peas. And gravy.

It is Sunday, and there will be a roast.

Getting back to the conservatory, where Ally, buttoned up to the throat, is watering the ferns, we see that between the conservatory and the garden, there is a passion-fruit vine. White stars, etched in purple and green, these are the passion flowers. And there are passion-fruit. Purple eggs of passion-fruit. They hang between the cool wet comfort of the conservatory and the murmuring haze of the garden where the bees are in the lavender. Their wings are glassy, and they carry the messages from the dark. The bees carry the messages from the under-world, the secret Celtic wisdom which is held deep in Daphne's heart.

Daphne is in the garden with the bees. With the lavender and with the bees. The aunts hope that she will not be stung. So many bees. At this time of year. Daphne is five. She is the daughter of the niece of the aunts. She is in the garden with the bees, and she has round pink cheeks, fat legs, a brown velvet dress, white pinny with windmills embroidered on it, and lace-up brown shoes. What a relief that the family failing of crippled feet has not been passed on to Daphne.

The world is feet. Daphne is five, and the world is feet. Little black boots, shiny boots, in the world of feet. Skirts swish and sway across the top of the boots. These aunts wear swoopy, swishy skirts of dark, dark, dark. The skirts are dark and secret and they smell. They smell of dust and boots and a little bit of piss. And lavender. There is some lavender in the smell of the aunts.

Out in the garden, there is lavender. And there is a pomegranate tree. On the tree, there are big globes of golden scarlet fruit. The skin of the fruit splits open. There are the seeds. Crimson seeds in shiny rows of crimson jelly. Juicy, juicy. The juice is clean and sweet. Crimson. There is crimson-purple on the edges of the seeds. The seeds shine with pomegranate. Daphne is eating the pomegranates.

Where are Daphne's mother and father? Well, they have had a baby, and they have brought Daphne here to stay with the aunts while the disturbance of having a baby settles down. Gosh. So Daphne is staying here with the surgical boots and the glass eye and the burgundy beret while the whole universe changes and her mother and father produce the new baby. Today is Sunday, day of roast dinners, and the baby is being brought to stay with the aunts while the mother and father go off to Mass. So Daphne, who is pushing her face into a pomegranate, juice running down her chin onto her pinny, is really waiting for her mother and father who will soon arrive with her baby sister. The baby sister is called Violet. Baby Violet is coming soon.

Yes, here are Daphne's mother and father and baby Violet. Mother is pretty, with a blue linen coat and a white hat. There are primroses, silk primroses, on her lapel. And Father is in his brown suit, with his yellow tie. He is all polished, and smelling of soap. His hair is spikey. They come up the path, the gravel path. The gravel path is edged with pink bricks. And there are bees and lavender. In a big wicker pram, under a mound of white satin and lace, is baby Violet. She is still and pink and good. She is a quiet baby. Baby Violet.

Daphne has pomegranate juice on her pinny. Her pinny with the windmills is stained with the crimson-purple of the pomegranates. She has been eating pomegranates again.

Baby Violet, in her pram, is put in the conservatory. It is so cool and quiet and shady and ferny and pitter patter ... in the conservatory. Mother and Father are going out to Mass. Baby Violet and Daphne, and Ally, and Sissy, and Mags will stay here. They will stay here until Mother and Father come home from Mass, and then there will be the Sunday roast—wing rib, tomato pie, mint peas, cauliflower cheese. Mags is in the kitchen, cooking the cauliflower cheese.

Mags is in the kitchen cooking the cauliflower cheese. She is wearing her burgundy beret. Sissy is in the parlour, polishing the piano. She is wearing her teeny weeny glass eye. Ally is in the conservatory, watering the ferns. She is in her long dark skirt. Ally, Sissy, and Mags are all wearing their surgical boots. Clop, stump they go about their business.

Daphne is standing under the passion-fruit vine. Mother and Father have gone to Mass. They will be back for the Sunday roast. Baby Violet is in her yellow wicker pram in the conservatory with the ferns.

Ally puts down the watering can. She pats her skirt. Then she turns on the heel of her boot and goes out the door. Ally goes through the doorway, under the passion-fruit vine, and down the side path to the lavatory. Ally is going to the lavatory. She shuts herself into the tiny cubby house. It is decorated with morning glory. The top of the green door is serrated. There is a big iron handle on the door.

Daphne is standing under the passion-fruit vine, covered in pomegranate. She looks at the pram. She tiptoes over to the pram. Outside, the bees are buzzing. Aunt Ally is going to the lavatory. Baby Violet is asleep. She is pretty. She is round and fat and pretty. Violet is wearing a white frilly bonnet. Her eyelashes are soft and sweet and golden on her cheeks. Daphne puts one pointy finger on Violet's round pink cheek. Violet hums. She stirs. She hums again. Daphne pulls back the pram cover. She sees the baby's hands. They are nearly transparent. Little pink fingernails. Slowly, softly, quietly, Daphne peels back the covers. There is Violet. She is a baby in a dress. She has booties and a bonnet and a fine white bib. Baby Violet.

Being very careful, Daphne pulls Violet from the pram. She is holding her. She is standing very still and she is holding the baby. In the conservatory, there are ferns and cool and damp and Daphne is holding the baby. The baby hums. Daphne tiptoes round the conservatory. She is a very naughty girl.

'Put that baby down, you naughty girl!'

Ally, named after the beautiful Queen Alexandra, is clomping and stumping down the path, gravel rolling under her footsteps.

'Put that baby down at once!'

Daphne is frightened. Her hands let go. With what seems like no noise, the bundle of dress and bootie and bonnet and baby falls to the floor. It is the floor of the conservatory. The floor of the conservatory is black and white. It is black and white marble. The baby is lying on the floor of the conservatory, and she is crying. Baby Violet is screaming. Well, at least she is alive.

Everyone is suddenly there. Mags grabs the baby. Ally grabs Daphne. Sissy is wringing her polishing cloth in her hands. Scream, scream baby. The baby is screaming.

The floor is marble. She has dropped the baby on a marble floor. The baby will die. The baby will be an idiot. The baby will have a broken spine, a cracked skull. The baby will be a cripple.

The world is little black boots, little flying black laced boots.

Daphne has been beaten around the legs with a walking stick. Violet is back in her pram. She continues to cry. Daphne is shut in a cupboard under the stairs until her mother and father come back. They come back; she is released; the story is told; the baby is fed and pacified. Everybody goes to the dining room for the roast dinner which Mags has been so busy preparing all this time. Nobody has the heart to play the piano.

Now we drift into the past tense again.

After dinner, Mother and Father took the children home— Daphne and baby Violet. Mags in her beret went back to the kitchen to wash the dishes. Sissy and Ally went for a little walk in the garden. So there were the three sisters, in their boots, together in their home, after the terrible excitement of the day. What would become of the baby, they wondered. What would become of the awful Daphne?

It was getting dark. The bees had gone. The two sisters in the garden passed under the passion-fruit vine, went through the conservatory, and into the dark house. All the dishes were done, and the house was quiet. The three ladies sat down in the parlour with their knitting.

You will be wondering whether Violet was damaged by the fall. The only effect we know of was that she grew up to be very fond of ferns. But that may have been coincidental.

Ally, and her two sisters, died. We can suppose that they were buried with their boots. Certainly the glass eye. Perhaps even the beret. The passion-fruit vine (it was a Nelly Kelly) went wild.

And bees, descendants of those very glassy bees who witnessed the dropping of the baby on the marble floor, still hover over the lavender. Humming.

A Modern Snowhite

Vicki Viidikas

SO it is for this you would bury your wisdom stone under a pile of ashes, in some solitary place overlooking the sea, with no boat in sight, no creatures cluttering the landscape with their inane activities? With nothing more than the clink and clatter of a handful of whitened bones drifting memories away on the wind, memories carried nowhere in particular, no preordained heaven or comfortable horizon ...

Would you, in your right mind, perfect this emptiness of death while still breathing in the body? Social reject, decay of innocence, maladjustment. Pyramids of sensation snowballing you into despair.

She stared at the white powder with its crunchy rocks cut with a film of sugar, resting in a glossy square of cut-up *Penthouse*. It (the chemical) said nothing, benign and without judgement, the substance claimed to be nothing but what it was: a painkiller, a narcotic to calm the senses when they registered distress, when the map of human flesh was trying too many directions at once. A powder for Snowhite to turn her life into that of a waif's ...

And the dwarfs would be her helpers, when she was sick they would feed her the White Lady, half a teaspoon at a time, with the curtains closed tight against the natural light, and her daily menu to a minimum. Snowhite, in her tranquil interior, would not notice the passage of days, the stiffness in her bones, the limp quality of her skin, or the slow footfalls of cold slipping

130

through her house. Pick Me Up, the chief dwarf, was so good at disarming her humour. She would giggle, curiously, as a child opening gifts at Christmas when she unfolded those packets of a dull white drug. Snowhite had come to believe she could celebrate all year round.

The White Lady gave heat which flushed through the body with crystalline clarity, she made Snowhite special, her power was reassurance, a slick detachment with a quiet confidence, the added interest of ritual. She was like perfume behind a woman's ears; that something extra concocted from a rare flower, the opium poppy, cultivated on terraces in exotic and faraway countries, where elevation cooled the flower's long throat, mountain breezes scattered the potent black seeds, and powerful sunlight nurtured her thick black sap. Later, when farmers had collected the dark essence in a pouch tied to the poppy's stem, ancetyline anhydride would be added to convert it into heroin, the deadly mistress, scag, the wicked hag.

Like any other product of capitalism, the use of it made the buyer feel important and appeased. The hype of taboo made it essential and exclusive—you always wanted more, your satisfaction was never complete, your joy was realised in strictest privacy. Your need of this substance invited approval from other users, you were instantly recognisable to each other, the product ensured bondage to a specific activity and image. You compared gratifications and talked of bargains, when really you just had to keep buying. You moved in a sub-group which believed they had a unique edge on reality, your knowledge of that product made you superior. As you satisfied your desire individuality was submerged in the mythology of the product.

After a few months there was no need for Snowhite to hold forth with any opinions—with a look or a woozy nod she was part of a secret order, a club filled with renegades and romantics who fancied themselves adventurers. She teetered on the peaks of a thousand exotic nights, and crawled the underbelly of backrooms where waiting to score was a beggar's nightmare. She gave up wanting to spend money on other products, and was content to focus on the intimacies of the White Lady. Nothing else could gratify like that sudden catch in the throat, as the chemical entered her bloodstream, or those gentle hours afterwards of dream and enchanted wanderings.

She grew used to the sight of red swellings under the skin, flesh dotted like a pointillist canvas into curious markings of the chosen. Snowhite visited the caves of the damned, the lairs of ravenous jackals, the plateaux of exhalted birds which only sang at night. She swam in deliriums of circus tents and feather beds. She translated the ravages of abuse into metaphors of character, and mistook cruelty for acts of conviction. She witnessed feudal systems where, if supply was cut off, the serfs would murder, or drop with disease. The White Lady demanded total co-operation, she'd have no truck with dabblers or weekend trippers. It was a full-time quest to be full of that white heat.

She filled glasses of water with blood and watched tiny clots drift through aeons of quietude. Her sedentary existence seemed full of activity, her passive surrenders like the quintessence of passion itself. Her nights were amplified with the brilliance of remote stars, and her days kept busy with subtle gestures over wobbly cups of tea. Her castle could not be reached by those who weren't in the secret order. Her life was circumscribed with the absolute of ritual. She felt immortal . . .

It was for the essence of a poppy that Snowhite took to working the streets; wearing a mask of indifference she landed men in cars like they were ravenous mullet. She made her exchange as brief as possible, her exits protected by the loyalty of her dwarfs. She stashed her earnings in the medicine cabinet, along with swabs of cottonwool and anti-bruising cream for her arms. She identified with her white-skinned body, believing its substance dependent on warmth in her bloodstream, just a harmless 'tolerance', an eccentricity not an illness. She retreated after each work session to her castle of dream, Queen of the poppy's poison, with her highheels kicked off, the belt slacked from her waist to loop around one arm. She felt a peculiar detachment growing inside her, along with a complacency towards the world in general, and her stupid customers.

Somehow each experience was gobbled up by the White Lady's appetite, nothing appeased for very long. She was aware of shadows and whispers in her empty house—the precise bang of a customer's car door became the impatience of waiting for water to fill a syringe. Thirty seconds at an intersection for the lights to change was a century to endure. She hated the noise of the kettle boiling water to sterilise her dope gun. She turned her mouth away from restaurant meals, only lollies and chocolates gave her a thrill, they rushed with an energy as artificial as something else. She almost dreaded waking up, the weather was never any good. With anxiety and caution, she applied cosmetics in the bathroom mirror, pressing her lipstick to a face gone pale with sugar and chemical. She felt the curves of her body flatten into a devastating sameness. Asexual. A new purity with the absence of orgasm. Only the powder was always on weight and on time.

So it was for this Snowhite turned her face away on the pillow from the morning's golden light. She felt as if her head was some brutal New Guinea mask on a stick, bobbing in a festival for the blessed outcaste. Her life was a barbarous rite—she touched herself, blood flowed, and she was alone. The horizon was empty, the chattering of the marketplace was unreal and heartless. When she rendezvoused with her secret order it was going commercial, letting too many tourists in. The magic was leaving the original members—no one maintained confidences, the quality of the powder was going down. The elegance of glass had changed to plastic. Beauty was a layer of carefully-applied paint over a cool in-the-know expression. Dynamic conversation was now a few clichés before the speaker nodded out with blood trickling down one arm. There was no class anymore to being a raider of the imagination.

Christmas brought no surprises, she waited like a waif on hungry street corners. The relativity of experience was dumped like a worn-out fit in a garbage tin, along with foils, bent spoons, and scraped-bare glossy packets. The wisdom stone dropped it absolute at death's door. The right mind of a pretty girl became the wrong end of a permanent need. Consume or die. Depend or be frozen out. Snowhite, in reverse, like the negative of a refugee in ashes, refused the kiss of the real one who fed her: spirit, fulfilled destiny, the invisible changer of tides . . .

The Lang Women

Olga Masters

*L*UCY was a thin, wistful wispy child who lived with her
mother and grandmother and had few moments in her life
except a bedtime ritual which she started to think about
straggling home from school at 4 o'clock.

Sometimes she would start to feel cheerful even with her
hands still burning from contact with Miss Kelly's ruler, and
puzzle over this sudden lifting of her spirits then remember
there was only a short while left to bedtime.

She was like a human alarm clock which had been set to go off
when she reached the gate leading to the farm and purr away
until she fell asleep lying against her grandmother's back with
her thighs tucked under her grandmother's rump and her face
not minding at all being squashed against the ridge of little
knobs at the back of her grandmother's neck.

Her grandmother and her mother would talk for hours after
they were all in bed. Sometimes it would seem they had all
drowsed off and the mother or the grandmother would say
'Hey, listen!' and Lucy would shoot her head up too to hear.
Her grandmother would dig her with an elbow and say: 'Get
back down there and go to sleep! Lucy was not really part of
the talk just close to the edges of it.

It was as if the grandmother and the mother were frolicking
together in the sea, but Lucy unable to swim had to stand at the
edge and be satisfied with the wash from their bodies.

Lucy made sure she was in bed before her mother and
grandmother in order to watch.

It was as if she were seeing two separate plays on the one stage. Carrie the mother performed the longest. She was 26 and it was the only time in the day when she could enjoy her body. Not more than cleansing and admiring it since Lucy's father had died five years earlier. Carrie was like a ripe cherry with thick black hair cut level with her ears and in a fringe across her forehead. She was squarish in shape not dumpy or overweight and with rounded limbs brown from exposure to the sun because she and the grandmother Jess also a widow and the mother of Carrie's dead husband worked almost constantly in the open on their small farm which returned them a meagre living.

Carrie was nicknamed Boxy since she was once described in the village as good looking but a bit on the boxy side in reference to her shape. When this got back to Carrie she worried about it although it was early in the days of her widowhood and her mind was not totally on her face and figure.

Some time later at night with all her clothes off and before the mirror in the bedroom she would frown on herself turning from side to side trying to decide if she fitted the description. She thought her forehead and ears were two of her good points and she would lift her fringe and study her face without it and lift her hair from her ears and look long at her naked jawline then take her hands away and swing her head to allow her hair to fall back into place. She would place a hand on her hip, dent a knee forward, throw her shoulders back and think what a shame people could not see her like this.

'Not boxy at all', she would say inside her throat which was long for a shortish person and in which could be seen a little blue throbbing pulse.

She shook her head so that her thick hair swung wildly about then settled down as if it had never been disturbed.

'See that?' she would say to her mother-in-law.

Jess would be performing in her corner of the room and it was usually with a knee up under her nightdress and a pair of scissors gouging away at an ingrown toenail. She never bothered to fasten the neck of her nightdress and it was an old thing worn for many seasons and her feet were not all that clean as she did

135

not wash religiously every night as Carrie did. She spent hardly any time tearing off her clothes and throwing them down, turned so that the singlet was on the outside and when she got into them in the morning she had only to turn the thickness of the singlet, petticoat and dress and pull the lot over her head.

Carrie did not seem to notice although she sometimes reprimanded Jess for failing to clean her teeth. When this happened Jess would run her tongue around her gums top and bottom while she ducked beneath the covers and Lucy would be glad there was no more delay.

It was only the operations like digging at a toenail or picking at a bunion that kept Jess up. Sometimes she pushed her nightdress made into a tent with her raised knee down to cover her crotch but mostly she left it up so that Lucy hooped up in bed saw her front passage glistening and winking like an eye.

The lamp on the dressing table stood between Carrie and Jess so that Lucy could see Carrie's naked body as well either still or full of movement and rhythm as she rubbed moistened oatmeal around her eyes and warmed olive oil on her neck and shoulders.

The rest of the little town knew about the bedtime ritual since Walter Grant the postmaster rode out one evening and saw them through the window. It had been two days of wild storms and heavy rain and the creek was in danger of breaking its banks. Any stock of Carrie's and Jess's low down would be safer moved. Walter on his mission to warn them saw Jess with her knee raised and her nightgown around her waist and Carrie's body blooming golden in the lamplight for they were enjoying the storm and had left the curtains open. Walter saw more when Carrie rushed to fling them together and rode home swiftly with his buttocks squeezed together on the saddle holding onto a vision of Carrie's rose tipped breasts, the creamy channel between them, her navel small and perfect as a shell and her thighs moving angrily and her little belly shaking.

After that the town referred to the incident as that 'cock show'.

Many forecast a dark future for Lucy witnessing it night after night.

136

Some frowned upon Lucy when she joined groups containing their children at the show or sports' day.

The Lang women's house had only one bedroom, one of two front rooms on either side of a small hall. The hall ran into a kitchen and living-room combined which was the entire back portion of the house.

It would have been reasonable to expect them to make a second bedroom by moving the things from what was called the 'front room'. But neither Jess nor Carrie ever attempted or suggested this. The room was kept as it was from the early days of Jess's marriage. It was crowded with a round oak table and chairs and a chiffonier crowded with ornaments, photographs and glassware and there were two or three deceptively frail tables loaded with more stuff. On the walls were heavily framed pictures mostly in pairs of swans on calm water, raging seas and English cottages sitting in snow or surrounded by unbelievable gardens.

Even when the only child Patrick was living at home and up until he left at fifteen he slept in the single bed in his parents' room where Carrie slept now. He was 50 miles up the coast working in a timber mill when he met Carrie a housemaid at the town's only hotel. They married when he was twenty and she was nineteen and pregnant with Lucy who was an infant of a few months when Patrick was loaned a new-fangled motor bike and rounding a bend in the road the bike smacked up against the rear of a loaded timber lorry like a ball thrown hard against a wall. Patrick died with a surprised look on his face and his fair hair only lightly streaked with dust and blood.

Jess was already widowed more than a year and managing the farm single handed so Carrie and Lucy without a choice came to live there.

Lucy could not remember sleeping anywhere but against her grandmother's back.

Sometimes when the grandmother turned in the night she fitted neatly onto the grandmother's lap her head on the two small pillows of her grandmother's breasts.

She was never actually held in her grandmother's arms that she knew about. When she woke the grandmother's place was empty because it was Jess who was up first to start milking the cows which was up to twenty in the spring and summer and half that in the winter. Carrie got up when the cows were stumbling into the yard seen in the half-light from the window and Lucy waited about until 8 o'clock when they both came in to get breakfast. Lucy was expected to keep the fire in the stove going and have her school clothes on. She usually had one or another garment on inside-out and the laces trailing from her shoes and very often she lied when asked by Carrie or Jess if she had washed. Carrie did little or no housework and Jess had to squeeze the necessary jobs in between the farmwork. Carrie was content to eat a meal with the remains of the one before still on the table, clearing a little space for her plate by lifting the tablecloth and shaking it clear of crumbs, sending them into the middle of the table with the pickles and sugar and butter if they could afford to have a pound delivered with their empty cream cans from the butter factory.

Carrie trailed off to bed after their late tea not caring if she took most of the hot water for her wash leaving too little for the washing up.

Jess grumbled about this but not to Carrie's face.

Once after Jess had managed on the hot water left and the washing up was done and the room tidied she said in Lucy's hearing that she hoped Carrie never took to bathing in milk.

Lucy had a vision of Carrie's black hair swirling above a tubful of foamy milk. Her own skin prickled and stiffened as if milk were drying on it. She left the floor where she was playing and put her chin on the edge of the table Jess was wiping down waiting to hear more. But Jess flung the dishcloth on its nail and turned her face to busy herself with shedding her hessian apron as the first step towards getting to bed.

This was the life of the Lang women when Arthur Mann rode into it.

Jess and Carrie inside following their midday meal saw him through the kitchen window with the head of his horse over the fence midway between the lemon tree and a wild rose entangled with convolvulus. The blue bell-like flowers and the lemons made a frame for horse and rider that Jess remembered for a long time.

'It's a Mann!' Jess said to Carrie who did not realise at once that Jess was using the family name.

The Manns were property owners on the outer edge of the district and they were well enough off to keep aloof from the village people. Their children went to boarding schools and they did not shop locally nor show their cattle and produce at the local show but took it to the large city shows.

But Jess easily recognized a Mann when she saw one. When she was growing up the Manns were beginning to grow in wealth and had not yet divorced themselves from the village. They not only came to dances and tennis matches but helped organise them and there were Manns who sang and played the piano in end-of-year concerts and Manns won foot races and steer riding at the annual sports.

They nearly all had straight dark sandy hair and skin tightly drawn over jutting jawbones.

Jess going towards the fence got a good view of the hair and bones when Arthur swept his hat off and held it over his hands on the saddle.

'You're one of the Manns', said Jess her fine grey eyes meeting his that were a little less grey, a bit larger and with something of a sleepy depth in them.

Arthur keeping his hat off told her why he had come. He had leased land adjoining the Langs' to the south where he was running some steers and he would need to repair the fence neglected by the owners and the Langs neither of whom could afford the luxury of well-fenced land.

He or one of his brothers or one of their share farmers would be working on the fence during the next few weeks.

'We don't use the bit of land past the creek', said Jess before the subject of money came up. 'The creek's our boundary so a fence is no use to us.'

Arthur Mann's eyes smiled before his mouth. He pulled the reins of his horse to turn it around before he said there would be no costs to the Langs involved. He put his hat on and raised it again and Jess saw the split of his coat that showed his buttocks well shaped like the buttocks of his horse which charged off as if happy to have the errand done.

Jess came inside to the waiting Carrie.

Lucy home from school was playing with some acorns she found on the way. Jess saw her schoolcase open on the floor with some crusts in it and the serviette that wrapped her sandwiches stained with jam. Flies with wings winking in the sun crawled about the crusts and Lucy's legs.

'She's a disgrace!' Jess cried trying to put out of her mind the sight of Arthur Mann's polished boots and the well-ironed peaks of his blue shirt resting on the lapels of his coat.

With her foot Carrie swept the acorns into a heap and went to the mirror dangling from the corner of a shelf to put her hat on. Jess took hers too from the peg with her hessian apron. She turned it around in her hands before putting it on. It was an old felt of her husband's once a rich grey but the colour beaten out now with the weather. It bore stains and blotches where it rubbed constantly against the cows' sides as Jess milked. Jess plucked at a loose thread on the band and ripped it away taking it to the fire to throw it in. The flames snatched it greedily swallowing the grease with a little pop of joy.

Lucy lifted her face and opened her mouth to gape with disappointment. She would have added it to her playthings.

'Into the fire it went!' said Jess. 'Something else you'd leave lyin' around!'

She looked for a moment as if she would discard the hat too but put it on and went out.

It was Carrie who encountered Arthur Mann first working on the fence when she was in the corn paddock breaking and flattening the dead stalks for the reploughing. Almost without thinking she walked towards the creek bank and stood still observing Arthur who had his back to her. He is a man, she thought remembering Jess's words with a different inference. His buttocks under old, very clean well-cut breeches quivered with the weight of a fence post he was dropping into a hole. He had his hat off lying on a canvas bag that might have held some food. Jess might have wondered about the food and thought of a large clean flyproof Mann kitchen but Carrie chose to look at

Arthur's hair moving in a little breeze like stiff bleached grass and his waistline where a leather belt shiny with age and quality anchored his shirt inside his pants.

He turned and saw her.

As he did not have a hat to lift he seemed to want to do something with his hands so he took some hair between two fingers and smoothed it towards an ear. Carrie saw all his fine teeth when he smiled.

'Hullo ... Shorty', he said.

'No ... Boxy', she said.

She was annoyed with herself for saying it.

He probably knew the nickname through his share farmers who were part of the village life and would have filled the waiting ears of the Manns with village gossip. Carrie did not know but he had heard too about the nightly cock show.

Arthur thought now of Carrie's naked body although it was well covered with an old print dress once her best, cut high at the neck and trimmed there and on the sleeves with narrow lace. Carrie was aware that it was unsuitable for farm work and took off her hat and held it hiding the neckline. She shook her hair the way she did getting ready for bed at night and it swung about then settled into two deep peaks against her cheeks gone quite pink.

'Come across', said Arthur, 'I'm stopping for smoko.'

Carrie nearly moved then became aware of her feet in old elastic-side rubber boots and buried them deeper in the grass.

She inclined her head towards the corn paddock as if this was where her duty lay. Still holding her hat at her neck and still smiling she turned and Arthur did not go back to the fence until she had disappeared into the corn.

Carrie spent the time before milking at the kitchen table in her petticoat pulling the lace from the dress. Lucy home from school with her case and her mouth open watched from the floor. When Carrie was done she stood and pulled the dress over her head brushing the neck and sleeves free of cotton ends. She swept the lace scraps into a heap and moved towards the stove.

'Don't burn it!' Jess cried sharply. 'Give it to her for her doll!'

Lucy seized the lace and proceeded to wind it around the

naked body of a doll that had only the stump of a right arm, its nose squashed in and most of its hair worn off.

A few days later Arthur rode up to the fence with a bag of quinces.

Lucy saw him when she looked up from under the plum tree that grew against the wall of the house. She was on some grass browning in the early winter and her doll sat between her legs stuck stiffly out. Arthur raised the quinces as a signal to collect them but Lucy turned her face towards the house and Arthur saw her fair straight hair that was nothing like Carrie's luxuriant crop.

In a moment Carrie came from one side of the house and Jess from the other. They went up to the fence and Lucy got up and trailed behind.

Arthur handed the quinces between Carrie and Jess and Jess took them taking one out and turning it around.

She did not speak but her eyes shone no less than the sheen from the yellow skin of the fruit.

'The three Lang women', Arthur said smiling. 'Or are there four?'

Lucy had her doll held by its one and a half arms to cover her face. Ashamed she flung it behind her back.

Arthur arched the neck of his horse and turned it around.

'I'll buy her a new one', he said and cantered off.

Neither Jess nor Carrie looked at Lucy's face when they went inside. Jess tipped the quinces onto the table where they bowled among the cups and plates and she picked one up and rubbed her thumb thoughtfully on the skin and then set it down and gathered them all together with her arms.

Then she went into the front room and returned with a glass dish and with the hem of her skirt wiped it out and put the fruit in and carried it back to set it on one of the little tables. Carrie's eyes clung to her back until she disappeared then looked dully on Lucy sitting stiff and entranced on the edge of a chair. She opened her mouth to tell Lucy to pick up her doll from the floor but decided Jess would do it on her return. But Jess stepped over the doll and put on her hessian apron and reached for her hat. She turned it round in her hands then put it back on the peg.

Carrie saw the back of her neck unlined and her brown hair without any grey and her shoulders without a hump and her arms coming from the torn-out sleeves of a man's old shirt pale brown like a smooth new sugar bag. Then when Jess reached for an enamel jug for the house milk Carrie saw her hooded eyelids dropping a curtain on what was in her eyes. Carrie put her hat on without looking in the mirror and followed Jess out. She looked down her back over her firm rump to her ankles for something that said she was old but there was nothing.

In bed that night Lucy dreamed of her doll.

It had long legs in white stockings with black patent leather shoes fastened with the smallest black buttons in the world.

The dress was pink silk with ruffles at the throat and a binding of black velvet ribbon which trailed to the hemline of the dress. The face was pink and white and unsmiling and the hair thick and black like Carrie's hair.

Lucy lay wedged under the cliff of her grandmother's back wondering what was different about tonight. She heard a little wind breathing around the edges of the curtain and a creak from a floorboard in the kitchen and a small snuffling whine from their old dog Sadie settling into sleep under the house.

Lucy marvelled at the silence.

No one is talking she thought.

Every afternoon Lucy looked for the doll when she came in from school. On the way home she pictured it on the table propped against the milk jug, its long legs stretched among the sugar bowl and breadcrumbs.

But it was never there and when she looked into the face of Jess and Carrie there was no message there and no hope.

The following Saturday Lucy could wait no longer and sneaked past the cowyard where Jess and Carrie were milking and well clear of it ran like a small pale terrier through the abandoned orchard and bottom corn paddock to the edge of the creek. Across it, a few panels of fence beyond where Carrie had first encountered him, Arthur was at work.

Under her breath Lucy practised her words: 'Have you brought my doll?'

She was saying them for the tenth time when Arthur turned.

143

She closed her mouth before they slipped out.

Arthur pushed his hat back and beckoned.

'Come over', he said.

Lucy hesitated and looked at her feet buried in the long wild grass. I won't go, she said to herself. But the doll could be inside Arthur's bag hung on a fence post.

She plunged down the creek bank and came up the other side her spiky head breaking through the spiky tussocks dying with the birth of winter.

Arthur sat down on some fence timber strewn on the ground and reached for his bag. Lucy watched, her heart coming up into her neck for him to pull the doll from it. But he took out a paper bag smeared with grease which turned out to hold two slices of yellow cake oozing red jam. When he looked up and saw the hunger in Lucy's eyes he thought it was for the cake and held it towards her.

'We'll have a piece each', he said.

But Lucy sank down into the grass and crossed her feet with her knees out. Then she thought if she didn't take the cake Arthur might not produce the doll so she reached out a hand.

'Good girl', he said when she began nibbling it.

The cake was not all that good in spite of coming from the rich Mann's kitchen. It had been made with liberal quantities of slightly rancid butter.

Lucy thought of bringing him a cake made by Jess and imagined him snapping his big teeth on it then wiping his fingers and bringing out the doll.

'I should visit you, eh?' Arthur said.

Oh, yes! He would be sure to bring the doll.

'When is the best time?' Arthur said folding the paper bag into a square and putting it back in his bag.

'At night after tea? Or do you all go to bed early?'

Lucy thought of Carrie naked and Jess with her legs apart and shook her head.

'Why not at night?' Arthur said. 'There's no milking at night, is there?'

Lucy had to agree there wasn't with another small head shake.

'What do you all do after tea?' said Arthur.

Lucy looked away from him across the paddocks to the thin drift of smoke coming from the fire under the copper boiling for the clean up after the milk was separated. She felt a sudden urge to protect Jess and Carrie from Arthur threatening to come upon them in their nakedness.

She got to her feet and ran down the bank, her speed carrying her up the other side and by this time Arthur had found his voice.

'Tell them I'll come!' he called to her running back.

Carrie was in bed that night with much less preparation than usual and even without the last minute ritual of lifting her hair from her nightgown neck and smoothing down the little collar, then easing herself carefully down between the sheets reluctant to disturb her appearance even preparing for sleep.

To Lucy's surprise her nightgown hung slightly over one shoulder and she was further surprised to see that Jess had fastened hers at the brown stain where her neck met the top of her breasts. Carrie had not cavorted in her nakedness and Jess had not plucked at her feet with her knees raised. Lucy looked at the chair where Jess usually sat and pictured Arthur there. She saw his hands on his knees while he talked to them and curved her arms imagining the doll in them. An elbow stuck into Jess's back and Jess shook it off.

'Arthur Mann never married', said Carrie abruptly from her bed.

Jess lifted her head and pulled the pillow leaving only a corner for Lucy who didn't need it anyway for she had raised her head to hear.

'Old Sarah sees to that', said Jess.

Before putting her head down again Lucy saw that Carrie was not settling down for sleep but had her eyes on the ceiling and her elbows up like the drawing of a ship's sail and her hands linked under her head.

Jess's one open eye saw too.

Lucy had to wait through Sunday but on Monday when she was home from school for the May holidays she slipped past the dairy again while Jess and Carrie were milking and from the bank of the creek saw not only Arthur but a woman on a horse very straight in the back with some grey hair showing neatly at the edge of a riding hat and the skin on her face stretched on the bones like Arthur's. The horse was a grey with a skin like washing water scattered over with little pebbles of suds and it moved about briskly under the rider who sat wonderfully still despite the fidgeting.

Lucy sank down into the tussocks on the bank and the woman saw.

'What is that?' she said to Arthur. Then she raised her chin like a handsome fox alerted to something in the distance and fixed her gaze on the smoke away behind Lucy rising thin and blue from the Lang women's fire.

Lucy had seen Arthur's face before the woman spoke but he now lowered his head and she saw only the top of his hat nearly touched the wire he was twisting and clipping with pliers.

The horse danced some more and Lucy was still with her spiky head nearly between her knees staring at the ground. The woman wanted her to go. But Lucy had seen people shooting rabbits not firing when the rabbits were humped still but pulling the trigger when they leapt forward stretching their bodies as they ran. Perhaps the woman had a gun somewhere in her riding coat and breeches or underneath her round little hat. Lucy sat on with the sun and wind prickling the back of her neck.

'Good heavens!' the woman cried suddenly and wheeling her horse around galloped off.

Lucy let a minute pass then got up and ran down and up the opposite bank to Arthur.

He went on working snip, snip with the pliers until Lucy spoke.

'You can come of a night and visit', she said.

Arthur looked up and down the fence and only briefly at the Lang corn paddock and the rising smoke beyond it.

'I've finished the fence', he said.

Lucy saw the neat heap of timber not needed and the spade and other tools ready for moving. She saw the canvas bag on top, flat as a dead and gutted rabbit.

'I know why you didn't bring the doll', she said.

'Your mother won't let you.'

146

Waiting For Colombo: A Close-Up

Finola Moorhead

*T*HE body was there. When i opened the door, the body was there. Even as i opened the door the body was there. It was still, it was hunched and it had slumped. From the door it was not possible to see more of the head than some curly black hair. I see it there, curling greasily over the suit collar, the sort of hair an elderly mother would tell her middle-aged son to have cut, and cut nicely. Mmmm. I will not say i touched the body, certainly not. I retreated. My back foot took a backwards and downward step to the mat. I closed the door, and brought the other foot to the mat as my hand reached for the keys. The keys now in my palm made a little music, and somewhere in my knee i felt a trembling, but mostly i was still. I stared at the shut door that was immediately in front of me. I was a soldier at attention at a silent door innocent of street noises except for far distant ones, a siren of a police car in the next suburb and the air brakes of a semi-trailer on the Great Western Highway. I was rooted to the spot until the brakes and siren receded, and then i pulled myself together, shook my leg with the knee and then the other one for balance. The keys in my hand took their customary jump and were caught like jacks, and i found the right one.

The body was there when i opened the door, slumped and hunched in the hallway with its back to me. It happened again. It had happened before. I wondered if flowers still grew on his grave. There was a grave, a man's grave and flowers grew on it. Wild and subtropical flowers grew on this man's grave in the cemetery.

Colombo would be the man to investigate, thought i, with my back to the open door and outside there a sun–drenched street and neighbours home-coming with shopping, hair done or school–books. Could be, i heard no one, not even the cat moved to welcome me. The cat would have had to execute one of her high elegant leaps to greet me where i stood. The body was in everyone's way in the passage. There was nowhere i could go except retrace my steps, and i had done that by now.

I must admit that my avoidance mechanisms were fully operational. If i opened my shoulder bag and brought out my packet of cigarettes and dug around for the lighter it would mean that i had begun thinking about the problem. I did not do it, therefore did not realise that my shoulder bag was not with me. I was not worried about my shoulder bag at this point. The superior avoidance mechanism was a concentration exercise which had made my vision fuzzy. So my eyes were probably crossed. One has to breathe. There were two of us, and the other one wasn't. Well, i have to breathe as i was the witness. I was witnessing a stillness in my hallway, and when i breathed i even heard myself. Such was the tyranny of stillness. This particular stillness was also an obstacle and it had a suit on, socks and shoes, the soles of which slanted up at me.

Now is the time for disciplined observation as the car investigates. I resist my longing to hug her and say 'Pussy-toots, whatcha bin doin'?' because she is busy poking her nose under greasy black curls. I need conversation. I say to the cat, croakily, 'Do you recognise him, puss?' The croakiness of my voice alerts me to the extent of shock i am feeling. But i was not feeling it, i was suffering it automatically. The cat, as suddenly as she arrived, backs away with a pert little rear onto her hind legs and goes about her business beyond the body. She did not execute the clear leap over the bulk which i know she is well capable of doing. No, she is out in the garden chasing butterflies, cabbage moths.

Writers have imaginations that bother them. The more bother the better, but when dealing with the law enforcement authorities on the telephone it is difficult to get down to tin tacks. They think you are making it all up. I, myself, had to execute the leap i thought only the cat of our household was really equipped to do. I fell over, twisting my already weak right ankle. But worse than that, far worse, here was i hunched and slumped on the floor face to face with a dead man in the hallway of my home. I struggled in the end to the telephone and i panted into the handpiece. I thought i was on television, i said i wanted homocide. They started asking questions which required answers that were farthest from my mind. I said i didn't need another homocide as i already had one. In my hallway. Where? Well not far from the front door. Your can see it almost *as* you are opening the door. I thought on the phone that that was a real tin tack, the preposition 'as' implied that the body was there *before* i, or any consequent entrant, came in. How long? The question made no sense to me whatsoever. I said, quite frivolously i admit, i bet it's a 172 centimetre one. They all seem to be these days.

It was rather like ringing the NRMA, and it was rather like the body itself between my front door and the back, that is, images of stillness: waiting for Colombo.

The self is a dreadful thing when it comes to stillness. One just buzzes with senseless activity, putting the kettle on for a cup of tea you don't feel like, and when it whistles wishing it was still coming to the boil, having to admit failure while turning it off. Failure so deep and intrinsic it has nothing to do with whether to make a cuppa or not, failure causing a need for nicotine and showing its intimate relationship to panic, its violent brother. My bag, i'd lost my bag. I searched every nook and cranny, the tiniest places and underneath the bedclothes, every possible where on the telephone side of the body, before i admitted to myself that it was probably stolen as it was probably left out on the veranda in full view of passers-by who would probably see the opportunity as a godsend: a full wallet, a couple of bank-cards, my identity in various forms. Yes, later torn and scattered all over the vacant lot. I peaked around the door from the living-room over the body in the hall and discovered to my horror that the front was closed. Who closed it? Am i losing my mind? Perhaps i blacked out: during a black-out it is possible not to remember being a murderer. There may well be a part of myself so repressed and angry, so hidden and denied, so strong and malicious as to actually kill. I am so nice and ordinary, how did i do it?

So it was one long wait, me, a body and an inexplicably shut front door. My car/door keys right there on the floor near the dead man's thumb, too close to him for me with paralysis to touch. The suspense was unbearable. I longed to drop in lotus and om myself to peace, but i cunningly thought that would look or sound ridiculous when Colombo actually did arrive.

He rings. I can't get to him. I shout, 'Here I am, inside'. They ring again, the NSW police. How can i make them see the genuinely intriguing thing that *as* you open the door the body is there.

When i open the door i can't explain to them how difficult i find it, leaping over a body of a big man in a narrow hallway without disturbing him. I simply couldn't explain my footprint on his back, the suitcoat being of a colour and weave that takes dust as it finds it. I should have removed my shoes, but that too might have been suspicious. So there it was, my footprint on the victim, white dust on navy blue wool. But that wasn't it. They were investigators and i wanted to know who shut the door. Two things happened at once: as i opened the door they saw the body, and as i was explaining my problems i noticed that no one had stolen my shoulder bag. The lady cop was holding it up asking, no, interrogating me, was it or was it not mine? I had doubts for a moment whether to admit to my own identity for during my wait-panic-failure i had questioned the very grain of my own moral fibre and i wasn't sure. 'It could be.' I sounded like a tease, and i was so pleased to see them i was grinning with pleasure. I know because there are all sorts of mirrors in the consciousness that i looked like the cat when she has killed a mouse and expects a bit of praise and appreciation.

'I'm a writer', i confide to the lady in blue, 'sometimes my etymology, my epistemology, my imagination et cetera run out of hand, i mean get out of control . . . ' I was trying to explain why i had been so frivolous on the telephone to Emergency about the 'as' and the length of time being the length of body. 'I really couldn't tell if he was a 172 centimetres, you see he's all

150

hunched up. He's blocking my passage!' I shouted a little, appealing to her as a woman, even though her being in uniform indicated that she was a junior, the social worker of the three. She stood steadfast, grasping my bag as if it were hers. I turned my attention to the gentlemen. I could see in their eyes that they believed i did it. Already, quite obviously, they were convinced.

'The body was there', i began calmly. 'When i opened the door, in fact, as i was opening the door i saw it.' 'Which time?' the taller man barked. Yes, he barked. And i responded indignantly, 'Well, each time, of course'.

Then through the corner of my eye i saw what they were looking at. The number of footprints on the hulk's back had multiplied. I pretended not to be nonplussed. The cigarette burnt between my fore- and ring-fingers. Now i was confused. The policewoman still held my bag.

I speak out, saying i am the one who is dead, he you can see but you are looking through me as if i weren't one of this crowd in the doorway and i know it's the right address, my address. I am she who telephoned and gave you this address. I am the hostess of this investigation and you treat me like a criminal it has taken your nous and resources to discover. Well, uncover me, find me, hear my incessant chatter. It's not only nonsense. I fall down on the body, my companion in suspense, and weep.

The policewoman speaks in a voice not hers, a bleak voice. She says, i hear her say, 'Did you love him?'

It is important now to have a cup of tea and a cigarette and to take my bearings from my shoulder bag: that is, have it by me in case i need my money, my bank book, my reading glasses, my lighter, a phone number, a bill, whatever the hell's in there, my identity. Then i can think . I can separate subject and object and sew them together with some imaginary incertitudes, relax, stare into space, focus on nothing more than the cat in the yard chasing white moths.

But she will not give it to me. She has opened it wide and she is peering inside. That is not really me, i long to plead, but i'm too proud. I step on his back and go into the kitchen, put the kettle on and i hear them mumbling among themselves, sorting out the contents, i bet. I must look. They are examining a pearl-

151

handled revolver, a little gun. She is using a tissue to dangle it upside down while the smaller of the men is sniffing the barrel.

Damning evidence, i realise, but that is the trap. To admit their evidence into my consciousness is a trick. It takes the mind away from the self and the self's interests. One begins imagining what they think, and then you have to start your sentences with 'but' and that immediately puts you on the defensive. And that is the more disadvantageous of the two sides. I am the subject and he is the object. Which is not to say I killed him. Or I anything him.

None of the three had made the leap. I could see why they were loathe to put their footprints with mine on his back. They stand there on the other side of the body bunched at the end of the narrow passage. I bring the teapot into my living-room and sit down. I refuse to beg for my own smokes, so i go to his cigar box. Most are stale, but i light one anyway. It is their turn to make decisions. She has gone. I note the change of tone.

I am suddenly so revolted by this creation, the fact of death and the corpse. The obstacle was once a person. His humanity turns beatific as i gaze at his shell and smoke his cheap havanas. I am thinking now, meditating on sweet feelings of sorrow and regret, concentrating on the ring of keys near its thumb. If he entered and was shot as he came down the passage, someone must have been ready for him, pistol cocked. There could have been no hesitation. The bullet must have pierced his stomach or groin or liver, because he doubled over, knelt, bowed before he expired. There was no aggression in his final movement. There is submission, contrition in the shape of his bulk. I am weeping so quietly. Soft tears recall that grave in the cemetery where bright flowers grow untended.

'I like you in pink. I like you in black. I like you in the colours that you wear', he said once. I don't remember him ever repeating it. I am as you see me, spots and lines of many thousand colours, so close, so tiny; the vanishing point of a square cone. And yet i have changed. I am basic now, in black. My legs are mottled under grey stockings. The fabric is crêpe, and slightly too warm; my cheeks are therefore a heightened peaches and cream. A French Impressionist blush. And that day in the cemetery by the sea comes to mind, when i stole the flowers from his grave. I plucked the flowers off their stems and placed them lengthwise in my cane basket, and whispered the rationalisation of my beauty in that setting in words something like 'the dead don't need them now'. There is a certain maturity in the lines on my face. In my face you will have already seen that i have lived some time in the world. I make this impression, i wish to convince you of my grace. I am now i dare say becoming an aesthetic part of yourself. You are terrified for my predicament. My calm allays your fears as it intensifies them.

As it intensifies them, there is a commotion in the hallway. My god, they're putting the body in a plastic bag. It's likely to be gone before he arrives. In my distress i turn my eyes away. I gaze unseeingly at the TV, which reflects me and the lighted parts of the room and parallel surfaces. The video cassette recorder is gone from the top of it. I blink. The VCR has disappeared. At first i register no connection between its absence and the presence of a body in my hallway. It seemed to me that it had just disappeared, as recently as my blink, as recently as the arrival of the plastic bag, heavy duty, body-sized. Poof. A magic act. A puff of smoke. With surprising speed they have removed the object, the obstacle, but i am still floundering this side of it. I have no curiosity as to the nature of the vehicle they are using to transport it to wherever they are going. I wait.

I suspect a chemical imbalance. I have had too many cups of tea. There is agitation inside. I am method acting, becoming the hysteric. The script falters, send up the credits, bring on commercials. I am asked to improvise in the interim.

At the cemetery then my ankle is bandaged, my eyes too are seeking another grave. I seem to have lost weight in the last few days. Was there an inquest or is it yet to come? How did he die, the man from whose rotted heart grows a floral abundance amidst the concrete and marble and common weeds? Does it rain? Do we have black umbrellas against a sombre sky? Am i still waiting, or has the part changed? Is it a full-length movie or an hour show? Where is Peter?

When he comes his cunning style slays me. I like his working-class values. He doesn't smell, which means he is cool. He's

153

been away on a love-boat cruise, sending up the idle and fey. He wears a visitor's badge on the crumpled lapel of his trench coat as he walks through Prisoner's set. He chews a cheroot at the corner of his mouth, and his eyes are smiling. He chooses a bare room with a barred window, an officer at the door and a table between us for his dénouement. We all respond with concentration as he begins his revelation, the workings of a truly honest detective mind. I am intrigued. He lets my wave of incessant chatter break and recede before he begins.

'Well, you couldn't have done it.' He raises his eyebrows, and i, inappropriately, ask, 'why?'

'It is your address, your home. It is even your cat. Why would you climb over the back fence into your own house?'

'Why did i have to?'

'Because he was shot from the inside before you got home.'

'But the footprints on his back ...'

'Go from the inside to the other side of the body, but why would you leave your handbag outside if you were already home? No, *as* you opened the door, the body was there.'

The Scenery Never Changes

Thea Astley

AT 32, 3, 4—think of a number between 30 and 40 but prithee not to say it, and you would have Sadie Wild, not too old, but again, not too young. Good looks had been dragging one foot off the bus since the last stop but one. In atonement, the chi-chi of frockery and hattery played two-part inventions on the still lush body, although certain disappointments that by now had assumed the bland stare of inevitability hardened her maxfactored mouth, and lay cautiously at the back of her eyes alert to anticipate the premonitory flare and flicker in the male. At each new shuffle about the backblocks into yet another staff-room, with possibilities hitching their crumpled pants before the dinner-break bell, a late spring glow widened those weary brown orbs, and parted the starlet mouth, and then she would say to herself, 'O, God, I mustn't play it wrong this time. Not this time. I'll handle it like a wren's egg. I won't look eager, sound eager, or even think eager.' But of course she did while she was still young enough not to know; and even as the years passed, and she should have learned what some precocious buds know at ten or eleven, a miscalculation of the crystal moment— seconds too early or seconds too late— would shatter it before her wincing eyes, and there she would be, brave and bright, seeing it through with a new handbag or dashing hat or a week at the Barrier, that August on an island packed from reef to peak with career women *en fête*.

Once or twice she had been in love, in those tensely young years when the disposition of a parked car or a café window or musical fragment or elusive relationship between roof and spire and park could evoke such nostalgia she would be incapable of subtlety. Their repetition these days merely feathered the surface, for tenderness is as difficult to recall as pain. Consequently, each new amorous venture contained its own wry and inward assent to the dismissal that came within two or three months of that introductory and brilliant smile.

Last time it had been particularly bad. Rattling along on a rail-motor somewhere southwest of Bundaberg, recollection nagged busily and painfully. Every prop in the jerking landscape outside the window reminded: classicism of eucalypt disposition along whistle-stop branch lines to nowhere but that two-storeyed pub, the pedagogue chatter, the claustrophobia of coastal hills—all had their own heartbreaking italics for the loveless last occasion that had so nearly been it. Her quivering submission to self-designed treacly situations had not been entirely feigned. He had at first, she recalled bitterly, regarded her with the warmth of need, accepted her physical tribute, grown a little tired of her sexual zeal, and finally had held her off at blackboard pointer's length to examine the possibilities of a union.

He was nearly 50. He was suitably divorced. He drove a large older-model car, played dull golf and lived in a rented room. That was the killer. The rented room. Descending from the shared bathroom each day, touchingly untidy flecks of lather dried on the lobes of his hairy ears, he would accept Miss Wild's late débutante gleam-paste smile and I-understand-you glance across the yellow leather eggs. They would exchange nods, world-weary, pub-weary, job-weary nods of long suffering, and their hands might brush sufficiently as they both reached for the salt.

With that speed which should always have been a warning to her, golf for one became golf for two. They inspected local tourist bait in his car. They drove dustily up and down the coast, and swam, she more coy now in her costume, for time had caused a muscle slackness and varicosity that her clothes normally concealed. She merely toyed with the water, tickled a brine-line with one salmon-pink toe, and laughed. 'I'm no swimmer!' she confessed gaily. (He was the type of man who wanted his women helpless, she estimated, but of course could not be entirely sure, as she scuttled back to the protection of her wrap and the umbrella, that this was the right thing to do.) Beer-soothed, at a later interval in another setting, unheeding the warning tuckets, he looked slyly at her above his glass rim, and said with an emphasis she liked to embroider:

'This is pretty good, isn't it?'

Like any slick-tongued starlet she had agreed. The shore, raggedly aloof below the headland slope, was all the loneliness of fifteen years of solitary pub rooms and dinner gongs and commercially travelling grogs to fill in the time. Tears, milked out of that purpling inturned tide, banked up behind the blue rims of her exotic eyelids. Out there on the lawn patch before the beach hotel with its fungus sprouting of empty tables and chairs, the drenching grey scrub north towards the headland and the ego-shrinking coolness of evening breeze, they could both believe in happy endings and knew an impulse to confess to this. An orchard of citrine bulbs fruited the main street; in the twilight, long phosphorescent parallels crept across the sea, and shattered, and rose again far out, and crept back to the pandanus cliffs and the picnic shed where sets of initials described unspeakable relationships. A bicycle squeaked along the road to collapse at the newsagency. There was about this place a deathlessness that could perceive a century of staggering bikes, and sandboys in freckles and shorts, and isolated blue-grey evening cries across paddocks or pub yards or from council-donated swings in the cliff-side park.

Impelled by timelessness such as this, and the quality of serenity these pockets of rustless regress yield, Dan had leaned across the table, and taken her hand.

'What are you doing at Christmas?' he asked.

Alert always for implication, for even the harmonics of wedding chimes, she had almost choked on her heart as it bounded up to shove gaucheries from her lips.

'I don't know yet', she admitted, holding his eye. She hoped her own did not glitter. 'Why?'

'I've plans for once', he said. (Look into him, her mind

ordered. Hold his gaze until the trial of the moment is over.)
'But I don't know whether they'll suit you.'

'Am I involved?' It came out with shocking sprightliness that
had not been her intention, so that something in the timbre of
her voice frightened him a little. He pulled on his cigarette, and
ran a finger down the side of his nose.

'In a way.' Twilight softened everything. Her face, his
intention, outlines crumbled. 'Thought you might like to come
down the coast for a bit. I'm going down for a couple of weeks'
fishing south of Bega. You'd like it. Pretty restful after a hell
year.'

Oh God, she thought. Wrong. But what do I say? Do I
protest propriety? Do I accept on the off-chance that . . .? Why
was nothing ever cleanly limned for her? Predicaments constantly presented themselves, but without timorousness. They
swaggered. They strode back and forth waggling their rumps.
Oh, again and again and again, it seemed for ever, chances
would slide away.

Her hesitation embarrassed him.

'Never mind', he said, gulping down the last of his middy,
and depleting the magic. 'It was only a suggestion.'

Frightened of putting a word wrong, she resolved on the
measures of the desperate—a cool indifference coupled with a
bright surface of interest in almost everybody else. But he
appeared untouched by this device and was as friendly as ever,
as if the abstraction of her person meant nothing. It was she who
approached him in the last days of barren weather, and asked
false-sunnily:

'Is that offer still open?'

It was, but not as enthusiastically, although his good nature
made slovenly attempts to conceal this. But time had dealt so
poorly with Princess Klein, she could sense the pea of indifference beneath layers of mattresses.

She made every effort, but that is the most that can be said for
the gingham-minded nightmare of strategy to make herself
indispensable. There were flurries of *bonnes bouches*, little appe-
tisers culled from the pages of women's magazines, fluffy
mousses, asparagus flans, anything but the full-blooded steaks

158

he craved. She emptied ashtrays as soon as they were sullied. She talked too much. Even when she was silent he found something twittering about her, although she tried to dissemble with sporty outdoor-girl cussing on the fishing trips, and noggin-knocking of formidable duration. As the fortnight told its agonising beads for them both, her despair carried her beyond the caution that had kept her suspended on a maritally pegged tightrope and, suddenly ceasing to care, revealed a loneliness and despair that moved the man—but to pity only. Even physically his conventionality found her just a shade too enthusiastic.

It was with the most terrible tenderness on that last dreadful day that he told her he would not be coming back to Sydney for another week and that, in fact, he probably would not be seeing her at all in the new year because of a transfer. He omitted to say that he had applied for it. Her hopelessness would not even permit her to ask where, although her agony wondered. They lay side by side on the sand. Her soul trickled out through the opened pores of her ageing brown skin. Below them on the shelving beach, wave percussion rocked and rocked to the cries of gulls.

'I suppose I had better get back and pack', she said.

'No hurry', came the worst of casual answers. 'You've got a good four hours yet. You want to make the most of this sun.'

She rolled over on her back at that and began to laugh and laugh, creakingly, harshly. Dan put out one enormous oafish hand to pat her shoulder.

'Come on!' he protested. 'I'm not that funny, am I?'

The laughter went on, and he repeated his words, stretching out his arm once more to pat her; but his hand found space and, turning, he saw he was addressing the hollow left by her body in the loose sand. She was already halfway up the dune where beach-grass grew in a wind-blown agony all over the crest. Curiously he watched her graceless stride aggravated by her rage, and observed impersonally the stringy quality of her brassy hair glued into salty curls. For a few seconds he was tempted to call her back, and if she had once turned to look at him might have done so, but at last she was gone, and he dropped his face again into the safety of his arms. When he got back to the flat every trace of her had been removed with a scarifying fanaticism that was almost frightening, and while she examined the shrivelled pod of her pride on the station platform he dozed through the cowardly afternoon, listening to the crash of the surf.

Even now as the rail-motor took her through the most sealess of landscapes, sea burned bluely, acidly, at the back of her mind. Across this gauze, station names registered automatically and, through the pain of recollection, she noted there were still three to go before she got out. Never again, she told herself. Not ever, ever again. But she could see herself all the same. There it would all be as it had always been. The station and the back-chatting clerk. The hotel with its veranda brim pulled well down over its eyes. The dirt road. The half-dozen stores. The school with its moth-eaten fox fur of pepper-trees. Another station went by, and the absurd optimism that was her special poison began to secrete. Outside the window, tide was on the turn. The acid-blue waters were receding in direct proportion to the speed with which this rackety carriage crashed towards the town. And by the time it shuddered to a halt, and she was opening the door, her smart new leather case in her hand, the sea was nothing but the thinnest of violet lines on a horizon she could never touch. There she would be, she knew in her ashamed and humiliated heart, walking through that door on the Monday, looking around her with her bright eyes and sophisticated smile, sensing him by instinct and moving to her martyrdom like a saint.

Vida's Child

Freda Galloway

'*T*HEY'RE here! I'm off! I'm off now, Mum!'

I see through the open window my aunts are waiting for me. Their worried, anxious eyes peer from the old square car. Their coarse brown coats are up to their ears. They feel the cold, my aunts. They are very old.

'Goodbye! Goodbye! Goodbye, Mum!'

I grab my suitcase, race to the door. My mother is coming down the hallway. I debate. Will I kiss my mother? I decide I won't ... No ... I won't kiss her. Why? Really I don't know! Not really. Perhaps it is because I am my aunts' girl. Yes! That is it! I belong to them. I am my aunties' Lindy Lou. I am going to live with them and Benjamin, the hired man, on the farm at the foot of the hills, with the cats and the dogs and the sheep, forever! And ever! Well, until the end of the school holidays.

'Coming, Aunts!'

I am at the gate. I ... I ... My legs stop ... refuse to go! I can't move! I have seen my mother's face. It is stricken! She knows! She knows! I think my mother was snared on a loganberry bush in the Garden of Eden. I go back. I give her a kiss. A rough hug. But she knows. I trace a thin cruel streak of red upon her cheek ... blood!

My mother knows. She is a scientist. No, don't get me wrong. There are no framed certificates hanging on the wall. Not even thumbed on with a drawing pin! She is a lay scientist. She takes the pulse. The life pulse with her sensitive fingers. The temperatures ... the respirations. My father thinks it is interfer-

161

ence, so would my aunts, if they thought at all.

'Don't spill that tub of water, Lindy, Lindy Lou. It's for Benjamin's working trousers.'

'There's plenty more water, Aunties.'

'That's all there is!' They are very upset. 'There's no more!'

'There's plenty', I argue.

'There isn't, child.' They are tight-lipped.

'The world's full of water', I cry. 'Hot water . . . cold water . . . soda water.' I can be very cheeky to my old aunts.

To them it is the only tub in the whole wide world, and Benjamin has only four pairs of working trousers.

I race off calling, 'You can wash in lemonade if you want to! Ha! Ha! Ha!'

They get quite dithery when I go on like this. Aunt Priscilla drops a baked custard on the brown linoleum of the kitchen floor.

My aunt drives the car like a thoughtful maniac.

I watch from the back seat.

My Aunt Priscilla (sometimes I call her Pris) sits solid in the front seat. She looks, looks, looks over the rim of the earth into a galaxy upon galaxies, into eternity. Or . . . or at a grasshopper that leaps over a lucerne patch.

We have left the highway. We turned off where the sign said Upper Creek. We are on a gravel road and the dust is like a smudge of burnt sienna where we have passed.

My Aunt Priscilla does the dusting at the farm. I saw her last school holidays flicking a pair of my Aunt Flo's pink bloomers over the sideboard that's got the wedding photos on it. She is very sober, my Aunt Prissie. I think she was put on earth to wash grey socks, mend sheets, cook at a large black fuel stove and to tie up the sagging scarlet runners. I think that is what God intended for her. Also I think he must have said, 'Don't laugh Priscilla. Don't play. Definitely you must not be frivolous! When the oven smokes and your pies are slow, scrape out the black soot with your bare hands and generally Priscilla keep your largish nose to the grindstone, because you were very wicked last time madam, my word!' She can't remember her mind goes blank, confused, when she tries to recall her former misdeeds. For she is a good woman this time. Ah! Good is my Aunt Priscilla!

I study the hair that sprouts from a mole on her sober chin. I return my advancing hand.

'How's Timothy?' I ask. Timothy is the cat.

'He's all right', says my Aunt Priscilla.

'He'll sleep on your toes tonight, Lindy Lou', sings my Auntie Flo. She is always cheerful, well usually. She is younger than my Aunt Pris.

'Goody! Goody! Goody!' I cry. I am very young despite my age. Do you understand? I feel the years tied up in bundles with pieces of twine, in my legs, in my arms, and in my chest. Sometimes it makes walking very difficult.

'And how is Rosamunde?' She is the cow. 'How is Pretty?' She is the bantam. Well, she is my favourite bantam, for there are lots of bantams on the farm. 'How is Mrs Tulip?' She is the pig that lives in the sty near the buddleia bush.

'Everything's good', tones my Aunt Flo.

'Nothing's changed', quavers my Auntie Pris.

Nothing's changed! It will never change. It will always be there. My aunts. The farm. Benjamin. They are immortal. An Old Master! The paint will fade. The varnish crack but it will remain. I am glad.

We bump over the rough roads. I open and shut gates. My auntie crashes the gears as situations demand. We stop at a neighbouring farm about a mile from home. The back door is shut. I pick a privet leaf and break it into one hundred pieces before the door is opened. It is very dark inside. An older woman is in the background near the stove.

'Come in', says the daughter-in-law.

We go into the kitchen. The remains of a meal are on the table. It has been a frugal meal. Usually I adore eating in other people's houses, but I have no appetite in this one.

'We've just finished tea', says the old one. She blesses the table. A preying mantis! Her arms and legs stick out. Her body follows reluctantly when she moves. Her hair is light and dry. Her eyes are full of cold challenge.

'We can't stay', cry my aunts. They never intrude. The

daughter-in-law is watching my aunts. She has big unhappy eyes. They are deep, deep deep brown.

There has been a row. Charged words still fill the room, the bedrooms and refuse to settle. The hands of the two small imbecile children are limp. Too tired, too hurt to play. A plastic doll lies dead on the floor.

'You've been to town', says the Preying Mantis.

'Yes', says my Aunt Flo. She hands the younger woman a parcel. The daughter-in-law is grateful. She holds a cardigan to one of the children. The child looks at her uncomprehending. Oh my children! My children! She sobs to herself. Her tears would fill the dam at the back of the house. Her unshed tears would flood the creek . . . the gullies for miles around. One tear fell on the red cardigan. She didn't know I saw.

The mother-in-law is watching with cold, blue insect eyes. Phhhhh! She made mad children, this daughter-in-law! She'd told her many, many times. 'The kids are mad! Mad!'

The words filled the cupboards, the open fireplace, they overflowed into the next room, into the bedrooms.

The son comes in. He is his mother's son. 'Afternoon', he says curt to my aunts. He senses the atmosphere. He says nothing. Resignation is on his face. But how he wishes his mother away . . . away . . .

He would say, 'Can't you go and live somewhere else, Mother?'

'Where?' she'd retort.

'Anywhere', he would answer. 'In the town! Somewhere!'

'This my home', she would say and walk away. Out of the front door, down the garden, down to the citrus trees.

'Would you like some lemons?' she asks my aunt.

'Well, my lemon curd is getting down', says my Aunt Pris gratefully.

'I'll get you some', says the Preying Mantis. Legs transport her from the room.

I lean against the table. Twist one foot around a chair leg. I put my index finger in my mouth and with the spit I write on the scarred linoleum. Lindy . . . Lindy L . . .

Aunt Flo gives me a shove. 'Out you go and play.'

They want to talk alone with the daughter-in-law. The son has returned to the dairy.

I uncurl my foot from the chair leg, wipe Lindy Lindy L off the table and slowly drag myself from the kitchen to show my aunts I am going of my own accord.

There is a silence until I leave the room and then the conversation commences like a hand of cards being cautiously dealt.

I creep outside and around the corner. A mean garden runs down the side of the house. I see one chrysanthemum in bloom. A tawny colour. I love tawny chrysanthemums best of all. The raging sea is in my nostrils, my arms ache, the lighthouse throws a golden light on my fair hair.

'I will rescue you, my love', I cry. I pick the bloom and stick it down the front of my blouse.

'I will put you in a vase. My Auntie Pris will give you fresh water', I add, 'if she remembers'.

I skip to the front of the house. The Preying Mantis is picking lemons. She drops them into an old felt hat. I run down to her. She keeps on picking. She pretends she has not seen me. I go quite close. I clear my throat.

'Has this tree got thorns?' I ask.

'It's a lemon tree, isn't it?' she snaps.

'Are they poisonous?' I touch a branch with studied timidity.

'Get scratched and see', is all she says. I move to the other side of the tree and calculate my next move.

'My mother makes lemon jam', I offer.

'Marmalade', is the tart reply.

'She', the Mantis reflects, 'had a craving for lemons when she was expecting you'.

Oh well, I indicate by my swagger, they have done a good job!

The Mantis is rather impressed.

'She', looking meaningful at the house, 'could have done with a few'.

'What?' I query. I put on my innocent look.

'Can't you tell?' she asks.

I continue my innocent look.

She regards me keenly. 'Those kids are mad!' Her eyes narrow. 'I told her this morning, they're hopeless. She might as well know.'

The chrysanthemum stalk jabs my tummy button. I watch the Preying Mantis.

'They want me to live somewhere else', she hisses.

'Do they?' I ask.

'But I won't!' she says. She gives a lemon a savage tug.

'No', I prompt.

'Why should I?' she asks.

'I . . . I don't know', I stammer. I hitch my bloomers to shift the chrysanthemum.

'Would you?' and her voice is rather shrill.

'No', I say, traitor.

'I'm not done for yet!' She comes towards me. She is going to tell me something. She is going to tell me what she has planned. We watch each other warily. She is forming words with her thin lips.

'Mother!' It is the son on the veranda above us. We turn sharply towards him. 'Mother!' he says again. She does not reply. There is an ugly look on his face.

'Mother', he repeats, 'Could you get me my riding boots?'

He knows where they are. He wants to terminate our conversation. He knows his mother is talking about the row in the kitchen. His hair is untidy. His face is unloved.

He watches his mother come towards him. There is dislike in his eyes. She is his dry school-lunches eaten alone. She is his trousers, smelling of the dairy. She is the jeering children. She is his mother waiting in the sulky after school, while the other kids go with their tennis mothers, lipstick mothers.

She pushes past him. He has won this round. He watches without conceit. He is the victor, but she is not done for yet, there will be many more rounds.

I go back to the garden. I take the flower from my blouse, I push the stalk hard into the earth.

My blistered eyes will see the holocaust and survive. My seared lungs will gasp the poisoned air and my scorched hands will lay the last tribute on this doomed planet.

'Lindy! Lindy Lou!' It is my aunts.

'Coming', I call, 'Coming!'

'Come on', they say. 'We've much to do. Calves to pen and eggs to gather ...'

'But Benjamin?' I say.

My aunt's hands tighten on the steering wheel.

Benjamin!

Aunt Priscilla is out of orbit between the Milky Way and the tilting Saucepan! Emergency! Avert the catastrophe! Ground stations alert! Quickly Priscilla, press some buttons!

'His fingernails are grimy', I say in my thin voice. I can be quite irritating. I see these things.

'It's his work', says Aunt Flo, softly. Why softly, Auntie Flo? He's only the hired man!

'They're men's hands', says my Aunt Priscilla reverently. 'Working hands!' Why reverently, Aunt Priscilla!

'Work!' I scorn.

'He shoes the horses. He brings the ewes from the back paddock to the flats. He brings the lambs to the sheds', my auntie chants. The Bible shuts with a soft thud!

'If he were Moses', I say, 'he'd wave a wand and make a tunnel under the hill paddock and the sheep would come out round about the orchard and then he could sort them out!'

My aunt turns slowly and fixes her sober eyes upon me. I draw my breath. I have offended the Gods. Of course Benjamin is Moses! His horse is Foam! I shut my eyes. I ask forgiveness. 'Please God let me do something nice for Benjamin.' I am silent for a time. I am thinking.

'He should be on one of the big stations. He wouldn't have to live in an old tin shed.'

'That'll do, Lindy', says my Aunt Flo. The car seems a bit unsteady.

'Why?' I snap.

'Because ... because ... because ...' They are quite distressed.

'Because', says my Auntie Flo triumphantly, 'we're at Muddy Gate!' She throws the car into neutral. 'Can you manage?'

I flex my arms. They are very thin. The gate I remember is

167

heavy. 'I'll manage', I say. I am a bit cranky. I've seen them struggling with tin openers when Benjamin could have done the job in a few seconds. I say to myself, Pris could have opened the gate. It's too heavy for a child!

I jump out. Wrench open the sagging gate. Tiptoe around the mud hole. I stare at the slush. I bend closer ... closer ... closer. There is something yellow down there. It looks as if Mum has miscut the collar of my new yellow dress!

'There's no fish in there!' yells Pris as they drive through the mud. I think she must be dying to go to the lavatory.

I jump back so that I don't get splashed. 'No, but there's mice', I grimace to the back of the car. 'You ought to know, Pris!'

We're nearly there. Nearly home. The chimney doodles preoccupied above the farmhouse roof.

'He's a good man', says my Auntie Flo when she sees the smoke. He has lit the fire for the aunts to cook his tea!

The birds flute homewards to the coming night. The scissor-cut mountains are pasted to icy blue. We would be very cold if we didn't have our coats.

'Down Rusty!' snaps Auntie Pris. She misses his grin by half an inch. We kick through the strips of bark on the creek flat. We cross the wooden bridge to the orchard. We pass the walnut tree, the mandarin, the loquat, we are here. Home!

Benjamin comes to the front veranda. He raises his right hand when he sees me. He is a solid man. He wears a flannel shirt. His hair is grey and he needs a shave.

'How's Lindy?' he says to me.

'Good', I answer. Suddenly shy.

'Ready for work?' he says. I squirm because I don't think it is a very nice thing to say to me when I am on holidays.

'You'll be on the blades tomorrow', says he.

We sit down to tea when my aunts have unpacked their parcels and set the table. I keep my eyes on the chequered tablecloth. My hands won't move. They are clenched on my lap. My knife and fork are anxious for me to pick them up. They want to start.

'Eat up!' they say. 'Eat up!'

I look at my aunts. Our eyes are level and then one of the brackets give way and then my eyes fall on to the cloth again. On the yellow and red squares.

'Come on! Don't be shy! Lindy, Lindy Lou!'

I am very unhappy. The tears are not far away. I want to go home. They'll have to take me home. I want my mother. I am at someone else's dinner table. Someone else's food is in front of me. My aunts are strangers. They don't know me. I am Vida's child! I just want to go home straight away. I want a cup of tea in my Toby Jug. I want to stretch for the bread, cry at my mother she has served me less than my sister, clean out the rice pudding dish . . .

'Pass the bread, Benjamin', says my Auntie Flo.

I grab the fur on Timothy's stomach with my bare toes (I have taken off my shoes), receive the offered bread and start off.

The chops from the lamb that Benjamin killed are good. The lettuce, the tomatoes, the onions from my aunt's vegetable garden on the creek flat are much nicer than Mum buys.

My Aunt Prissie watches my skinny arms. My word the child is thin. Look at her arms! She needs a good feed. Building up! I suppose Vida . . . well Vida would feed her I suppose but not the sort of food that she, Priscilla, would give her. Vida was careful . . . Vida . . . Vida was a little mean. If she had Lindy, Lindy Lou for a few months, say two, she'd make a difference. And she placed apple pie after steak and kidney on the warmed place in front of me. If . . . if I had been her child. Her child!

She looked at Benjamin quickly. His child! She fingered the ruby my cousin, Hilda, had bought her last August from Woolworths. My aunty was 57 last birthday.

It was warm in my bed. Timothy slept on my toes and I was afraid to move lest I waken him. The plates clattered in the kitchen as my aunts washed the tea dishes. The newspaper rattled as Benjamin read by the fireside. The frogs held choir in the chilly night and I thought I could hear the water slipping around the large stones near the wooden bridge.

I don't remember going to sleep, but I must have, for I didn't hear a tall dark man in black tights slip in when my aunts and Benjamin had gone to bed. He must have come in through the side door, where the tweediana climbs the wire-netting near the veranda post, then up the steps. Because he sneaked into the kitchen and was eating my Aunt Priscilla's steamed pudding with a long thin knife that had a jewelled handle. He ate and he ate! He'd cut the pudding into slices and then stick the point of the knife into the middle of the slice and put it in his mouth like that. I don't know why he didn't pierce his throat but there was no blood. He ate and he ate! I didn't think he would ever stop. (My Aunt Priscilla is a tremendous cook). He grew larger and larger. The walls of the kitchen bulged. The door creaked. I woke up. I tried to scream. No sound came. A door squeaked at the end of the hallway. It was him! He was going out!

I'd have to get up. Tell my aunts . . . Benjamin! I crept out of bed. My heart was pounding thickly in my chest.

'Aunties! Aunties!' I tried to scream. No sound came.

I tiptoed to the door and peered into the dark hallway. Auntie Flo was creeping through the door. Her hand was on the door knob. She shut the door gently.

I could tell she didn't want to frighten us.

'Where is he now?' I whispered.

She almost jumped out of her skin. She didn't know I had heard. 'Where is he?' I repeated. She advanced towards me, fingers on lips.

'Shhhhhhhh!' she said.

'Did you catch him?' I asked.

'Shhhhhhhh!'

'He had a long thin knife with a diamond handle', I cried.

She looked startled.

'And he ate Aunt Prissie's steamed pudding with all the sultanas in it, plus six meat pies!'

She looked relieved. 'Did he?' she asked softly.

'Yes', I whispered, 'did you catch him?'

'You've been dreaming, Lin', she said gently. 'Go back to bed, there's a good girl', she came closer, 'Don't wake Auntie Pris'.

There was a faint creaking in my Aunt Prissie's bedroom. My Auntie Flo turned startled eyes on me.

'Shhhhhhhh! Go back to bed, Lin.' Her voice was urgent.

'I can't sleep', I said stubbornly.

She watched me fearfully, biting her lip. 'Wait a moment!' She disappeared into her bedroom, leaving me standing near the doorway. A few seconds later she returned and pressed some sweets into my hand. 'That'll fix you up!'

I popped two into my mouth. There was a noise like splintering glass.

'Lin! Lin! Eat quietly! Don't make that noise!' She looked fearfully towards Aunt Prissie's bedroom. I didn't want to go.

I said, 'Aunt Flo, did you and Aunt Pris catch these?' I indicated the deer heads with the long antlers above the bedroom doors.

'They're plaster of Paris, Lin', she stifled a laugh. 'You didn't catch them?' I am disappointed. 'I thought you and Auntie Pris went out one moonlight night and caught them near Muddy Gate!'

'No', she giggled slightly.

I could see the two of them out with big black bags roaming about in the moonlight amongst deer like those in the large pictures in the drawing room. I could hear a scuffle, rather terrible, and then my aunts returning hysterically to the farm house.

'What have you two women been up to?' It is Benjamin at the doorway of his old tin hut. The noise had woken him up.

'We've got them, Benjamin!'

'Got what?' His voice is sleepy, irritable.

'The deer!' shriek my aunts.

He comes to take a closer look. 'My God, so you have!'

'Where'll we put them?' they ask laughingly.

'Above the bedroom door', says Benjamin on his hands and knees with his pocket knife.

Their laughter is infectious. He seems a bit amused too.

My Auntie Flo says, 'I went alone', and she giggled and disappeared.

I went back to bed. We must have disturbed my Auntie Prissie for the bed squeaked. But she couldn't have been awake, she didn't call out. Although, I thought I heard another sound.

171

It sounded like weeping ... but I know it was the sobbing of
the possum in the loquat tree.

I woke when Auntie Prissie went past the bedroom door. It
was still dark. I think it must have been about five o'clock.
I jumped out of bed and followed her to the kitchen. I sat
huddled in my nightdress hugging my knees. I was very cold,
but I loved watching my aunt lighting the fire. The way it
crackled and the way the flames danced for pure joy.

'It's showing off', I told my aunt. She didn't seem to hear.

'Don't you love lighting fires in the morning?' I asked.

She shoved another length of kindling on.

'Those little flames like lizard's tongues, Auntie Pris?'

She prodded the fire with a poker.

The kettle hissed, then sang, then finally boiled over. My
aunt made the tea in a big brown teapot and jammed the old
stained tea-cosy over it. I love my tea sweet. I had two cups
straight, one for each leg.

There were shadows everywhere. Outside there was only a
slight hint of day. Timothy's fur was still cold from the night's
frost.

'Don't you love the mornings, Auntie Pris?' I could see the
faint outline of the oak trees now.

'More tea?' was all she said.

'One for my stomach', I replied. She poured the third cup.
She fed the cats, she put on a big saucepan of porridge, she
swept the hearth.

'Auntie', I said, 'can you really imagine that the creek runs all
night? Even when we're asleep! Not watching!'

'What?' she said and cracked an egg into the sizzling fat in the
frying pan.

She didn't enthuse about being up early at all!

Benjamin came up the back steps as she was laying the table.
He cleared his throat. 'Morning.'

My Aunt Prissie was too busy to hear him, so he knocked
Timothy off his chair and sat down. My aunt handed him a
bowl of porridge. He shovelled on the sugar as if it were
cement.

'Got an offsider this morning', he commented.

'Yes', said my Aunt Pris.

'Wish I had one', he said, 'What's she like? Any help?'

'Not bad', was all my aunt said. She passed him a plate of eggs and bacon and two pieces of fried bread. He was watching me intently.

'My word', he paused and removed some food from his teeth with a matchstick. 'She's Vida's child!'

I crept from the kitchen. My legs were watery and it wasn't the tea! What did he mean? Vida's child! Didn't I have a father? Wasn't my dad my father? I must be ... I must be illegitimate! Illegitimate! What a disgrace! I dressed quickly. What if the kids at school found out I was ... illegitimate! I raced quickly up the hill that rose sheer from the back of the house. I was still sore from the shock but the grass was ruffled velvet in the far paddocks and there were spring flowers at my feet. I looked at the house below and the diminished figure of my aunt as she shook the tablecloth out the back door.

I waved. She waved. I waved again and she waved. Then she went into the house again. Timothy slipped in too, just before she shut the back door.

Away, away in the distance smoke lay over the town where my mother lived. I could see the people stirring. I could see the shop girls putting on their dark frocks, nibbling their toast as they dressed. I saw them walking in the cold windy street. I saw them smiling in their mirrors at lunchtime when they were putting on their lipstick. 'He'll kill me', they told their image, 'if I look at anyone else.' I dug a stick in the ground and twisted. It would probably save a tired ant a bit of trouble. Nobody would ever love me like that. Never! No one would ever love Lindy Lindy Lou like that. I made the ant-hole deeper in case the ant had rheumatism. Why? Why not? Because ... because ... the answer came flying back from the birds that flew overhead. Because ... because you're Lindy Lou Lou ... you've got straight hair and blue eyes and you're illegitimate ... that's why ... that's why ... you're Vida's child ...

I feel a bit better after a while and anyway I love the mornings at the farm. I can't be unhappy for long. There is so much to do. So much to see. I search for walnuts in the fallen leaves. I am a dragon in the bamboos. I am a heavy bumble bee in the petunias and I catch the gudgeons in the deep pool round the bend of the creek.

'Lindy! Lindy Lou!'

'Coming, Aunts!'

It is Aunt Priscilla. 'Lindy, we'll feed Mrs Tulip. You take the bread. Careful now! Don't tip it out of the basket!' I carry the bread and my aunt carries the heavy bucket up the steep hill. She has a few rests and I wait near the buddleia bush and stick my nose into a spray of flowers. The world spins round.

'What are you doing, child?' says my Aunt Priscilla.

'Ah gee, Auntie Pris', I say, 'Ah gee!'

'You'll end up with hay fever if you go on like that!' She picks up the bucket and struggles on. Mrs Tulip is lying down but she is not asleep. She gets on her feet when we arrive.

'Would you like to be a pig, Auntie Pris?' I ask.

She empties the bucket into the trough. 'Watch out!' Her face looks funny.

'I would call you Mrs Pig.'

She scratches her arm on the barbed wire and grimaces with pain. 'Would you have babies, I wonder?' I lean against the corner post and watch. She hasn't been listening, she's been too busy mixing up the bread. When we go back our hands are free. I take the hand that is next to mine. It is covered in tears.

Wet clothes are slapping in the stiff breeze. A big cumulus bundles across the sky. My Auntie Pris is making pink and white blancmange and stirring some soup with the other hand. My Auntie Flo is sweeping big balls of fluff and toffee wrappers from under the bed. I roam around the orchard, the sheds. There is a noise from the stinging nettle near the saddle shed . . . I go closer . . . closer . . .

'Aunties! Aunties!' Frantic. 'Aunties!'

They fly from the house like startled birds.

'What is it child?' Their hearts in their mouths.

I can only sob. 'You'll never guess!' A snake! Yes Lindy Lou has been bitten by a snake! A red-back maybe! Gracious! What do you do! What do you do for a snake bite! Oh heaven help them! Heaven help them! Vida's child! 'It's . . .' I am too helpless. Breathless from running. But my Auntie Pris knows. Ah! Now she knows! It is Benjamin! He has lost his hand! Severed at the elbow by the shearing blades! She waits for confirmation and bandages the splintered bone with the patched sheet, that was too far gone, from the ironing basket.

'There ... there ... Benjamin ... there ... there ...' And rueful Benjamin says, 'Only for you Pris I'd be in hospital and they'd be drenching the daylights out of me'. Afterwards she would build him up! Lemon meringue pies ... sago ... apple dumplings ... tapioca ... 'You'll have another slice of this plum duff, Benjamin?'

'Just one more slice if it's not too much trouble Pris and fill up the old pannikin to go with it.' When the last crumb has disappeared, 'By Jove ... by jove a man's got a lot to be thankful for, even if he has lost his right arm'.

God is perverse at Upper Creek.

'It's Pretty!' I gasp.

'Pretty' they echo. 'Pretty? The bantam!'

'Come and see.' I get each by the hand and run them on their thick old legs to the nettle bush near the hay shed. We fall on our hands and knees and peer into the green shadows. The baby chickens are peeping through their mother's feathers. They are so safe. So safe with their fierce little mother. We stare at them like lady tigers.

The days fly by. I help my aunts weed the carrots. I pick a bunch of wildflowers for my dressing table. I knit my sister a crimson purse. I search for gold in the bed of the creek.

'Lindy! Lindy! Benjamin's morning tea!' There is coffee in the thermos and hot scones at the bottom of the basket.

I cross the gully to the shearing shed. Benjamin is working with the sheep this morning.

'Morning tea, Benjamin!'

'By Jove! You're the girl!'

'The coffee's hot!'

'Doesn't matter! Pour it out.' He reaches into his pockets for his tobacco. He watches me pouring the coffee. I don't like people watching me. I get nervous. I don't like this look he's got on his face either! What is it? I've asked Mum. She won't tell me. It starts with A! it's ... ad ... adu ... adultery! Yes, that's it! Adultery! The kids at school told me. I run from the shed ... adultery ... adultery ...!

I race into an old chook shed. I frighten a big black hen. She flies in the air and crashes down on a nest of eggs in the corner. She forgets all about me and gobbles up the golden yolks. I think she only wanted an excuse to break those eggs!

The days fly by and the nights come. The wind blows and then is still. The sheep are lost, then find each other and the herefords in the waving grass are like knitted toys from a church bazaar. There is an empty house where the creek bends and finds its source at the foot of the mountains.

One day my cousins come and we walk up the creek to the empty house.

'Is there anyone there?'

'No.'

'Some rabbiters lived there once', I say.

'Murdered', informs my cousin. I shudder.

'In their sleep.'

'Oh!'

'Serves them right', says Patricia and looks in my direction. She doesn't go much on me. She is a hard little thing.

I don't cause my cousins much trouble that day. But then I am a naturally tractable child.

We follow the creek. There is debris high in the oaks where the floods have been.

'Does this creek flood?' I question. I don't like to take many chances.

'Sure.'

'Much?'

'Course!' A kookaburra has a stick thrown at him in contempt.

'It would be over our heads! We'd drown!'

Patricia rolls her eyes.

'If', I say more calmly, examining a sapphire, 'if this creek flooded and I was swept through my mother's town hanging onto a slippery log', I rub spit over the stone, 'I wouldn't wave.'

They stop open mouthed! 'Good for you!' they say. They are full of admiration for my stoicism.

'I would just get swept out to sea and drowned. I,' the jeweller would be interested in this stone, 'would leave my mother just crying and waving from the creek bank.'

I think I went up in Patricia's estimation after that. Although we never became real friends because she couldn't stand that stupid look I get on my face every now and then.

I am a very friendly person myself. Anyone can come into my life or thoughts at any time. Just knock upon the door. I am a very open person. Although sometimes I feel embarrassed if people enter without knocking. Mum knows I like to be alone, sometimes.

There is a tree fenced off near the empty house. The trunk is brown, the leaves dark green and the fruit is the colour that is near the red in my paint box. Orange. Oh, and small brown spots used straight.

'Freckles', I say.

'Fly droppings', says my cousin.

They are delicious those oranges!

The house looks as if it has been raped and then murdered. It is very sorry for itself. The wreaths have seeded. Seedlings grow where the sheep have not access. There are obsequious snow-drops (they must have been there that night) careless old marigolds (prostitutes) and red geraniums. I am a butterfly. I touch their smiling faces as I flutter round. There is a rose, pink, loose-petalled, fragrant.

'Beautiful! beautiful . . .' I whisper in my quivering butterfly voice. 'I will love you forever. For ever and ever. I will never forget you. Eternal love.'

We explore the slab wash-shed. We crush the leaves of the citronella on our mosquito-suspicious arms.

I am the Mistress! I am the Mistress of this enormous mansion. I am slim and dark and I laugh a lot. I carry a silver tray to my famous guests. No! I am fair and reserved. I give quick nods and slip away.

We find a bottle of kerosene and light a fire. We bring in armfuls of bark from the gum trees.

'Come on! Let's do some exploring! The billy won't boil for ages yet!'

We go to the sheep dip. I pretend to fall in. My cousin grabs my waist. He keeps his hand there. We stand together. Close! Patricia has her back to us. My cousin tightens his grip. The sun is a hundred times brighter. A huge paint brush, vivid with colour impastos my gaze ... the gum trees ... the mountains ... the roof top ... there is a brush mark on one of the ranges ... titanium.

'Lindy! Lindy!' he is urgent.

'Yes', I whisper, 'Yes Lester?'

He swallows, 'One of these days I'm going to take you and Patricia to the Burning Mountain.'

'Gee!' I say.

'When you're bigger.' I was just going to ask whether it was the vertical or horizontal measurements that I would get Mum to run the tape over, when Patricia calls, 'Let's play hide and seek in the woolshed'.

Lester and I jump to the ground. We avoid each other's eyes. The doors of the shearing shed are locked. We crawl up the runways. There are squares of sunlight on the big open floor. Patricia and I race around singing. 'Here we go gathering nuts and may' while Lester examines an old engine in the corner.

Afterwards Patricia hides her head and counts to two hundred by fives while we look for hiding places. I wriggle into an old brown sack and am not found. Patricia gives up looking for me. I am very disappointed but I can still feel Lester's arm around me when I pretended to fall in the sheep dip.

'We'd better see if the billy's boiling', says Patricia. Gee, she's a spoil-sport! I drag after them slowly. Just my luck not to be found.

Lester stands on an antbed near the house and the ants run up his legs. He yells like mad and Patricia and I double up with laughter and roll on the ground. I forget I am disappointed.

'Lester?' I ask, 'Are there any giants in the Burning Mountain?' These modern times are not much good to me. I like witches and goblins and things.

'Giants!' He is incredulous.

178

'Yes', I say, 'like Jack and the Beanstalk'.

'It's a seam of burning coal', he says. 'A bushranger lit a fag and chucked the match into a crack in the hillside.'

'It was a silly thing to do', sniffs Patricia. She'd know of course!

'Crazy!' agrees my cousin. 'You wouldn't get me up there if there were giants, Lindy Lindy Lou.'

I decide I mightn't go to the Burning Mountain even when my measurements are big enough.

The fire has gone out. My cousin piles a heap of newspapers on it.

'Be careful!' I cry.

'Sook!' jeers Patricia. She throws on another newspaper. I pick up the kerosene bottle and tip the remaining fluid on the fire. I jump back before the explosion.

'Now you've done it!' screams Patricia. She uses her ugly voice.

'That's torn it', says Lester resignedly.

We look at each other with sudden dislike, then fear. We hear the sound of a vehicle approaching. Brakes screech! Footsteps! We race to the window. A utility has drawn up near the wash house. It is too late to hide. We are strangely dumb.

A man in working clothes strides into the room. 'What the hell are you bloody kids up to?' He glares at us. 'Eh?' We don't know what to say.

'Trying to burn the place down?' He brings his fist down hard on the mantle shelf.

We don't say anything. Our eyes lack focus.

The man says to Lester, 'I thought you had more sense! A boy of your age! You could have', he indicated Patricia and myself, 'burnt them to death!' I give Lester a scorching look but Patricia stands isolate in her asbestos suit.

'Go on, you'd better clear out!' the man shouts. 'Out you go!' He shoos us out like Aunt Pris does the hens when they get into the garden near the house.

Another man comes into the room. 'This coulda been pretty!'

'I wish', snarls the first man, 'that the old man would buy

them out'. He throws his arm in the direction of my aunts' property.

We walk home another way. Lester throws stones at the magpies.

'Lester', I ask, 'did that poor innocent magpie do you any harm?' I am not a member of the Gould League of Bird Lovers for nothing!

'Ach!' he spits and mumbles something about 'soft sheilas'.

Patricia has her nose in the air as usual. Miss High and Mighty!

Auntie Pris makes us a cup of tea. I wish she wouldn't put so many raisins in the fruit cake and I wish she'd put the pink icing right to the edge of the sponge cake. And, they always know at home I'd rather have apricot jam than plum for a filling.

I go home tomorrow. I have packed. I have unpacked and repacked several times. Everything is neatly folded. I am a bit excited. I will see my mother again. I will sew the bias binding on my apron. I embroidered it at school. I will pump up the tyres of my old bike and fly around the lanes.

Timothy comes into my bedroom. I give him a brief pat. The ducks are swimming in the still pool beneath the willow trees. I go to the window and look out. They are made of cardboard.

Auntie Flo comes into my bedroom. 'You've packed!'

'Yes', I say. I hold my breath. She might ask me to stay. Auntie Prissie comes in 'You're ready to go!'

'Yes', I mumble. There is a silence. They taste the hollow hours when I depart. They dare not look at each other.

I go to the wooden bridge and swing my legs over the cool stream. I drop mandarin peelings in and watch them bob away out of sight.

That night I heard the door open softly in the corridor, footsteps, my Aunt Prissie's bed squeaking.

I heard the clip clop of a big white horse called Moses down by the oaks; clip tock, clip tick, tick tock. I heard the teardrops fall from the loquat tree, drip drop, tick tock, and I heard the desperate sobbing of the possum in the pear tree next to mine.

The Book of Life

Leone Sperling

*I*T is Kol Nidre night. Tomorrow is the Jewish Day of Atonement, the day on which God decides whose name will be written in the Book of Life for the following year.

He is 83 years old and he wants to live for another year. Not only does he want to live; he must live. It is his sacred duty to stay alive to look after his wife. His wife is eight years younger than he is and physically fitter but she needs looking after, none the less. They have been married now for 50 years. There was a time when he thought he might not make it to his golden wedding anniversary, but he did make it and now he needs to go on living for at least another year.

His wife has lost hold of her memory. It has flittered out of her grasp. She has entered a twilight timelessness where minutes and hours, days and dates, months and years are meaningless. He must be her constant clock. He is her timekeeper, guardian, father and friend. He unravels her confusion and imposes pattern and order onto her chaos. Without him she could not function in the real world.

He has lost his faith. He has lived his life in goodness, guided by the sure knowledge that God the Father looked down upon him and blessed him. But his wife's deterioration has changed all that. If there is a God, how can He have allowed such a thing to happen? Such a clever woman! Incomprehensible. He has lost his mate, his friend, his 50-year companion. She has retreated, contracted. He cannot crawl for comfort into her inner world.

He has gone through all these married years in peace and

harmony. No fights in this marriage; no disagreements; no harsh words. But lately he's been getting impatient, irritated, losing his temper. She must ask him the same questions over and over again in her enormous effort to engrave the answers on her sliding mind. Sometimes he cannot control himself. The irritation builds and mounts and, before he knows it, he explodes in anger. And then she cries and he feels guilty. He keeps reminding himself that she can't help it. It's not her fault. He manages to stay calm most of the time. The thing that upsets him most is the enormous effort she makes to please him. She warms his pyjamas on the electric blanket every night.

He has lost his faith but it is Kol Nidre night and the habit of ritual is strong and, after all, how can anyone be so certain? Maybe God exists. Better to be safe than sorry. Better to go to the synagogue tonight and again tomorrow. Better to fast, better to pray, better to ask for another year of life—just in case.

She is waiting for him in the lounge-room. She is wearing her fur coat. She is always cold. She even wears her coat when she sits outside, eating fruit in the sunshine. He does not know how to keep her warm.

If only that fire hadn't burned his business down. He'd planned to keep working for another six months but thieves had broken into his shop and, finding no money, they'd expressed their frustration by setting fire to the whole place. Too old to start again. Too late to rebuild.

Retirement. Strolling with her each day around the safe, known streets; letting her tell him, over and over again, the names of all the flowers and plants; walking slowly up the hill to the Scoop grocery store to buy a few cartons of yoghurt, a litre of milk. Going to the bridge club twice a week. The only thing that keeps him sane. But how much longer can he go there? She's an embarrassment. She can't remember even the last five minutes' play. The other players won't tolerate her too much longer. What will happen to him then? They've had to give up playing bridge at home. The anxiety caused by having to provide people with sandwiches and cups of tea is too great for her to bear. They buy all their meals from the gourmet food shop.

182

He remembers her as she used to be. Chief pharmacist of a large hospital. How proud of her he had been! He wouldn't let her work, not for a long time. Not his wife. His wife didn't need to work. After all, he earned enough money, didn't he? Enough to support her and the children—all quite comfortably. But she wouldn't give up. She pestered and begged and finally he'd let her go back to work. What a difference it had made to her! She could whip through her day with lightning precision; dash home with swift steps, feet flying; cook dinner, wash dishes, iron clothes, help the children with their homework. Phenomenal! Her momentum propelled her through the days, the months, the years. No one could keep pace with her.

And the Friday nights, the family dinners, children and grandchildren spilling around the swimming pool. How can it have come to this? Now, now when he needs her companionship, her friendship, her understanding; now when they should be enjoying the rewards of his hard-working life. He thinks of his children. All successful, thank goodness. All well-educated. No like him. No reliant on the business world. And yet, he'd done well, hadn't he? Comfortably off. Not rich, but comfortable. 'The whitest man in the rag trade.' That's what they'd called him. Too honest to be rich. And too much given away to charity, so some people would say. But isn't that the most important part of being a Jew? Doing mitzvahs— giving to those less fortunate than yourself. They could have gone on a world cruise if only she'd managed to keep hold of her mind.

He looks at her, sitting in the lounge chair, waiting for him. Frail now. So thin. Her upper lip trembles. Her gloved hands grasp her handbag very tightly. He tells her it won't be long. Soon the taxi will arrive to take them into the city.

They are walking down Elizabeth Street towards the Great Synagogue. It is 5.45 p.m. He knows that the service begins at 6 p.m. but he has to get there early. He is a man of extreme punctuality. If he is not 15 minutes early, then he considers himself to be late.

It is difficult for him to walk quickly because the arteries in his legs no longer function properly and he suffers from angina.

Her pace slows down to match his. The wind claws into her. If she did not have her fur coat on, she would surely die.

They reach the synagogue and find that the gates are closed. Not only are the gates closed, but heavy, locked chains hold the gates together.

'We must be very early', he says to her. 'I must have mistaken the time. Perhaps the service doesn't start until 6.30 p.m.'

'It's so cold, dear', she complains. 'I can't just stand still. I'll have to keep walking.'

'Come on, then, Mummy dear, we'll walk round to the Castlereagh Street entrance. It's bound to be open.'

By the time they walk around the block to the back entrance of the synagogue, it is 6 p.m. The tall, brown doors are closed and locked. The street is empty.

'Let's walk back to the front, dear', he says. 'By the time we do that, they must be open.' He walks swiftly now and her pace quickens to keep up with him. He should slow down, he should be calm. He knows that if he gets upset his angina will get worse but his agitation is beyond control.

The front of the synagogue is still locked. He moves away from her and stares at the gates in disbelief. She pulls the collar of her coat up around her chin. 'There must be some reason, dear, why the synagogue is closed', she says. 'I don't know what that reason could be, but there must be a reason.'

He does not hear her. Where are all his fellow Jews? Don't they know, as he does, that they must begin their fasting and their atonement on this night? Why are they so late opening the synagogue? He goes to the gates and rattles them. He pulls at the chains. His mind is mathematical, decisive and precise. He never makes mistakes about dates and times. The synagogue must be open. It must! No other possibility is tenable. He grabs the heavy iron gates and shakes, shakes, shakes them. 'Open the gates!' he cries. 'Open the gates and let me in! God, let me in! Put my name, my name ... down—my name, write my name in the Book of Life!'

She stands apart from him, waiting, whipped by the wind. She folds her hands into the sleeves of her coat.

He stops, lets the gates go. His hands drop, head sags. He

stares at her in blank confusion and a tear spills out of the corner of his eye. He takes her arm and they lean against each other, tightening themselves against the wind, shuffling through the darkness, along deserted Elizabeth Street.

Never the Right Time

Betty Johnston

PLAY it.

Children, parents (divorced), birthday party, other children, other parents, old house, evening.

And the father says, Well, I want to go now. Where are the children? They are coming with me?

The mother says, That's right, I'll find them for you. And walking away from her half-drunk cup of tea, away from the dying cake and through a sea of burst balloons, she seeks through the old house for her children. One is playing doctors and nurses in the bedroom, the other is outside playing soccer. She says to each one, it is time to go now, your father wants to go. And each one says, oh not now, can't we stay? And she says, your Daddy loves you too, he needs to see you. Reluctantly each child leaves the game. What do you want? says their father, lifting his head from the newspaper. Oh you want to go now? Hang on a minute while I finish this. He reads his article, looks for his keys, finds them on the mantelpiece. I can't have them tomorrow afternoon, he says, I'm going out, I'll drop them off on the way. He goes.

The mother sits down with the other people of the house to her cold half cup of tea. I'll make a fresh pot, she says.

Play it again.

The father says, Well I want to go now. Where are the children? They are coming with me?

Yes, says the mother, cupping the tea mug in her cold hands, I think they're in the other room.

The father goes to the other room. Time to go, he says. Oh not now, can't I stay, says the little one, and the father returns to the party room, to the blue icing on the cake, to the spilt Coca-Cola. She won't come, he says, picking up the newspaper.

The mother slowly puts down her tea and stands up; she walks to the other room. Little one, she says, it is time to go with Daddy. Oh Mummy, says the child, can't I stay? No, says the mother, I need a night of my own, and tomorrow night you can play the game again. And both children come with her, reluctantly.

You're ready at last, says the father, shall I bring them back for lunch or for dinner?

We're having roast for dinner, says the mother, come back then. She hugs the children goodbye and puts the kettle on. A proper cup of tea this time she says.

No, play it again.

The father says, Well I want to go now. Where are the children? They are coming with me?

Yes, says the mother, but I don't know where they are. She is drinking her tea at the table, surrounded by half-eaten frankfurters and crumpled chips.

The father walks through the old house to find his children. Time to go now, he says to the little one. Oh not now, can't I stay, she says, I'm a mother having a baby. And the father walks back to the room where the party has finished, and people are quiet, drinking tea. She won't come, he says, picking up the newspaper.

The mother puts down her tea, slowly.

No? she says.

You ask her, he says from behind the newspaper.

No, she says.

What, he says, what do you mean?

I mean no, she says, I mean I won't ask her to go. No.

People are looking at them. He says, Don't fuss, we'll talk some other time.

No, she says, no, this is the time to talk.

It's not the right time, he says.

The time is never right, if you wait, says the mother, this time will do as well as any other.

But I want to go, he says.

Well go, she says.

But I want the kids to come, he shouts.

Well *tell* them that you want them, she shouts back, have you ever told them that you want them, that you like them, that you miss them, that you love them? Have you?

They know I do, says the father.

How? cries the mother, how do they know? When all you do is sit behind your newspaper and grunt at them to go to bed? How do they know? Hundreds and thousands are sticking to her cup as she lifts it from the table. She is crying.

The father is quiet. He walks back along the veranda to the sound of voices. Come on kids, he says to each child, it's time to go. Oh not now, they say, can't we stay? No, says the father, I need you for a day, I miss you when you are here. He puts his arm around the older child, strokes the little one's hair. Come on, let's go, he says. They run to their mother, hug her. See you tomorrow, they shout, running out to the car. The father looks for his keys; he says, how about if I have them till evening?

If they could be back for dinner, says the mother, we're having a roast.

I'll drop them in about six, he says, see you.

The mother puts her head on her arms on the table and weeps. Someone brings a fresh cup of tea.

I'm all right, she says, I really am all right. I've just wanted to say that for so long, such a little thing and so hard to say.

The cats weave round her legs waiting for food and from far off there is a rumble of the television where the other children lie, tired after minty hunts and hide-and-seek, after presents and candles and wishes.

The woman curls up in the large old chair, with the newspaper and her cup of tea, content, alone for a while.

Dropping Dance

Kate Grenville

*W*HEN Louise thought about her life, at night, the pillow became slimy. Why does no one want me, she cried. What have I done to deserve this? In the morning she put on scorn with her clothes and turned the pillow over before she left for work.

I am alone, she said to herself and shredded her bus ticket. I am alone. Why me? When the inspector climbed on the bus she saw how his lips were mauve with effort, and how he was panting. She smiled a great deal so he would not be cross about her shredded ticket. *There is a fine*, he said, but she saw his sad mauve lips and knew that this was a sick man who would never fine a smiling face. He waited for the bus to stop completely before he climbed down, and she heard a grunt as if he had been struck when his foot touched the kerb.

At the office she smiled at Myra the silly receptionist who got everything wrong, but it was not the same as the smile she had given the bus inspector. *Mr Trink is waiting for you*, Myra said, and Louise prepared a smile for Mr Trink.

I am sending you to Italy, Mr Trink said. For a moment she wanted to jump up and touch the ceiling, but then she remembered that she was all alone. Even Italy is not much fun alone, she thought, but remembered the way her mother always said, *you never know who you might meet*. Mr Trink did not care if she had no boyfriend or twenty of them, although at the Christmas party, after the third or fourth glass, he had held her against him as they danced and told her she was a fine figure of a woman. Mr Trink lit the stub of his cigar and puffed blue smoke

189

as he spoke, and she had to concentrate hard on what he was saying. The brown smell of his cigar made her remember how she had not always been all alone. The way the smoke gave a soft edge to Mr Trink's face and desk made her remember that she had had a happy childhood, full of cigar smoke and the steam of threepences being boiled. Everything in the kitchen had become dewy and friendly when the threepences were being boiled. The steam had billowed up from the pot and everyone's face had smiled through steam, because everyone had enjoyed the business of boiling the threepences. Something went wrong, she thought as Mr Trink talked about Italy. What went wrong? Mr Trink was handing her a plane ticket, maps, brochures. *It is some new ski place*, he said, *in that place that is like a disease, Dolomites*. He puffed, coughed, and said, *Or perhaps Dolomites is the cure*. She smiled her Mr Trink smile, the professional smile that said, You are right to rely on me. *It will be a little while away for you*, Mr Trink said, *and you will write them a good piece. You have been looking peaky*. She felt a tear swell in each eye and thought of how she would like to say, oh yes, I am peaky, I have been left all alone again, I am very peaky indeed, but in spite of the cigar, and the way it made everything look sympathetic, she knew that Mr Trink did not want to hear why she was peaky. *And no scorn*, he said as she was opening the door to leave. *None of that scorn like in the piece about Isles of the Aegean, understand?*

When they arrived at the village where people were going to come for the skiing, many people were waiting for them, and Louise smiled at them all but thought, there is no one for me here, although most of them were from her own country, and tried not to scorn. There was a fat man and his thin wife, who ran the hotel where the skiers would stay. *We have given you the best room*, the fat man shouted, *so you better write a good piece about us*, and his thin wife shouted too: *We will make sure you have a fine time*. A man called Scotty was not a Scot, but was going to teach the people how to ski, and was joking now, and doing knee-bends, as if getting in practice. *I am that hungry*, he told Louise, *I could eat the crotch out of a low-flying duck*. Everyone laughed and Louise laughed too, but falsely, feeling her face ache. I am showing too many teeth, she thought, and closed her mouth. Now perhaps I am looking glum, she thought, and hoped the fat man or his thin wife would suggest she go to her room to unpack. *He is the clown of the place*, the travel man said to her. *That Scotty is a laugh a minute.* Marigold was a pretty girl with glossy hair and a fine bosom. *I'm that excited*, she told Louise. *Never been out of Thin Ridge before and I've made that many friends already.* She joined Scotty in knee-bends so they looked like a pair of things on springs, but giggled from her red mouth and had to be grabbed by Scotty when she lost her balance. Franco tried to grab her but he was too slow and had to smile out of his square face while Marigold clung to Scotty. Franco had a flat face like a rock with small crevices for the mouth and eyes. *I am the guide of the mountains*, he told Louise. *That is a fine profession*, Louise said, looking at the slab of his face. She could imagine him beckoning the mountains. They were all around them, but she had tried not to look at them until now because they made her feel as if nothing much mattered. But she looked while Franco told her about them, and tried not to think about nothing mattering. The mountains were jagged like a page ripped out of a book, and were moving steadily against the sky towards them. There was a little early snow on the peaks, but not much. Franco told Louise what each mountain was called, but could not stop watching the way the last rays of sun made Marigold's hair look like something good to drink.

I am more alone than ever, Louise thought in her room, and watched herself in the mirror. The more people there are, the more I am alone. She sat with her face on her fists, staring at herself in the mirror. She tried to pretend that the reflection was not herself, but someone else, and had almost succeeded when there was a sneeze behind the reflection. She got up quickly in case the mirror disappeared and she would have to look at pretty Marigold, leaning into the mirror plucking her eyebrows and sneezing.

What did the parson say to the choirboy? Scotty shouted down the table at dinner, and everyone laughed. *Why did the elephant cross the road*? he yelled, and everyone laughed again. The fat man and the thin woman were kept busy filling everyone's plates and glasses. *What's red and blue and collects stamps*? The laughter beat back from the walls. Marigold looked as if she would wet herself laughing. Her bra was made of black lace and could be seen through her blouse. Louise was shrivelled and lonely against the wall, and the wine sat cold in her stomach like unhappiness. *Why did the dago have his head up a bull's bum?* Scotty cried, and had to add, *No offence intended Franco and none taken I'm sure.* Louise was sick of laughing and the bald travel man's close-set eyes were making her queasy. I am miserable, she told herself, and not understood by anyone. It seemed that no one could come to her rescue.

Next day Franco took them up a mountain. In the beginning it was easy and Louise kicked through drifts of dead leaves and watched how the top of the mountain hung weightless in the morning sun. I am alive and well, although alone, she told herself, and at present climbing a mountain, and heard with scorn the fat man panting behind her. But the path became steeper and steeper and soon she could not hear the fat man's panting, but only her own. Ahead of her and always further up, Franco walked on and on in his square boots and she began to hate the way his feet came down one after the other without stopping. I hate this, she began to think, and had to remind herself, this is not a plot. When the path stopped being a path and became a stony place where water must rush down in spring, she thought Franco might stop. If she had not been aware of the fat man grunting behind her as he laboured up behind her, she would have sat down on a rock until her blood cooled and her chest stopped burning. It came to her that she was not sufficiently alone at this particular moment.

Marigold was just behind Franco, and began to squeal so that he looked around at last and everyone was allowed to rest. The top of the mountain did not hang in the air any more, but loomed over them. It was not weightless now, but ponderous and unfriendly. There were no trees up here, only prickly bushes and tussocks of grass, and there was nowhere much to sit, and only the grey stone of the mountain to look at.

After they had rested as long as Franco let them, they went on, and the path became more difficult. Louise had to grasp at rocks and sharp grass to pull herself up, and felt the stones roll out from under her feet. Her ankles were tired from so much twisting on the loose rocks, and her neck ached from looking up for the next place to step. There were patches of snow, iced-over and hard, that her shoes slithered over, and a long steep slope of chips of stone that was like dandruff on the shoulders of the mountain. Nature is vile, she was beginning to think, when she saw that Franco had stopped and was staggering with Marigold in his arms around a cairn of stones. They were at the top, it seemed, although mountains still surrounded them.

Scotty shouted to hear his voice vanish into the air, and rolled stones down the slope for a while, to see how gravity snatched them, and the fat man lay on his back and wheezed. The thin woman put a stone on the top of the cairn and spat on it: *Instead of champers*, she shouted. Her spit dried quickly on the stone so it seemed that it had never been there. The thin woman looked around at the empty sky and the mountains, and began to wind her watch. There was too much air up here to fill, and too much mountain to look at. When everyone stopped talking at the same moment they could all hear the thin woman's watch being wound.

Louise had taken off her shoe to get out a stone when Franco shouted *Down!* and everyone began to leap down the slope after him. Louise got the stone out of her shoe and was comforted by the hot rising smell of her sock. I am not completely alone, she thought, no one is completely alone who has the smell of their socks. When she had put the sock and shoe back on she stood up and was suddenly dizzy. The mountain was so silent it deafened her. Silence roared at her. It surged into her ears and made her want to hide but the mountain was grey in the shadows now, and there was nowhere to go. Suddenly she was not sure which way was the way down, and she could see two valleys both full of the same dark green trees. She could not be sure which way the others had gone, and could not hear anything except the silence in her ears.

Sunlight was sliding off the peaks around her. She watched as it slid like water up a rock and left darkness behind. *Help*, she tried to say, but had to cough. *Help!* she tried again, but the

193

silence was like a waterfall in her ears. *Help me*! she shrieked, and a bird made a creaking sound with its wings as it flew along below her. I have been abandoned, she thought, and tried again: *Help*!

She began to pick her way down one of the slopes, but her ankles would not hold her up and her shoes twisted and slipped on the steep rocks at every step. She sat down and began to cry. She wanted her white pillow and her quiet room more than she had ever wanted anything, but had only sharp chips of grey rock to cry on, and they were quickly becoming cold. *You swine*, she began to screech, *you pigs*. Her voice cracked but she went on shouting. *You rotten lumpish buggers, you vile toads!* She stopped and listened, but could only hear silence ebbing and flowing in her head. *Rescue me*, she called, and heard her tears break up the words. *Save me.* She waited a long time, but no one came.

When she had waited a long time she began to go down again. She limped and whimpered and made small moans of distress. *You don't care and you don't give a damn*, she whispered and her feet slipped and twisted. *You bastards have left me here alone to die.* Dusk was deepening and she had to look hard to see where she was going. I could break my leg, she thought, or my neck, and she ran a few steps down the slope. I am asking for trouble, running, she thought, but she kept running and jumping down from rock to rock. She hoped she would fall and break something, and when the search party found her they would have to carry her down carefully on a stretcher, and give her brandy to drink, and wrap her in warm blankets, and keep up her spirits with jokes all the way down the mountain.

The mountain was flying past under the feet like something flowing, and the air rushed up against her face. She opened her mouth so the air could come into her mouth and she could hear the music of air and speed in her head. Under her feet the grey stones were a blur and out of the corner of her eye she saw white banks of snow pouring past. Around her the whitening sky filled with mountain, as she ran further down into the valley. *There, there, there, there*, she began to shout as each foot landed and sprang and she felt her hair blow out behind her. Stones that were loosened by her feet kept her company, rolling down after her, but they could not keep up. Faster and faster she swallowed the mountainside. Like a bird, she thought, I am like a bird now. Free as a bird. Her arms made arabesques in the air around her as she sprang down. She felt as though she had invented a language and was writing it on the air. I am a bird, she thought, or the wind. I could run like this all the way down every hill to the sea.

When she reached the hut at the bottom where everyone was, she stopped, but did not want to go in. The windows of the hut were filled with yellow light and she could hear everyone talking and laughing, and a tinkle of glasses. Someone threw a log on a fire and sparks leapt red out of the top of the chimney. She did not want to go in and be with other people, but would have liked to go on running and watching the mauve light in the sky that was slowly turning into night.

The fat man came to the door of the hut with a big pot between his hands. *You are there*, he said. *We were wondering.* Silhouetted in the doorway, his size was stupendous and he was wrapped in a halo of lamplight. He stood there with the pot in his hand, staring up at the mountain she had just danced down. *I have always been afraid of heights*, the fat man said suddenly, and began to drain water from the spaghetti in the pot. The steam gushed up suddenly and swirled around him as he bent over it, concentrating. The shape of his body was made soft and luminous by so much steam lapping around him. He finished draining the water and stood looking at the sky between the treetops. *This is my first mountain*, he said, and Louise could hear that he was smiling. *My first mountain*, he repeated, and the rising steam enveloped his head as if it would carry it away into the night.

The Death of the Fat Man

Penelope Layland

T HE figure was still there when the party left the restaurant in a swill of hot air and cognac.

One of the party, a fat man with greedy eyes, who would have a heart attack later that night, alone in his flat, turned to stare at the figure.

'They found one of your kind last week, you know? In the Bois. Cut up in pieces and put in a suitcase. Some crazy Japanese fellow did it—told the police he was Jesus Christ.' The fat man peered into the shadows. 'Hear me?' Then he spat.

'Pascal, the taxi's here. What are you doing?' The woman's voice was glassy. She peered too into the shadows and swayed perceptibly on her brittle, sophisticated heels. Later, in the taxi, she would wind down the window, feel the air inflate her lungs, vow never to drink champagne again. She would go home with her husband, the sullen man who was now beckoning impatiently from the taxi. She would dream about her husband's American friend, to whom she had made sharp, insulting remarks at dinner that night.

She was not happy, and the sight of her friend, the fat man Pascal, who would die that night, alone in his rooms, disgusted her. The knowledge of that figure in the shadows revolted her.

'Come, Pascal.' The woman advanced the top half of her body towards her friend.

'Come on, you two', cried the woman's husband, leaning from the taxi and burping discreetly. Later, his indigestion would become more severe and he would lie beside the living wall of his wife, wishing he was dead.

He watched his wife now as she concentrated on the cobbles, her ankles absurdly thin. Pascal hobbled after her, looking ill and colourless under the fizz of street lights.

'Perhaps if we go your way first, Pascal', said the woman. 'It's probably quicker. Or cheaper at least.' She laughed, amused by the suggestion that they could be concerned over a taxi fare, they who had just dined in luxury. She remembered her witty, callous remarks to the poor American, the friend of her husband, and her cruel contempt of the greediness of the man beside her, Pascal, who would die tonight.

Pascal was silent as he heaved his legs into the taxi after his shapeless torso. The taxi driver demanded an address, inner-cursing these drunken people, envying their ease. Pascal gave his address and got confused with the address of a flat he had owned years before, before ... but he couldn't remember and the woman at his side looked cruelly at him and said sweetly, 'You've drunk too much, you silly old fool'.

Later, before going to bed, the woman would have a fight with her husband. He would accuse her of flirting and she would grow angry as the throb of champagne ebbed to leave her cold. He would go to the bedroom, pretending to be asleep when she came in. He would be relieved when she entered the bed too far away for accidental contact and indigestion would burn pinpoint holes in his heart.

'Ten francs.'

'We'll settle', said the woman and felt annoyed when Pascal refused to recognise the gesture, not that it mattered, of course. She watched him hesitate at the door of the building, groping for keys in the stuttering light, his face grey. The taxi jerked away.

The fat man, Pascal, was to wake, later that night, for no reason he could think of but with a nagging tip-of-the-tongue awareness. The pain was not to strike at first and when it did he would wonder at the mediocrity of all previous sensation, wonder how he could ever have thought he had lived, so feeble would all things seem, compared to this. The pain would be strong, embracing and overwhelmingly suprising.

So during those moments, the ones in which his life rapidly changed into merely other people's lives, he would lie quietly, as if that would help.

Later, too, the woman would wake, would say 'Pierre? Did you say something?' She would sigh, move restlessly in the territory of her half of the bed. Then Pierre, her husband, would sigh.

'Perhaps if you just tried to go to sleep . . .' Pierre would roll his head to look at his wife. Her skull, leaning against the headboard would seem as fragile as a snail's shell, her hair twisted in green–brown grain across it. 'If I lit a lamp behind your head', he would think, 'the light would shine right through.' But he would not say so, he would say instead, 'Why don't you sleep?'

Her skull would appear to be trying to scale the headboard, a pulse would move in her slug-neck.

'I slept with your friend. The American', she would lie.

'I know. I don't care. Do whatever will make you happy', he would also lie.

Outside snow would begin to fall, big wet flakes rough around the edges from the heat of the city. They would melt as they hit the roads. A few blocks away the fat man, Pascal, would just be awakening, with something on his mind.

The Shot

Vasso Kalamaras

Translated by Vasso Kalamaras and June Kingdon

NIGHT had fallen at last.

Beniamino was lying down in his clothes loosening his belt. His bed was made of old planks resting on four rickety wooden boxes. He had made the mattress himself, stitched the hessian bags, and filled them with hay. For a pillow he had a thick Tasmanian overcoat, carefully folded in two, and on top of this a dirty towel. His blankets, originally colourful, now resembled discarded hides.

Beniamino closed his eyes, exhausted from the day's hard work. He started thinking. On the left of him lay Bridgetown, to the right, Pemberton. His thick fingers, like overstuffed sausages, fumbled blindly over his chest, unbuttoning the rough flannel vest with difficulty. He belched, stretched out, and farted loudly with satisfaction, then spoke quietly to himself.

'Yes, left Bridgitowni, right Pembertoni, in the middle Manjimupa.' He wanted to write to his son in Italy. Salvatore was a novice studying at a Catholic monastery. In his last letter, written in a round clear hand, he had asked, 'Father, just where do you live over there? They are teaching us Australian geography at school right now—Salvatore.'

Beniamino was already snoring. His lips, so thick they looked swollen, were vibrating. They were like a garnish on the round fat cheeks that looked like over-risen unbaked cottage loaves.

Outside his hut the frogs made a deafening noise in the swamps around the edges of the paddock he was clearing. Some charcoal was still burning from the firewood, turning to ash in the wood stove, which was made of corrugated iron, long narrow and low, daubed with grease. On it stood a blackened frypan with leftover food.

He had built the humpy himself. Two strides in width and two strides in length, the ceiling so low you had to stoop to go inside. It was made of unplaned first cuts, which the mill threw away. He had picked them up here and there, nailed them together and hung sugar bags for a door. As if he needed to lock up his wealth and possessions! Doors and keys are for those who need them.

The only precious things there were a radio from a second-hand dealer, the stove, the kerosene lamp and his suit which he wore for special occasions. He did not bother to light the lamp when he was alone, but lit the place with a little oil lamp. He had forgotten to blow it out, so it was still burning, the flame flickering in the air.

He kept his food in a wooden vegetable crate. Nestles milk, sugar, coffee, matches, methylated spirits, salami, Kraft cheese, macaroni. There was always bread. Above his head, hanging from a beam, were half a dozen sausages and a plait of garlic. In a corner on the earth-floor was a heap of onions and a half-full sack of fried red beans.

He was snoring with gusto.

Before we arrived at the door this sound could be heard from a distance.

Leon called out, 'Hey, anybody in?' He had left the car lower down. It was a bad track and unknown to us, full of soft earth. We did not want to be bogged at night.

We were walking and calling.

'Beniamino! Beniamino, is anyone there?'

With his short hair standing up straight around his head, Beniamino appeared in the opening looking surprised.

'Oh, come in, plissa come inside.'

He put two wooden boxes on end for us to sit on. Hurriedly

he pulled another pair of trousers over the ones he was wearing, and buttoned only the waistband. Unbuttoned in front, the other pair showed through. Both were roughly patched with unmatching pieces of cloth and thread. All this stood out distinctly in the half-light.

He started to light the kerosene lamp whose glass edges were chipped and black from smoke and lack of washing.

'Don't bother with the lights, Beniamino, we've only come for a moment.' We sat down and he offered us his home-made wine in two teacups, one without a handle. As he offered them to us I thought his hands trembled, those puffy hands, that looked swollen, with their short stubby fingers.

Was he pleased or annoyed by our unexpected visit?

Was I too afraid or too embarrassed to look at him?

I glanced out of the corner of my eye at the shape of his head, like a round rough stone. His hair was cut like a convict, and this evening he was unshaven.

'Scusa me', he said as if reading my mind. 'I no manage to shave today. I find too much work in the paddock. I'm clearing it to plant olive trees.'

We told him about our cow. He listened carefully, then spoke slowly, trying to make us understand him. Like us, his English was not good.

'Everything is monee monee, we do everything for money. I know this very well.'

Then, referring to the sick cow. 'The cow need a gun. Why you keep her? These vets, they take all your money. Not man not beast feela sorry for them. Monee, monee, monita, all they want is your money.'

Leonidas explained to him, he could not shoot it. Not after the way the cow had looked into his eyes.

Beniamino laughed heartily, his short, heavy fat frame was shaking, while a row of large white strong teeth made his fleshy lips beautiful, though his nose was short and fat, as was his whole appearance.

'Ha ha ha', he stirred the air with his two hands, the fingers spread like those of a strange prehistoric dinosaur.

201

'Me, Leonardo, I don't look at their eyes; only the girls, I look in their eyes and at their bottoms.' He made a sly gesture to convey the shape of a woman's backside.

He called Leonidas, Leonardo.

We explained to him. 'Tomorrow we are leaving at dawn for Perth at 4 o'clock.'

'Eh, so letsa go.'

He stood up first. There was a hoar frost, the temperature dropped quickly in the evenings at this time of year, by morning everything would be frozen. The paddocks looked like glass, with a dull gleam. The ice on the new grass crumbled like crystal in your hand.

He picked up the short overcoat from his pillow and put it on, puffing.

His fatness and obstinate energy fought each other noisily. He left everything as it was, the little oil lamp shining, the kerosene lamp alight.

Then he turned back and blew out the flame of the lamp noisily, saying, 'Eh, my friends, oil is a very 'spensive these days'.

We got into the car, he sat in front. We stank of dung and dogs, he of moist earth, kerosene and dirt. He was chatting as if he had not just woken up, his two hands were holding the gun by the barrel, the butt between his legs. He held it like a living creature in his embrace.

He read my mind.

'Missis, I have fight many years in the mountains of my country.'

'Do you want to go back there, Beniamino?' I asked him stupidly.

'Me, Missis? Me, Missis?'

He was disturbed, the colour rose in his face, at every word, first one then the other hand left the gun, spreading out and expressing more than his words.

Now the prehistoric reptile with the strange, lively wings groped in the darkness in front of him, digging for beloved faces that he entertained only in his dreams.

202

'Missis, my wife no want to come here. You see, she a very religious woman, she loves very much the priests. She do only what the priests tell her. The boy, he'sa good boy. His momma give him to the school. He study to be priest. My son, he'sa called Salvatore.'

'Bravo, bravo, Beniamino, everything is for the best.'

'Leonardo!' He expressed his disappointment as if he wanted to say, 'Where do you see all this good?'

Then again, after a silence.

'Eh, my friends, you must understand, because you are my friends. You're Greek, not like the bloody Aussies.'

'Bah!' I said.

'Yes, Missis, they're not all bad, we have some good and some bad in Italy.'

'It's the same here, Beniamino', I replied, 'Australia has good and bad'.

'Um!' he nodded his heavy round head bitterly. 'They don't want us.'

'Huh, what of it? They'll want us in time. They'll understand Beniamino, don't let it get you down', I said, without believing it myself.

We arrived at our own farm. The three of us got out. The cold stung us and we huddled in our clothes. I think we were shivering. I was wearing a white, fringed head scarf with an old brown beanie on top, trousers under a loose check skirt, and a fifteen-year-old shaggy woollen jacket. I felt uncomfortable with Beniamino, I was trying to forget why we had brought him here. He turned to me earnestly, pointing to the house.

'You better go, Missis. Thisa man's job.'

I did not look at them, an unimaginable weariness and sadness clutched at me.

'Goodnight', then in Greek, '*Thee mou!*'★

I went through the small porch in the yard towards the house. Leonidas was talking. The two of them walked towards the hay shed where we had fixed up a place for the cow that had not

---

★ My God!

203

been able to get up for two weeks. One of them stopped, then both stopped. Leonidas held a torch, switching it on and off so that the beam spread and dissolved in the thick darkness.

I heard Beniamino's voice again, it was strong, with a strange resonance like an echo coming from that spot.

'Leonardo, I know this very well, when my time comes, I will go to die in Italy, there in my own village. I want to die with dignity. My friend, you can live and work like an animal, but when you die, this must happen as it should for a human being. Here I'm an animal.'

His laughter, bitter as bile, sounded strange, resounding like the groaning of a wild beast in a cage.

I turned to look at them. Beniamino was pointing to himself with one hand, and with the other he was waving his gun in the air threateningly.

'Leonardo, you see me, here me, Beniamino, I'm worth nothing to nobody. I not even worth a bullet. They wouldn't even give that to get rid of me from this country. My friend, I want to die over there', he pointed with his thick finger. His hand appeared more swollen in the darkness, becoming to my eyes, a special force, a living black bird caught by the foot.

The gun gleamed in the torch light.

'I go there to die. There I make my bed as I want, my friend. My size. I go when I want, you understand? Italy is the country of Beniamino.'

Now his laughter sounded more bitter, stronger, it turned into a cough.

The sound of their steps began again. He coughed and laughed. They turned at the first tobacco kilns.

Silence.

A bleak silence. It was unbearably cold. Winter in the depth of the bush, covered with fog like a black cheesecloth, a veil, hiding all the various parts of the landscape. Some poor chilly wandering stars bathed in an atmosphere of milky fumes. The black trees stood out here and there, fantastic mythical silhouettes of gods.

The gun shot shattered the frozen silence.

The noise startled the frogs and my heart.

Our dogs began to bark angrily, then to howl horribly. I covered my ears.

Holy Mother, what a terrible waste. Her eyes were still before me, they looked at me with a moist human pleading. Life! Big brown eyes with an infinite sweet sadness.

Leonidas has said, 'I can't do it. She looks into my eyes.'

Summer of a Stick Man

Kathryn Stone

*F*ROM a distance it was like this: one fat line for a plain, and a curved one for a hill. Several heavy scratchings of lead for dead trees, and an accidental thumbprint smudged to the right for the faltering town. As a picture this place had no balance. On the edge stood a long stick person of thin strokes—the last of the tourists. Not that this place was any better than a handful of other dead or dying towns in the mid-west, but he had long since cultivated an eagerness for faith. Appearing out of the smudge, the stick man took a house on the outskirts for two weeks. It had a peculiar Summer Window that seemed to show him everything. Straight ahead was the playground alongside the old brickworks, and behind these the newly closed brewery. If he stuck his head out the window he could see a house on the hill. Of course from a distance everything was simple.

The first time he saw Hetty, it was from the Summer Window on the hottest day of the year, and he had a feeling something wonderful was going to happen. He practically insisted on it. From his bedroom he watched her walk through the old brickworks into the playground, swinging a piece of wire above her head that a dog occasionally jumped for. Peterson smeared his thinning hair off his forehead. He could not explain the feeling she gave him, the little jump of surprise and recognition at the same time, but it seemed as if her moral self was heightened by her distance from his window. It was the anticipation of a heart that had little more than preparation.

As he watched, the caretaker, a full circular man, waddled in with a handful of letters he had just picked up at the town post office, and put them on Peterson's dresser. He wheezed and spluttered to testify to his overexertion in the heat.

'Who's that girl over there?' asked Peterson, pointing to the brickworks. 'No, there. The one with the black dog.'

Baker leaned over, pressing his fat hands to the glass and leaving a large oily smudge.

'Hetty Jones', he mumbled through his loose teeth. 'She goes out wiv Bradley, who use ta work in the cappin' section.' His conversation was always padded out with facts about the brewery.

'Do you know much about her?'

'Only she lives in the house on the hill.'

'I wonder why she walks about there. Doesn't she go to school?'

Baker shrugged, and caught a sneeze in the folds of the curtain.

Sitting on the swing two days later, Peterson waited for her in an attitude of anxious prayer. He watched her clambering over the hollow smoke stacks and the first drafts of a ruin, the dog racing ahead to find the shade. Hetty was a brown spidery thing, in a long green dress with dark stains under the arms, and scuffed black school shoes without any socks. A pair of stockings were tied round her waist. As she swung over the fence into the playground, she took the smallest glance at the thin man on the swing.

At the monkey bars she tucked her dress into her bloomers, climbed to the top bar, and flipped over so she hung from her knees. A short whine escaped the dog as it ducked beneath the gate into the neighbouring brickworks.

'He don't like me doin' it', she said, still hanging upside down.

'I can see that.' He guessed her to be about fifteen, though she was very thin and small, not unlike one of those children who stare out of the pages of magazines appealing for famine relief. 'You're quite good at it!'

'This ain't anythin'. I could be a gymnast y'know.' And to

prove her point she executed a few elaborate flips and twirls on the top bar.

Suddenly she had somersaulted to her feet and was leaning against one of the vertical bars scrutinising him carefully.

'Why y'here?' she asked.

'It's a nice day ... and I'm renting just over there.'

'No I mean, why y'here!'

'Oh!' he pinched his chin thoughtfully. 'Well, a little while ago, someone very close to me died ... a great-aunt ... I thought I needed a holiday in a quiet place ...' He had no secrets.

'You came, an' tonight Bradley goes. Can't find work. Brewery's closed.' She tipped her face to the sky. 'Sun's white hot', she sighed, then looking back at him, 'd'you know Bradley then?'

She sat on the swing next to Peterson's and untied the brown stockings from her waist. 'Look at these. He got me these some ...' She tried to think when it was and unable to decide, finished off with 'some time ago'. She stretched the stockings to their full length revealing a large hole near the toe of the right leg. 'Dog did that—crazy! Can't wear them cause they give me hives all up here', indicating her inside leg. 'D' you know Bradley?'

'No. I haven't been out of the house much yet.'

'But y'know the fat man', she leant forward enthusiastically, 'the one with no buttons on the bottom of his shirt.'

'Baker?'

'Baker eh? Y'know why he's so fat!'

'I suppose he eats too much.'

'Oh', she sounded disappointed. 'I thought it must have bin glands. Baker eh?' She watched Peterson briefly then walked back to the bars to hang upside down.

'He's just a caretaker', Peterson snorted.

'He use ta work at the brewery.'

'What's so important about that place?'

'Well there's Bradley of course, an' there's me Dad who works in one up north. At least he use ta. He got this train now, so he lives in that.'

'Whereabouts?'

'At a railway station somewheres. It's closed down now so he don't get in the way. If they ever close this one down he can live here.'

Peterson rocked gently on the swing. 'They will close it down, they'll close down the whole town. I read it in a newspaper.' He looked up at her. 'I wanted to see the place before it died.'

'Have you met anyone who lived in a train?' she continued unperturbed.

'No.'

She sighed and let her arms hang down past her head till her fingers brushed lightly across the earth. 'What's y'name?'

'Sam Peterson.'

'Don't y'think Baker's a funny name for such a fat man, Mr Peterson? I do, I really do!'

Nothing she did could surprise him, it was all part of her earthy nature. He had read about her a hundred times, and seen her face in paintings and magazines. She was something deeply rooted in the minds of every city dweller. During that fortnight he learnt very little about her family, except that she had a nine-year-old brother, and a mother who left early each morning to work in the smudge. Hetty did the general cleaning about the house, got her brother ready for school, and took the dog for endless walks. Peterson often liked to imagine he was standing at the bottom of the hill looking up, and there she was, on the very top, the pale shadow of her chin, the soft rise of her cheeks. He didn't love her, it was something less personal than that.

His Summer Window was the only solid square in a house of weak lines. One day he sat at it all morning with his breakfast, framed by a thick black edge for anyone who cared to look in. Finally he left the remains of his cereal in a white china bowl and went outside, where the cereal was still with him, and scattered all about his feet. The yellow earth was cracked, and each uneven shape curled up at the corners from the rock beneath like a giant golden cornflake. Then suddenly he looked about him and there were cornflakes as far as the eye could see, and yet he

209

had never noticed it before. He strolled across the yard to the playground, intent on the crunching under his shoes, and the delicacy of his purpose which was quickly escaping him.

Mr Peterson had never told anyone he loved them. He was too sensitive to embarrass his friends. But he considered himself lucky to be in the midst of a bush love-affair between Hetty and Bradley. It was truer, and purer, than anything in the city. At the playground he inspected the swings for some evidence of their childhood romance: an etching in the crusty tree, two pairs of initials encased in a heart, a lost ribbon, a hanky, a piece of notepaper under the bars; but there was nothing. It was as if the playground was dropped from the sky *en route* to somewhere else, and no one had reclaimed it. The tourist, ageing every moment, leant against the tree and looked across the crazy tiled floor that held nothing for discovery, wondering where the bush children hid their love toys.

He stabbed the ground restlessly with one foot until a sudden jab sent his brittle toe-nails crumbling against the leather. Just under the surface was a cement slab, and he knelt to brush it off. He knew it wasn't from the rented house, so it was probably brought down from the pavement outside the house on the hill, but when he couldn't be sure. Across the slab were several brown stains no bigger than rain-drops, and one large stain in the middle, as though something dripping had been held over it.

Two tiny bare feet entered the top half of his frame of vision. He looked up to see Hetty twirling her hair about her finger, surprised at what he had dug up.

'Bradley had a nose bleed', she said, engrossed in the memory of the stains that were once bright red. 'The fat man carried him back to our kitchen.'

'How long ago was that?'

She shrugged. 'I can't remember which one it was.' She was sitting beside him picking a cathead out of her foot, and surreptitiously glancing at the slab as though it held an alarming power. 'I remember that now. We got the cement for hop-scotch. I forgot the fat man carryin' Bradley.' She started to count the blood spots, sticking her brown thread-like fingers on each stain. 'Eeny meeny miny mo', she sang tunelessly, her thin voice being carried around the playground, 'catch a nigger by the toe.' She stopped abruptly and grinned at Peterson, with a face that held a secret. Her fingers had unearthed one corner of the slab, as if she planned to take it with her. But then she let it go and stood up.

'He'd prob'ly have a better one anyhow', she said. 'That weren't the best nose bleed he ever had.'

So she left him, giggling about grabbing niggers by the toes and making them squeal, and somewhere in that she held a secret. Peterson lowered the slab and covered it up. He sat down like Hetty had done a moment before, his trousers riding up his legs to reveal two white shins. He looked like a man sitting in a bathtub after the water has drained out.

It was outside the cities in the bush where the real Australia began. In the rented house he perused the caretaker critically, assessing his capabilities to understand this important fact, but Baker had something else on his mind. He shuffled his feet on the spot, and sucked and puffed his cheeks nervously.

'But there's another thing', Baker interjected. 'Bradley told me the night he left about this story Hetty told someone.' He couldn't look at Peterson, but played with the empty button holes at the bottom of his shirt. 'He says she never met her father, doesn't know a thing about him. It doesn't really matter but ...'

They both pretended they didn't know who Hetty had lied to. Peterson tried to sound careless and rocked on his feet beside the sturdy window.

'I wonder why she said it, then?'

'It's not a lie so much', explained Baker. 'Well it's ... it's just a pretty thing.' He spoke as if something so pretty ought to be true. 'It's something Bradley thought up once.'

The lie wasn't important to Peterson but he still couldn't see her the next day. There was a strange tug in his chest that had nothing to do with her, but the changing frame within which she existed. When they did meet again he brought a box of ribbons wrapped in green paper. She squealed as she ripped it open and tied ribbons on herself. She put them in her hair and around her neck, a few were even threaded through the dog's collar.

Afterwards she took him for a guided tour of the brickworks. 'D'you wanna see some stuff I've collected?' she asked. 'It's garbage really.' She led him behind one of the largest smoke stacks in the centre of the yard, to a deep sandbox filled with twisted wire and rusting metals, and proudly pulled out a short silver pipe and stuck it upwards in the sand. As he followed her trail Peterson noticed there was something in the orphaned red dust that fed her heart with a thousand possibilities. She was bending over her treasures as if they were a shrine to life's potential.

'D'you know what Americans call garbage? Trash. They call it trash!'

For an instant he guessed it, before pushing it from his mind forever. Amongst it all, the tangled strokes and dashes of debris, and the rainbow ribbons blowing wildly about her face and neck, there emerged in Peterson a distant disappointment that swelled in his heart. She wasn't happy here, after all. She was not amongst her junk but at the head of a primitive airship made of salvaged odds and ends, and dreaming of a great redeeming north wind that would sweep all the earthy children to another hemisphere, and set them down in the middle of a great city.

He called Baker in from the kitchen, where he was shredding carrots into the sink, and tried to explain their earlier discussion in the light of what he now felt. 'You see what you told me the other day, about Hetty, well I can see how that fits.'

'Sir?'

'She's confused, she has the wrong perspective on things. City people are so coarse, but Hetty. Well, there are some people who are more fragile than ourselves, and are best kept out here. Sometimes I think they were born into the world by mistake.' He turned from the Summer Window to face Baker. 'I don't expect you to understand, you've never been to the city. But there's something fake about it. And if someone is so very fragile . . . don't you see? It's like an accident of birth.'

When the dog was killed by a delivery van, Peterson ran across the plane to the hill, and all the way up to Hetty's place. It was a simple weatherboard home without a garage or fence, and its outside walls had swelled in the heat and cracked in parts. The paint peeled off in perfect slivers.

A young boy answered Peterson's knock in a school uniform. A startling miniature of Hetty, though he lacked the same effort and determination in his face. Obviously the accident had given him a reprieve for the day. He squinted up at the crooked thin man through the wire screen door.

'Y'can't see her', he said without consulting his sister.

'Tell her it's Mr Peterson, will you. I'm a friend.'

'She don't wanna see nobody', he persisted.

'Would she like me to buy her a present?'

The boy shrugged. He was just about to leave when he remembered something important. 'Can you bury dogs?' he asked.

As they walked to the back of the house, Peterson discovered the little bloke was of the same stuff as himself, some accommodating bendable matter. The boy chatted as they carried the dog to a small twisted tree. He wanted to know if in the city the cars kept Peterson awake at night, and did the street-lights shine through his bedroom window. Peterson answered happily, standing on the empty square in the cement path, running from the back door to the toilet.

A little later Hetty wandered out and sent her brother for a glass of water. 'Let the tap run cold!' she said as he skipped past. Her eyes were red and puffy, but if she wanted to mention the accident she never did, except to say she thought cremation was best. A mug of cloudy water was set down at Peterson's feet.

'Jasper', Hetty said, not taking her eyes off the visitor. 'Mr Peterson knows the fat man's name. It's Baker', she cried triumphantly, 'ain't it!' Jasper jumped up on cue. 'Mum says he's got bad glands!'

She walked Peterson to the start of the driveway.

'I hope you're not too hurt?' he mumbled rather foolishly.

Hetty shrugged. 'But I'll have ta write Bradley, he gave me the dog, y'know.'

'No?'

'Yeah.'

213

Half way down he turned and waved, from a thin edge that would have broken under a better man. It would take a good imagination to make him more than a simple sketch; as it was, Hetty was constructing about him a complex composition of light and dark. She was too kind to point out the frugality of others. Walking the line backwards he called to her, 'You mustn't ever want to leave ... you don't understand the city at all!' The end of summer was hard on them all, especially Mr Peterson. So many would-bes that never are.

He spent the weekend alone in his room, contemplating whether to extend his holiday, which was up in a couple of days. There were a set of confusing contradictions he wanted to untangle first. A few days ago he had bought Hetty an icecream at Krandles, and told her about the fragile people. Walking past the school to the playground he was trying to explain her to herself, the whole idea of what he had entrusted to Baker, but they got caught up on trifling points. In frustration he sat quietly and rigidly on the swing. Her responses were often disappointing. There were many times when he was curiously dissatisfied with her attempts to keep on the edges of the matter. There were boundaries to her understanding that went no further than that of a young child. She learnt a fact and it became part of her, another detail to flesh out the body, but it didn't grow, it didn't lead to anything. Hetty had held the doomed dog in her lap and tugged playfully at its ears.

'What I'm thinkin' about is Bradley's animals, an' trains, an' trash.' She looked at him for his turn.

'I wish very much', he said, staring straight ahead, 'I wish you went to school like the other girls. I think I'd like to meet you outside the gate at the end of the day.' On their way out of the playground he asked her, 'Do you read? You should. I've always found it helpful to look back and see where I've come from, what's important, what we're all about', he took her hand briefly, 'it would clear up a lot of confusion you know.'

Had he met another child things might have been different, but it was too late now. Though it would always nag him, and keep alive a useless remnant of illusion. Later he would store up these memories till they became a lump in his throat, late at night, over a warm beer. A snatch of summer that might have been a lifetime for all the importance he gave it. At the moment he still had the Summer Window to give him perspective, even though it was in the process of changing seasons. The beginning of the week seemed solid and certain. The beds were changed and the dirty sheets were in the laundry.

Baker was depressed with the cool greyness of the day. He shuffled back and forth from Peterson's room with fresh linen, every so often stooping to clutch his knees with the horrors of an upcoming arthritic winter.

'Not like summer at all', he moaned, pressing past Peterson's wardrobe into the hall. 'Just waitin' for the snow', he said, returning to put on a fresh pillow slip. 'Wish I could go north now', he complained, though in truth it was still a very mild day. Peterson was reclining in a chair which he had moved, along with the dresser, beside the window. He blocked out much of the caretaker's babbling until a name dragged him back.

'What did you say?'

'He's back', said Baker with renewed importance, 'but not to stay. Just came back to collect his things, then he's goin' north. I saw them at the station on my way here ... he could never do much wivout her.'

Peterson ran to the station in a series of exhausted stops and starts, from shop block to shop block. There were bush people milling all about, but Peterson was a thousand miles away in another country town, and from that distance they were incidentals to composition. Straight ahead he could see Hetty sitting on the platform with a boy who must have been Bradley. The station was a stretch of cement laid for several yards along the track, with no roof or ticket office, and apart from the two angular figures and their meagre luggage, it was bare.

He tried to compose himself as he approached but contracted a stilted, formal style. He looked at Bradley first, and suddenly he knew Hetty's secret. Bradley was a black and shiny boy with watery brown eyes, and a nose that twitched in expectation of a cold. His thick hair was ruffled and long, and not knowing what to do with his arms he crossed them over his chest and buried a hand under each armpit.

They were going north, all the way to Queensland. Hetty looked up and smiled. Bradley rocked at the end of the bench.

'G'day Mr Peterson', he said, 'Hetty says you've bin nice t'her while I've bin gone'. He bit his lip, and thinking he had not done enough, jumped up and grabbed Peterson's hand. 'Thank you for Hetty!' Then as the last bit of vitality ebbed from him, he flopped down on the bench, and stared ahead at the empty track. His body disturbed him so he loaded it down with a couple of large suitcases.

Peterson turned to go then turned back. 'Queensland is very commercial', he said to Hetty.

'But Bradley's got heaps of relatives up that way.'

'And it's not enough to say you'll hate it? You'll be miserable up there?' Bradley cowered even more, chipping at his finger-nails.

'He got me this ticket', she said.

Peterson might have told Hetty it could be returned, he would repay Bradley any expense, but almost despite himself he played with the possible nobility of the moment.

'This is funny', he said fumbling with his collar, 'and I'm leaving only tomorrow.'

'Why did y'come, Mr Peterson?' she asked.

'I told you. My great-aunt? You know when I was little I used to sit on her settee and just stare at a painting on the opposite wall . . . a small town it was . . . a Drysdale print, do you know him? No. Well, it's not important. Of course he's a lot more impressionistic than the real thing . . . I mean his paintings evoke a feeling.' It told him there was something durable in the face of change. His voice shook and he pinched the end of his nose to keep himself sensible. 'You can write if you want, Baker will pass the letters on.' He touched her for the second time, a light pat on the shoulder. 'Yes . . . better write.'

'Mr Peterson', said Hetty with a significant movement of her eyebrows toward Bradley, 'I was thinkin' on what you said about breakable people.'

He walked to the end of the platform, but it was not until he had stepped off that he realised she would not be following, that she hadn't the faintest notion of how to conduct a proper farewell, and he had lost something of his vision. Later he would notice it had been a little too obvious, or a little too oblique for him to catch on to. There was a sadness in Mr Peterson that hinted at a far greater loss than leaving Hetty. From some idle promise that is made to little children he had nurtured, in his moments alone, a faith in what people might be. It was not concerned with success or money, but a hope in the tenderness of the human spirit.

Out in the open the smudge drew on his sadness and discovered the light dashes of soft grey rain. The two lines of the hill and plain blurred, realigned, but remained lines after all. His eyelashes matted as the last fragments of a summer melted away before him, and as it left he noticed the resilience of some things, of buildings and people, and kept it in his heart to tell Baker. It was then Mr Peterson crumpled, not a great deal, just a little on the edges, which a stick man will do every time, when he has set himself up for a brilliant summer.

Ring of Kerry

Rosemary Jones

*H*E stands at the doorway as though he's just blown in from the Ring of Kerry.

For a minute I do not recognise him.

'Yes?' I am about to say. 'Yes?' As though he's selling vacuum cleaners.

Until it dawns on me. That, and the fact that his top front teeth are missing. The false set. Knocked out by the police, he says later.

I try to look at his eyes, I search for his eyes which squint up at me. I'm not too sure of my movements and I hug him. He squeezes the breath out of me.

It's a surprising sort of day for a visit such as this, a free-wheeling wide day, the sky agape, spitting blue. I lead him into the garden clutching two wine glasses and then watch him, upright and alive. I had not thought to see him so. Not standing firmly on two feet wearing a clean shirt. I am surprised at these things, and so, I think, is he.

He looks thinner. Like a man who is convalescing, like one who has been to a bottomless pit and back. He speaks in an undertone so the neighbours won't hear (won't hear what, I wonder) and mumbles so I only get a whisker of what he says, just a morsel—of blurred days and vagabond nights, enough to chip away at any girl's heart. More than enough. He speaks as though it is all over and done with, finished. And yet he sounds like a man trying to fit a thousand smashed pieces together and make them work again.

218

I nod. 'Of course, of course.' And remain sceptical. He came round to tell me he loves me, he says.

Now it is I who squint, half into the sun, and away. He repeats it.

I tell him quietly he is a liar.

Not because I don't believe it but because it is no longer relevant. And because he talks in double-speak, two meanings at once, as though one bit of him tries to keep his foot in the door of reality, while the other shakes its head forlornly and wanders half-extinguished in some other land.

He's joined the IRA.

Not that he had to tell me. I had a hunch. His Irish blood squats under his heavy chest, rumbling. He's leaving for Ireland.

'When?'

'Soon.'

Except that he doesn't look exactly loaded with money. My eyes catch his odd socks, one blue, one brown. The same old style. Or lack of it. I screw up my face wondering where he got the new suede jacket that's thrown over the kitchen chair. And then shove it smartly into the too–hard compartment. Just curious.

'When was your birthday?' I ask for something to say.

He tells me, and then adds that he spent it in the watch-house.

'For calling a pig a pig.'

I wriggle my toes. He watches them. Next door somebody shouts and bangs doors.

'Why did you really come round. On a whim perhaps?'

He smiles and agrees. 'Yes, a whim.'

His sturdy legs stretch out on the grass. Slowly. He asks to kiss me.

I shake my head. Laugh it off.

'I must show you where to sit in the parklands', he says.

'Maybe I don't want to know', I reply a little tersely.

'It's magic, a little piece of magic in the middle of the city. Can I kiss you now?'

'All right.' There's a smattering of that old charm in him.

He puts his lips on my neck, once, twice. Sad kisses. Snippets of kisses. As though his jaw has been broken. I am lost for words.

'Do you see anyone we both knew anymore?'

'No.'

'Because you've gone too far—over the edge?' I dare to say.

'Over what edge? Whose edge?' He heads me off.

'Yours', I say after a bit.

'Great apricot tree you've got.'

'You've been to the bottom.'

'I've been further than you'll ever know', as if he takes a tiny amount of pride in that.

I shut up. There's no point talking this way. We look straight ahead, anonymous. Except I get hit with a bunch of faded memories, clamping round my head like a tropical rainstorm about to burst. A sort of wet-worn weariness.

'Have you still got my letters?' I ask stupidly.

'I ripped them up, along with everything I owned. I got angry.'

I nod. I imagine the scene all too well.

'You must meet my son again.'

'I wouldn't know what to say to him.'

'Neither would he.'

'Then what's the point? What I mean is', I take a breath, 'I don't want to get tangled up in your life'.

There, it's out, just in case he had thoughts in that direction.

'I didn't mean it like that. His life, your life, my life, are three completely separate things. You're my friend.'

'But every friend I have, I get tangled up with their lives to some degree.'

'It's up to you', he says gruffly.

'Sometimes you frighten me. I don't mean threaten me, but I'm scared of what's sitting there inside you.'

'I've crossed the major bridge', he says.

I shake my head with disbelief.

'There's more to come', I whisper in the direction of the fence.

He talks about the apricot tree again. And then he turns on me.

'Damn you, you make me tell the truth. Not that I'm not honest, I am, but you have to be careful who you tell the truth to.'

He's right there. Dead right.

'Where else can I kiss you?'

It becomes a game. 'Oh, maybe here', I point to my cheek suddenly light-hearted.

And there are eight toothless soft kisses.

'You smell so good, so good', he almost smiles.

I hug him for that, and a number of other reasons I can't quite put my finger on. I look again and again, scrutinising his green brown eyes, and see a remnant of that old magic, buried right down deep, so far under he'll need a tow rope to get at it when the time is right. If there is a time.

I enquire after his liver.

'That organ', he hastens to tell me, 'is in excellent condition. Excellent'.

His words slip out sideways as though he might suddenly break into a nameless tongue and he chastises himself, 'Speak English, speak English', he repeats. And then he breaks into mumbo-jumbo, talking a brand of politics which is neither left nor right nor logical but an incantation to private gods; it falls from his mouth like a delirium. I cannot even begin to discuss it. I sit very still as though I am perched on the edge of a telegraph wire waiting for a train to blaze past underneath.

He points to his heart. I relent. He buries his hair in the back of my neck like someone who has emerged from a jungle after twenty years, having forgotten what human touch feels like. For a long time he remains like that, passionless, sorrow-filled. 'I love you', he says again and again as if trying to hear what it sounds like. It wafts up the black trunk of the apricot tree.

'I've got a man', I say gently. 'I mean, there's someone I spend some time with.'

'Ahhh.'

And adds, 'I'm hungry, I've been hungry for two years.'

The words fall out vacantly as though he's drawing on a line he might have used a long time ago. It falls emptily into my ear. I know then he won't push too far. I realise I have no need to build defences. That was all done years ago, wedged in his memory like a poison dart. Whatever the cost, he doesn't want to be remembered as a man who uses women or damages them. Though I know, he knows, the damage has already been done. By something even greater.

'You look good', he raises his head, 'last time you looked—crazed.'

I am startled at that. So did he, worse, evil-crazed with a madness hissing just under the surface. It was my fear of him he saw then, fear that his weight would come crashing through my flat, bellowing at every skerrick of my life which could be labelled capitalistic, just as he had violated his own belongings.

'We will go out together', he decides, 'before I leave the country'.

'I have my own life,' I try telling him.

'What if we fall in love before I go', he drifts into fantasy, 'we'll have to wait until I get back.'

'I won't fall in love with you', I say, trying to bring him back.

'Won't you? I don't believe you.'

I know better but say nothing.

'You may not see me again', he says. Just as he did a year and more ago. He may be right. He may end up in prison.

'There's no point in telling you to be careful, is there?'

'No, none at all.' He ducks his face in at me as though poking it through a servery window.

I drive him to St Vincent de Pauls. He's helping out there. Maybe I believe him, maybe I don't.

'Lend me a dollar?'

I bat my eyelids quickly. Very neatly he negates the whole afternoon. And then I scrounge in my purse, tipping out the change into his waiting palm. He laughs uncomfortably.

'You make me hot', he says, getting out of the car. I watch him walk out into the square where the hoboes lie.

Maybe the IRA won't have him.

I watch his stride through the rear vision mirror. There's a queer black and green madness in the air, like the trees and the trunks and his eyes. He walks into his twilight world, across to the park bench where Big Jim lies sprawled, bottle in hand. As

222

he walks he bends his head a little as though searching for visions, someone else's symbols, someone else's knowledge. Or a 20 cent bit fallen from someone's pocket.

'I want to go home.' Those were his words.

'I want to go home.' To the land of his blood, to Ireland.

Even after he's gone I can still smell him in the kitchen—a sweet, heavy sort of smell as though he's left a bit of himself lying around waiting to be picked up.

I draw the blinds.

'Just one more kiss', he asked, 'on the lips?'

'Just one.' That's all. For the old times. Maybe I'll see him again. Maybe I won't.

Love's an Itinerant

Amanda Given

THE first time she fell in love my daughter was three. Well, she may have fallen in love with me when they threw her onto my belly, convex one minute, concave the next. No, I actually doubt it. Not the way I looked or felt. And she was really quite repulsive. Red, she, the subject of days' pain. I had the distinct impression at that time that she had preferred it on the inside, before the repulsing hostilities. We did, of course, love each other. At least a little later on.

That's it, you see. It was Evelyn Waugh who so poignantly indicated that distinction. You know, when Charles Ryder's wife, looking to pin down her unfulfilment, had put the question 'are you in love with anyone?'. He replied devastatingly (although we'll never know whether she understood, or indeed, whether he intended her to) 'no, I'm not in love with anyone'. It was something like that.

I've actually seen Jerry Lewis, a sagacious stooge, make that distinction as well. Presented with a neat embodiment of American collegehood, and reflecting that he'd always loved her, he added after a trial kiss, 'but I'm not in love with you'. My daughter summed that one up—'he thinks kissing tastes'.

Lots of people are in loving relationships; how many do you see in love? It's not necessarily true that they'd have to be with the object of their exultation; they could quite likely be alone. The essential thing about love is that it lasts about the same time as an orgasm and, likewise, happens many times in a life. Our tragedy is that we learn to deny its sporadic nature; efforming

224

sophisticated, twisted inscapes to cultivate regret. Love's an itinerant, a momentary obsession. It's distinctly recognisable, and so it was with my daughter.

There had been a busker around town. I'd seen him a few times. He was an enigma with the skill of Waugh and the comedy of Lewis; it was never clear whether he was a lunatic or whether people just fancied him so. He dressed in sort of tutu arrangements, often ripped, with lovely shiny stockings. At the end of his spindly, diaphanous legs were huge work boots. It was difficult to imagine how he was able to dance in them but he did and they clicked magnificently. He always wore hats. And he used to warble; you'd be hard pressed to call it singing. One of the facets of his act, there wasn't entirely a focus, was his puppets. Constructions of twigs, bound at various junctures, would dance to his tune things. He could really draw a crowd. But it wasn't the busker with whom she fell in love.

Sophie's godfather is a guitarist. He plays in a group. She was aware of his status and had often pleaded to be allowed to see him do it, to see what the fuss was about. After all, he was hers and she'd never seen him play. She'd never been to the pub, neither had Purply, her rag doll. I gave in, as parents do. On the appointed day she'd had a preparatory nap. I had sacrificed the notion of eight o'clock freedom in announcing that Wee Willie Winkie had granted special dispensation for such a worthwhile purpose.

Since she'd first comprehended her Mother Goose I'd noticed that Sophie was particularly receptive to the eerie omnipotence of Wee Willie Winkie. She would indurate at the mention of his name. Parents need effective tools. A squirm or a murmur from her room after bedtime and a knock on the wall heralded his presence. He worked like a charm, the benefactor.

She was uncharacteristically subdued, sitting on her mother's knee in awe of the music of her idol. She'd warmed up though, after he'd dedicated a song for her. There he was, lit up on the stage, and only the dance floor between him and Sophie in the first row.

'What's the time, Mummy?'

The hour of doom had long passed. It was a coup. Purply had decided that she wanted to dance. Sophie went with her. They moved with an uncanny registration of tempo and pitch. The crowd, if not engaged in exchanges of their own, were unperturbed; there was an absence of pretence in the child's appreciation of the music.

The itinerant moved to a corner of the dance floor. He sat there cross-legged, bedecked in a purple, high-topped hat and a green blanket which was punctured in the centre to accommodate the head. There were those boots. The man was transfixed; before him, Sophie and Purply, were two dancing dolls, his creatures in animation. His euphoric gaze drew attention to his fantasy. The child had not registered his presence. He wanted to dance with her: he needed to await an acceptance. He sat smiling through the song, that inane glaze which is the ass head of love's fall. During the applause he caught her eye to bestow an approving tip of the hat. She ran to her mother.

'Mummy, it's Wee Willie Winkie!'

She returned with privileged deliberation at once to test and tease him. The percussion had been augmented. A rhythmic, clicking sound punctuated the music. Staccato steps for Sophie. She and Purply continued their dance on the opposite corner of the floor.

Wee Willie Winkie proffered the purple hat. She glided to accept it. To avoid intimacy she placed it on the doll's head. Purply, eaten by the head gear, danced between them. He clicked on, twisting legs, abandoning arms, singing inside celebrations of his liberated puppets until his anticipation of regret built in the closing chords; his movements became stiff, deliberated, conclusive. He bowed to the child, donned the returned hat and left the bar.

'Hey, Mum! I just danced with Wee Willie Winkie!'

Since that compelling night, bedtime's been a nightmare. Parents have to be philosophical: it was better to have had him and lost than never to have had him at all. But that's an adult adage.

End of the Affair

Nancy Keesing

'*I* thought I'd like to see you and Richard again, before we all die' said the woman on the doorstep. She looked composed and self-assured; her denim suit, since her figure was slim and graceful, did not look unsuitably young; her greying hair cut like a cap, very sleek. But it was not what she had intended to say. And her real meaning was 'before *you* die', or, 'before you *both* die'. She was, after all, barely 45, whereas the woman who had just opened the door, and Richard whom the visitor really hoped to see, must be in their late sixties.

The woman of the house peered at the visitor without recognition. Her expression was expectant, in a dull sort of way, rather than puzzled or curious.

'I'm sorry', said the visitor with a confident half-laugh. 'You don't recognise me. I'm Valda Rushton now, but my maiden name was Blackford, Valda Blackford.'

The other woman shifted her lumpy body from one swollen foot to the other and said 'Oh yes' in a flat voice. She still looked blank, and placid.

Valda Rushton would have recognised her anywhere without question, even after nearly a quarter of a century. That flabbiness emphasised by age and a terrible cotton dress, but she was always flabby. That hair, now haphazardly dyed black but grey at the roots, had always been haphazardly dyed, though the long-ago colour was auburn. She tried again:

'You *are* Iris Green?' making it a question.

'Yes.'

So what now?

'Is Richard, your husband, at home?'

'Yes.'

'Well ... I wondered ... Might I see him?'

'Yes.'

But still she did not move. Had she had a stroke? Grown dotty? Stupider than ever? Against the unlit cavern of a large hall she stood immutable and immovable. Valda's eyes were becoming familiars of that gloom and remembered furniture; a massive oak settle against one wall, an Austrian table of wood tortured into thorn bushes against another, a carpet patterned geometrically in dark red and grey. So far as she could tell, the hall looked well-kept and tidy, as did the narrow veranda where she stood now, and the boring garden plot of grass and fleshy begonias behind her.

'Iris', Valda asked, being careful to keep any pleading sound from her voice, 'may I see Richard?' She was determined to do so. Iris might be merely dense. More probably she was being deliberately rude, or intentionally resistant. Valda glanced at her watch. I give her two minutes, she decided, then I ring the bell again, long and loud. Perhaps Richard is deaf. OK, I'll think of something else. At least I can walk down the side path and look for him in the back garden or try the back door.

Iris said:

'I'll go and fetch him.'

Pitilessly Valda watched Iris stump through the hall and turn out of sight round a dark corner. At least she knew Richard was not decrepit. Three nights ago, as she'd watched a TV news item describing his retirement, he'd looked old but hale. His white hair was unexpected but he still had masses of it and still the same grinning smile and quick movements. He'd deserved his honours, his retirement fêting, but not this. How would he endure an old age of Iris, day in, day out? His problem. Her curiosity had led in three days from that short news flash to this abandoned veranda. For what purpose? To display the fag end of her own youth? To test her confidence, even after a quarter of a century? Frankly, the decision to visit had come into her head

228

as a *fait accompli* the day before, mysterious to herself but not to be argued away. She was curious about that, too.

Iris returned through darkness.

'Come through.' Her expression as stolid as before. 'Dick's shaving.'

Valda stepped into the hall. 'Shall I close the door?' she offered.

'Might as well', Iris agreed.

The gloomy hall disclosed its pictures—the Landseer engraving of foxhound pups; the buttery oil in greens and browns of a church on a crag in, no doubt, Ruritania; the pthisic beauty in medieval drapes with sword and rose; two dour, Germanic ancestors. Down a right-angled passageway they passed the open French doors of a large formal drawing room. A glance confirmed the dreariness of contorted wood, unwelcoming upholstery, bulbous china and Benares brass. Someone took good care of it all. The inside air was dry and chilly.

Iris led to the back of the house to a glassed-in and louvred ex-porch. An ugly sun-room, but light and warm. She did not indicate any particular chair. Valda avoided ancient seagrass as inimical to stockings and broken-spined deep leather as hazardous to spine. She perched on a contraption of aluminium tubing and purple plastic straps; Iris subsided into its twin in orange, spreading her fat unstockinged knees. Above brown moccasins her legs were a webbed contour of bruised veins. She said evenly and agreeably, as if they had not already had a confrontation at the entrance door:

'Fancy you dropping in, Val. You've changed a lot, haven't you? That grey hair. I wouldn't have recognised you. You'll find Dick much the same, but. He don't change. He's retired, you know.'

'Yes, I saw a TV news bit.'

'Fancy. 's that why you thought of us, Valda?'

'One reason.'

'Can't say we often think of *you*. 'Cept if we run into any of the old crowd from the old days. D'you ever see Madge and Herb? They come here to tea now 'nd then.'

'I do, occasionally.'

'Yes. Well, 's a matter of fact we know that.'

Madge and Herb were Valda's only link with long ago. Cheerful idiots who relished a persistence of ancient gossip and never forgot to send embossed and tinselly Christmas cards or 'fix an evening' of reminiscent boredom once a year. They were reliable. Madge would offer her crumbs of Dick and Iris discreetly in her nylon ruffled bedroom while the central interest that kept Valda ribboned to their maypole remained a mystery to Valda's husband. One of her unaccountable 'things'.

Somewhere in the house a door slammed.

'Dick'll be here in a sec. You'd like a cuppa.' Iris got clumsily to her feet. 'I'll go 'nd light the gas.'

Within the house two voices. Then at the sun-room door, Richard.

'Valda! My goodness! What an unexpected event. Iris *is* delighted!'

'Is she ...?'

'And so am I. We were only talking over old times with Madge and Herb the other day. Last Wednesday week. As recently as that. You *do* look lovely. Here, of course, we're old folks now.'

He skittered about the cluttered room as he spoke, peering at her first from one angle, then another. Her eyes followed him. He had always looked young for his age and still did. When she was a girl, and he somewhere near her own age now, he'd seemed a man in his thirties. Most people had supposed him younger than Iris, though he was not. Now that Iris had flopped into ruin the discrepancy was far more obvious. He wore grey shorts and socks and a brown safari jacket open at the throat disclosing areas of tanned and healthy skin. His stomach was flat.

'I saw your retirement on TV, Dick. It made me feel ... old.' She heard an inane half-laugh in her voice.

'Really? Did you really feel old? But you're practically a girl, Valda. And you look lovely. I mean it. Lovely. Smart. You were always smart. Very good taste in clothes. You know, honestly, *I* don't feel old. I've great plans for my retirement. Such a lot to do.'

230

'Yes?' His voice was unaltered. Still high and brisk but with a curious whining undertone as if, perhaps, once he had striven not to drawl. He sat in one of the leather chairs.

'I shall write up the history of my family in Australia. I'm looking forward to starting that. I have all their papers. Letters, account books, journals, the lot, back to, oh, 1834 or so. All indexed, too. My mother's hobby.'

The reply she thought of was sarcastic, like 'I'll *bet*!' or 'You *do* surprise me.' So she said nothing. That dreadful, dreadful old mother with her stays and jet and Queen Alexandra frizz and her grandeur and haughtiness. No girl or woman good enough for her Richard, not because of Richard himself, but because all his large, long family came to an end with him. Then he'd married Iris, and had no children. Iris was too old.

'You met my mother, didn't you?' Richard asked.

'Once. In this house.'

'Yes, of course. I couldn't be *quite* sure. Did she seem to like you?'

'What an extraordinary question, Richard.' She laughed uneasily and fidgeted with her rings as she always did when nervous, a legacy from the time when her marriage to Jim Rushton had been such a blessed unexpected relief and they its talismans. She said:

'No. To be honest I think she hated me.'

'Oh', he said brightly, 'I'm sure "hate" is too strong. Though she probably didn't care for what you represented.'

'What I . . .'

'Oh, nothing personal to you, Valda. *My* wild oats. My last crop when she thought I'd finished and which I really had not intended. Actually my mother and Iris were great friends. I'm sure that surprises you.'

'It does.'

'Mother was a realist. She accepted the inevitable. Unlike Queen Mary. She knew Iris loved me completely and she thought I'd kept the poor girl guessing for quite long enough, on again off again for years and then you. Quite long enough. Mother was dead right.'

He stood up and circled the room, returning to the same

chair. Always restless, Richard. But he sat perfectly still to ask:
   'Why did you come here, Valda?'
   'Why? To see you, both of you, again. I had a fancy.'
   'Not to seduce me again, I hope.' He laughed jauntily at his
joke, though it was not funny. 'Valda, Valda, don't look so
outraged. You're a big girl now. You have a big successful
husband and charming children, I believe. We *do* know who
you are, you see. In our humble way. We do hear from other
people, from time to time. We haven't quite disappeared into
Dogpatch.'

She said, 'I think I'd better leave', and picked up her patent
leather clutch bag. Behind them Iris said flatly:
   'I thought the pot'd never boil. Give us a hand with the
trolley, Dick.'

Trapped by hospitality, Valda stayed where she was. Sounds
of rattles and squeaking reverberated in the bowels of their
cave. An ancient tea-wagon, pulled by Richard and pushed by
Iris did at last lurch into the sun-room, loaded with Richard's
family silver tea service in all its elaborate glory, its scrolls and
curls glowing with a mellowness that spoke of regular and
skilful polishing.

'We like to use our nice things; no one to leave 'em to', said
Iris, carefully straining tea into eggshell china cups, fragile and
transparent, but large.

'We're great afternoon tea folk', Richard confirmed, slicing
an engraved knife into a decorated cake that no one had
whipped up in taken-by-surprise haste.

'A real Darby and Joan', added Iris, handing Valda a starched
napkin of old, fine linen and moving a rickety small table to
hold her cup, saucer and plate of significant cake with a small
silver fork set parallel with the slice. 'We like our spot too, of
course, but not mid-afternoon like some do these days.'

'Really', Valda protested, 'I don't eat between . . .'

'Then you shouldn't of come mid-afternoon, dear', Iris said.
'Do you good. I have to admit', she continued, 'I was real put
out when I first seen you. I wasn't sure Dick'd be the best
pleased. But he is. As you can see. Me too. It does kind of round
things off, doesn't it.'

232

Well, yes. Round off one fleeing, unsuitable, callous fiancé. One clandestine baby placed for adoption (who'd be 24 now, somewhere, and well rid of family silver.) Close a circle on one lifetime of dishonest marriage. Her visit was intrusive and impertinent but inevitable. She was reproved but felt no guilt, or none that was not dispelled by the drinking of two cups of tea and the swallowing of two slices of cake. She need never see Madge and Herb again, thank heaven.

Richard kissed her smooth cheek coolly when she left. He stayed at the front door. Iris followed her to the gate and opened it.

'Well Valda', she said without moving her expressionless lips, 'bye-bye for now.'

'Thank you Iris', Valda farewelled.

'You never worried me', Iris said evenly and clicked the gate-latch behind the visitor.

Only a Little of so Much

Fay Zwicky

HELP me up with the last button, says Aunt Eva, my mother's youngest sister. According to the scales even Krupp the Murderer puts his personal signature on I weigh exactly thirteen and a half stones, she says. It never poisoned the spirit to see a bit of flesh. Too much, they're telling me but who listens? The same all my life—for this I should be bereaved? Why eat, says nurse, the Brünnhilde, with respect mind you. Why sleep is my answer to Miss Rheingold. Legs and arms were never wicked to us stage people. Or bosoms, bursting from the good life wherever it was. What's wickedness I'll tell you is something else. Don't let that button become your emotional problem—a safety pin does in this place! Here! Please God you wonderful younger generation won't drop the cheese when the fox says 'Sing!'. Plums all day if you want!

Your mother was the skinny one. Pickled in dill and vinegar like her cucumbers, stuffed into glass jars like stiff hussars. Living decently while the earth trembled, may she rest in peace! A ruin at 30 following you and that messiah, your brother, round with a Wettex. Your father couldn't come in the back door with his shoes on, and a colonel in the war! No wonder he looked other places, excuse me for saying so but you're old enough ... you needn't search your soul for answers either. 'What's a little dirt in a family?' I'd say, sorry as usual. 'You always were a fool', she'd come back like a tiger. 'You ought to know about dirt. You bring enough of it into this house.' Harsh you're thinking? She didn't eat enough for kindness ...

234

Your father liked his food, poor thing. A hedonistic streak going nowhere. I'd run up a chocolate soufflé for support and other reasons. I made one the day after the ad came in the *Chronicle*. 'A celebration! Hello cello!' I said, my breath coming and going. 'They don't need this rubbish', she shouted swinging open the oven door with a bang. The soufflé sank in the sudden cold like a dead creature. 'He's putting on enough weight as it is. And your fanny needs now a duet stool!' 'It can't be your doing then', I said under my breath, sharp fingers pinching my hammering heart. Don't look so worried, kid. *I'm* still here. Save worry for the final judgment. You're pretty enough for Miss Australia even if you are *her* daughter! A heap of cucumbers and four dead souls, 90 per cent water! Do you wonder I couldn't marry? Sisters! I could only take a little of so much . . .

It wasn't my first endeavour in the Personals, by the way. *That* was an Armageddon! The perilous primrose path any time but, remember, I was no vision according to the authorities. Plump however. Some said womanly but no man around to make sense of it. Everyone acting as if they knew a thing or two. And I believed! I believed. 'Always stuffing your face!' 'How much on truffles this week?' 'Get your fat bottom off my seat!' And so forth. A Goldilocks with bears and no porridge. A full life of nothing and me crackling inside my thin skin like a Christmas duck!

The first—that hiker and waltzer!—turned out a tuner and I'm not talking fish. A race dying for you lot with your televisions and nuke boxes rocking and rolling. No Beethoven but who is so lucky? Deaf he wasn't but blind, yes. That such a man could call himself special, humorous, substance and character and ready to match an attractive female—I wrote Rubenesque with the returnable photo—for refreshing interludes of levity. Levity! I used to think it was a Jewish word. Him, me and the guide god and your mother's Wettex chasing us into every corner—a collaboration!

And who was he to say the family piano was finished? Finished! It sounded always good to me. You won't find filigree flowers and candle holders like that any more. Straight from the

235

Fay Zwicky

Steinway factory in Leipzig with your grandmother, I told him.
Maybe the F sharp in the middle stuck a bit now and then.
I could still get off lots of runs in the Minute Waltz—just under a
minute in my prime—and plenty oompah and what-have-you
on the left in the Tannhäuser arrangement. I practised like a
fiend when your mother was out, pretending I never touched it.
She always had to slave over her fiddle! Hours of scrape and
scratch and for what? New hammers, he said, prodding away.
That'll cost extra, he said. Who asked about cost? I started
weeping like the fool that I was, thirteen and a half stones of
autumn dream streaming like Niagara!
      And what was Mr Substance and Character doing in the
middle of the flood? Building an ark for my bones? Why,
poking away at the F sharp stuck forever like it is today in spite
of my runs. Who notices, kid? Your mother showed him the
door. And to me, 'Don't bring any more of that trash into the
house again!' with other profanities I won't soil your ears with.
Screaming 'You need a psychologist!' and worse, waving her
soapy rubber gloves over my plait like Mickey the Mouse and
him still on the path to the gate with his dog. Sorry as usual,
I didn't bring anyone for a time, having trouble getting breath
back . . .
      All right, Miss Nosey. I promised no lies. The best last.
Water drop by drop will also split stone. I was on the way to
splitting when the colonel comes back from the war with his
boots and medals and I start on the soufflés, making no demands
on anyone. *Anyone*, mark you, patience my middle name
almost. What was is what will be is by now my philosophy so
no picture needed this time. Flesh may be flesh—how could I
doubt?—but spirit no gherkin regiment either, even if I did
believe everything for what it wasn't. I'm not religious, God
forbid, but if I was, then God would be a musician. Or maybe
an actor—Shakespeare only, with a little Schnitzler for luck!
This time, please, a real *Musikant*! Beethoven he doesn't have to
be. Never forget your musical talent comes from me, not your
scratching mother! My prayer, kid, was heard and noted. Even
a soufflé murdered couldn't wreck the day!
      Every word comes back. Handsome professional cellist. And

236

French! Twenty years under Toscanini. Warm and dynamic
calibre to share hopefully dancing. Sense of laughter. Legally
unencumbered. Photo appreciated but not essential—can you
imagine? Another late bloomer exactly my age and ready to
romp, the French culture a bonus. Ça va sans dire, Flaubert!
That surprises you, doesn't it? I took to languages like a duck to
troubling waters. Not educated like your generation but honoured, yes, honoured to match this person in intellect and
frolicsome invigorations. I hid the *Chronicle* from your mother
and communicated immediately. A woman of passions and
ideas, I wrote, and ready always for gracious dining and something personal.

I am in levitation hours after first meeting—a Jewish word I
told you it must be!—no questions in my mind. Size, shape, IQ
high or low, my fate was written in his fancy! Kismet come
true, my heart in throat and sleeve together! See for yourself the
picture—a life-member of the Pleasure Principle Club, isn't it?
Wonderful dancer and diner, a prince of eloquence—the entire
holus-bolus! A pity all those genius Jews took precious time
trying to make us better than we are—Misery Marx, Sad-Sack
Sigmund and the atom bomb person whose name I am for-
getting for ever. A woman has to measure things according to
pleasant or unpleasant. How it feels is her final standards. Still,
I am asking him to play me the sad Swan of Saint-Saëns and
occasional Kol Nidrei to curb enthusiasm for more frivolity!

Even your mother, smelling excitement in my life, is impressed. Enough to forget to tell the colonel to take his boots
off. The matter is not for laughing, kid! 'France my spiritual
home', she murmurs in her spotless kitchen, wandering round
his chair. 'Ah, Paris', she sighs, Wettex stranded on the sink.
'My dream place! Where men chase real women with life's
experience and leave minors alone.' 'Who is minor in this
house?' I say. 'Humph!' snorts the colonel waiting for his dinner
in the corner. No soufflés these days, alive or dead, poor man!

Before I can nip her bud, he is telling her what a lot of this and
that she has, a woman with life's contacts written all over her
face—her *face*, mind you!—fine children, loving husband and
military to boot, the works. 'Why so personal?' I ask. 'She's

only my sister, the eldest, and can't play the fiddle for peanuts.' Thinking, of course, of my under-the-minute waltz. 'My youngest sister here', she says, 'is only a baby in arms. She can't help it.' A baby? Thirteen and a half stones and 50 years? I want to shout but do not for fear of releasing my cat from the sleeping bag. My paramour is thinking 38 but since the word marriage has recently arisen I let the sleeping dog lie ...

What next you are wanting to know? So much so quick, my mind rocky with remembering. But never so dumb I couldn't tell who warned him off my grasses ..

The day before we were booked for Paris, I get a postcard with the Eiffel Tower in colour which says for all to see, 'I have missed for so long France. Now I must miss you for the remainder of my days. Thanks for all the good times, never so good with my legal encumbrance but duties call me home, *adieu.*' I go to my room and shut the door, very quiet. Outside, I hear your mother, *my* sister, saying to the colonel, 'All for the best. He did the right thing.' 'Always right if you say so', says your father, no smile in his voice. 'In this case, yes. It was for the best. She doesn't know her own good and never will!' *My* sister again.

I come out, swinging the door with a bang behind me. Ten feet tall and stronger than any tiger. '*You* asked him to stay away?' I say in a quiet voice unlike my own, coming slowly down the stairs. 'Yes', she says, backing away. 'And he agreed with that?' I say, still coming down, still quiet. 'Yes', she says again. 'And he just *agreed*? He didn't even *want* to see me again?' 'He said he would write to you.' 'What am I, then? A dead-letter office? And what', I scream, no tears, 'are *you*?' Then I leap at her skinny throat, a creature dying of pain. I know she was your mother, excuse me, but also my sister! And they say women stick together!

Turn on the light, kid. It's getting quickly dark these winter nights. Over the basin is the switch! There goes the colonel again in his silver lining! No, he didn't break, dear. Put him carefully back with the others and we'll celebrate. The tablets go down easier with a drop. They won't find out, don't look so worried! You remind me of your mother when you look that way. Miss Rheingold will be along soon with that tuft of dog-grass she calls dinner. No, I won't calm down! Calm isn't my nature. Why calm when I'm nearly dust? Tomorrow's almost behind me and yesterday's here already! So what's to celebrate? Something, maybe, missing the first time around?

Biographies

GLENDA ADAMS was born and educated in Sydney. She is the author of *The Hottest Night of the Century* (stories, 1979) and *Games of the Strong* (novel, 1982), both published by Angus & Robertson. 'Coral Dance', which is part of a new novel, was written wth the assistance of a grant from the Literature Board of the Australia Council.

HELEN W. ASHER was born in a part of Germany that became Polish after World War II. She came to Australia with her husband in the mid-1950s, and then moved back and forth between Europe and Australia before finally settling in Sydney. For a period she wrote for the German newspaper *Feuilleton*. Her novel, *The Childbearer*, is to be published by Penguin. Helen Asher has published other short stories in Australia, and has participated in art exhibitions with her wall hangings.

THEA ASTLEY was born in Brisbane and studied arts at the University of Queensland. In 1980 she retired from Macquarie University in NSW where she held the position of fellow in Australian literature and creative writing. Since 1958 she has published nine novels and a book of short stories. Three of her novels have won the Miles Franklin Award: *The Well Dressed Explorer* in 1962, *The Slow Natives* in 1965 and *The Acolyte* in 1972. In 1975 *A Kindness Cup*, another novel, won the Melbourne *Age* Book of the Year Award, as did *An Item from the Late News* in 1982. Her most recent novel, *Beachmasters*, was published in 1985. Thea Astley is now living and writing full time in Queensland.

INEZ BARANAY, born in Italy in 1950, is an ex-schoolteacher, activist, actress, barmaid, traveller, television researcher, spendthrift. She is currently working on a novel and a screenplay. Inez Baranay lives alone in Sydney with her answering machine.

CARMEL BIRD, born in Tasmania in 1940, was educated at the University of Tasmania. She is a teacher of short story writing at CAE and Holmesglen TAFE in Victoria. Sybylla Press is to publish her novel *Cherry Ripe* in 1985. Self-published works include *Births, Deaths and Marriages*, a collection of stories, and *Dr God*, a cassette of performed work. Carmel Bird is active in organising readings and performances of satirical work, and is an editor of *Syllable* magazine.

MARGARET COOMBS was born in Mudgee, NSW, but moved to Sydney at the age of eight. She studied philosophy and government at the University of Sydney, graduating with an MA in government. She received a Literature Board of the Australia Council general writing grant for 1980, and spent most of 1980–81 travelling with traditional (i.e. neo-feudal) English circuses. Her short stories have appeared in, among other publications, *Cleo*, *Luna* and *Southerly*. She lives in Petersham, Sydney, with Paul Fitzgerald and her two daughters.

FREDA GALLOWAY, born in 1928, spent her childhood in the small village of Parkville, NSW, and attended Scone District Rural School. She went on to do nursing in West Maitland. 'Vida's Child' was an award-winning short story at the Grenfell Henry Lawson Festival in 1975. Freda Galloway has also written several plays, one of which was broadcast by the ABC. She lives in Hazelbrook in the Blue Mountains, NSW, has two children, and has continued to both write and paint.

NENE GARE, born in Adelaide in 1919, was educated at East Adelaide Public School, the School of Arts, North Terrace, Adelaide and later at the Technical School, St George's Terrace, Perth with part of an arts degree completed at Murdoch University, WA. She has published five books, has recently completed a sixth, and her short stories have been included in various anthologies. Her novel, *The Fringe Dwellers*, is to be filmed in 1985 with Bruce Beresford as director. Nene Gare has also won several prizes for her paintings.

HELEN GARNER was born in Geelong, Victoria, in 1942. After studying English and French literature at Melbourne University she worked as a teacher in Victorian state high schools. She later worked as a writer and collective member on *Digger* magazine. Her first novel, *Monkey Grip* (1977) won the National Book Council's Book of the Year Award in 1978, and was made into a film in 1982. Her second book, *Honour and Other People's Children*, appeared in 1980. Her next book was a novelisation (with Jennifer Giles) of the film *Moving Out*. *The Children's Bach*, a novel, appeared in 1984, and a collection of short stories is to be published by McPhee Gribble/Penguin in 1985. Recently Helen Garner has worked as a freelance journalist, translator and theatre reviewer. She has also worked as writer-in-residence at Griffith University in Queensland and at the University of Western Australia; and has lectured on Australian writing in Tokyo at the expense of the Literature Board of the Australia Council.

AMANDA GIVEN left Ireland for Tasmania in 1967 at the age of thirteen. She has studied and worked in the fields of drama, education, welfare and law. Her writing to date has consisted mainly of short stories, but she hopes to work also in drama and children's literature. Amanda Given now lives in Sydney with her daughter.

KATE GRENVILLE was born in Sydney in 1950. She holds degrees from the University of Sydney and from the University of Colorado, USA. In 1984 her collection of short stories, *Bearded Ladies*, was published by University of Queensland Press. In the same year she won the Vogel/*Australian* National Literary Award with a novel, *Lilian's Story*, to be published in 1985. Kate Grenville works for multicultural television in Sydney.

BETTY JOHNSTON was born in Christchurch, New Zealand, in 1942, and teaches mathematics to primary school teachers in training. She has been writing poetry and short stories since the late 1970s, with occasional publication. She is married, with three children, and has been living in Sydney since the mid-1960s.

ELIZABETH JOLLEY came to Western Australia from England in 1959. She cultivates a small orchard and is a part-time lecturer at the Fremantle Arts Centre and the Western Australian Institute of Technology. Publications include three collections of short fiction and five novels, one of which, *Mr Scobie's Riddle*, received the *Age* Book of the Year Award in 1983. A sixth novel, *Foxybaby*, is to be published by the University of Queensland Press and Viking/Penguin USA in 1985.

ROSEMARY JONES, born in Adelaide in 1954, is a secondary school teacher. She was founding (and subsequent) editor of *Ash Magazine* from 1979 to 1984, and has had short stories published in literary magazines and broadcast on radio in Australia.

VASSO KALAMARAS was born in Athens in 1932 and came to Western Australia with her husband in 1951, where she lived on a small tobacco farm. She later studied fine arts at Claremont Technical College, WA, and has an associateship in fine art at the WA Institute of Technology. She has had two grants from the Literature Board of the Australia Council, and has won numerous awards for painting and writing. She has had ten books published in Greek and English, and six plays, and has produced work for a number of Greek, Greek-Australian and other Australian publications. Poet, playwright, author, sculptor, painter, Vasso Kalamaras also translates and lectures in modern Greek.

NANCY KEESING AM was born in Sydney in 1923 and educated at SCEGGS Darlinghurst and Frensham, Mittagong. She acquired a diploma of social studies at Sydney University in 1947, and has been active in writers' and community and educational organisations. Nancy Keesing was chairman of the Literature Board of the Australia Council 1974–77, and was awarded the AM for Services to Australian Literature in 1979. Some 23 publications include four books of poetry; two novels for children; two collections of Australian bush songs and bush ballads (with Douglas Stewart); a biography; works of criticism; and various anthologies. She lives with her husband in Sydney.

GWEN KELLY was born in Sydney in 1922 and educated at Fort Street High School and the University of Sydney. She has worked as a salesgirl, a clerk in the Commonwealth Public Service, a fellow and lecturer in philosophy at the Universities of Sydney and New England, and as a lecturer in the Language Department at Armidale Teachers College. She has also taught English and history to secondary students. From 1974 to 1976 she held a senior writing fellowship from the Literature Board of the Australia Council, during which time she wrote her novel *Always Afternoon*, published in 1981. Other novels include *There is No Refuge* (1961), *The Red Boat* (1968), and *The Middle-Aged Maidens* (1976). As well, she has published numerous short stories and some poetry, and has won the Henry Lawson Award for Prose at the Grenfell Festival four times, the Melbourne *Sun Herald* Short Story Award, and a number of others. Her work has appeared in Germany, Canada and America as well as in many Australian collections. Gwen Kelly lives in Armidale, NSW.

JERI KROLL was born in New York in 1946 and has survived degrees and jobs at tertiary institutions in the United States and England. She has a doctorate of philosophy from Columbia University. She came to Australia in 1978 and has taught at Flinders and Adelaide Universities. For four and a half years she produced 'Writers' Radio' and 'Authors' Proof' for 5UV, Adelaide's public radio station. Her first book of poems, *Death as Mr Right*, won second prize in the Anne Elder Award for 1982. Her second, *Indian Moves*, appeared in 1984. She has received two grants from the South Australian Government to complete a collection of short stories. Jeri Kroll lives in Adelaide with Jeff Chilton and their son.

PENELOPE LAYLAND was born in 1962 in Liverpool, NSW, but has lived for most of her life in Canberra, where she completed a bachelor of arts degree while working in the Public Service. She is now working as a journalist in Orange, NSW. Penelope Layland has had one story published previously, in the short story magazine *Inprint*. She has received neither awards nor grants but is open to offers.

Biographies

KATE LLEWELLYN was born at Tumby Bay, SA, in 1940. She has a bachelor of arts degree from the University of Adelaide. Her book *Trader Kate and The Elephants* (1982) was joint winner of the Anne Elder award in 1983. Her work has appeared in *Frictions* (1982), *Sisters Poets I, Meanjin, Overland, New Poetry, Poetry Australia, Refractory Girl, Compass*, the *Sydney Morning Herald*, the *Age*, the *Bulletin*, the *Australian* and *Southern Review*.

OLGA MASTERS was born in 1919 in Pambula, NSW. She started writing fiction in her late 50s, after many years spent working as a journalist. Her first book, a collection of short stories, was a winner in the National Book Council Awards for 1983. Her first novel, *Loving Daughters*, was published in 1984. Her next book, a collection of self-contained chapters about the inhabitants of a small country town, is due for publication in late 1985. Olga Masters is married with seven children, most of whom are in journalism or the electronic media. She lives in Sydney with her husband and youngest son.

FINOLA MOORHEAD was born in Victoria in 1947 and, having acquired a bachelor of arts degree, became a full-time writer in 1972 after being selected in the First Australian National Playwrights' Conference. In 1974 and 1975 she gained a half-year fellowship from the Literature Board of the Australia Council, and had short stories published in magazines, broadcast by the ABC, and a couple of plays produced in small theatres. In 1980 she was writer-in-residence at Monash University, where she began an as-yet unpublished novel. She is working on her third novel.

PENELOPE NELSON was born in Sydney in 1943 and, apart from a year in Berlin, has lived there ever since. She was educated at the University of Sydney and Macquarie University, and has worked in publishing, research, adult education, community relations and administration. She has had a number of short stories, articles and poems published, as well as a study guide on the poems of Les A. Murray. She was also a co-author (with Kim Vu) of a report on refugee services in New South Wales.

JENNIFER PAYNTER, playwright, was born in Sydney in 1944. Her play *When Are We Going to Manly?* was performed in Sydney in 1984 by the Griffin Theatre Company. She is married and has two children.

ROBIN SHEINER was born in West Perth, WA, in 1940. She left school at 14 and worked at Western Australian Newspapers and later at Princess Margaret Hospital for Children. After graduating in 1961 she obtained a midwifery certificate, topping the year at King George V Hospital in Sydney. She commenced writing in 1980 after matriculating and partially completing an arts degree. Her short stories have been published in various magazines and anthologies. Her first novel, *Smile The War is Over* was published in 1983. A second novel will be published in 1985. Robin Sheiner is married with three teenage children.

LEONE SPERLING was born in Sydney in 1937 and educated at Sydney Girls' High School and Sydney University, where she gained a bachelor of arts honours degree in English literature. She lives with her four teenage children, and at the time of publication she has been a full-time English teacher with TAFE for 12 years. Her short stories include 'The Clean Up' (published in *The White Chrysanthemum*, edited by Nancy Keesing, 1978, and in *The True Life Story of ...*, edited by Jan Craney and Esther Caldwell, 1981). Her novel *Coins for the Ferryman* was published in 1981. *Mother's Day*, a volume of two novellas, was published by Redress Press/Wild and Woolley in 1984.

KATHRYN STONE was born in Dublin, Ireland, in 1963 of Australian parents, and brought to Australia at eighteen months of age. The family moved about extensively before settling in Dubbo, NSW, in the late 1970s. After studying law for a year at Sydney University, Kathryn Stone enrolled in the communications course at the NSW Institute of Technology. At nineteen she won the Australian Society of Authors Under 25 Short Story Competition. Having completed her degree, with majors in professional writing, literary studies and advertising, she hopes to compile a collection of short stories for publication.

BRONWYN SWEENEY was born in Sydney in 1963, and has always lived there. At the time of publication she is finishing a bachelor of arts degree in communications at the NSW Institute of Technology and is working as a library assistant. 'Licorice lozenges. french safety pins. and jelly snakes.' is her first published work.

KYLIE TENNANT OA was born in Sydney in 1912. She has published some 20 books, and twice won the S.H. Prior Memorial Prize, first with *Tiburon* in 1935 and then with *The Battlers* in 1941 (which also won the Literary Society Gold Medal). Her play *Tether a Dragon* won the Bi-Centennial Prize for Drama. Kylie Tennant was a member for some years of the Literary Board of the Australia Council, and is a journalist, critic, and reader for Macmillans. Widowed, she runs an apple orchard at Blackheath, NSW.

VICKI VIIDIKAS was born in Sydney in 1948, left school at fifteen with her intermediate certificate, and has worked in almost every conceivable job since. Her first poem was published in 1967. For some eight years she was involved with *New Poetry* and *Free Poetry* magazines and readings in Balmain, Sydney, and also in 1969 with readings at La Mama, Melbourne.

She has recorded her work for the National Library in Canberra; and her poetry has also been recorded by Robyn Archer (Larrikin Records 1978). She has had three writer's fellowships from the Literature Board of the Australia Council, and her publications include *Condition Red* (1973, poetry); *Wrappings* (1974, prose pieces); *Knabel* (1978, poetry), and *India Ink* (1984, poetry). A short film was made in 1975 from a story in *Wrappings*, directed by Stephen Wallace. A further collection of short stories and a novel are to appear in 1985.

NADIA WHEATLEY was born in Sydney in 1949 and grew up in a middle-class foster family. She has an MA (honours) in Australian history, and has been a freelance writer since 1979, her main published work being labour history and children's novels. *Five Times Dizzy* (1982) was highly commended in the Australian Children's Book Awards and won the NSW Premier's Special Prize in 1983. *The House that was Eureka* is to be published by Viking/Kestrel in 1985.

FAY ZWICKY, born in Melbourne in 1933, is a poet, short story writer and critic. Formerly a concert pianist, she has lived and worked in Indonesia, America and Europe. She now lives permanently in Western Australia, and is currently senior lecturer in the Department of English at the University of Western Australia. Her publications include two collections of poetry, *Isaac Babel's Fiddle* (1975) and *Kaddish and Other Poems* (which won the NSW Premier's Award for Poetry in 1982) and a collection of short stories, *Hostages* (1983). She edited *Quarry: A Selection of Western Australian Poetry* (1981) and *Journeys: Four Australian Women Poets* (Wright, Harwood, Dobson, Hewett, published 1982). A collection of critical essays, *The Lyre in the Pawnshop*, is due for release in 1985.